*IN*ESCAPABLE

a ghost story

Stonehouse Publishing Inc. is an independent
publishing house, incorporated in 2014.

Cover design and layout by Elizabeth Friesen.
Drawing, Aimee en déshabillé, D.K. Stone
Printed in Canada

Stonehouse Publishing would like to thank and acknowledge
the support of the Alberta Government funding for the arts,
through the Alberta Media Fund.

National Library of Canada Cataloguing in Publication Data
D.K. Stone
Inescapable: A Ghost Story
Novel
ISBN 978-1-988754-46-8
First edition

*IN*ESCAPABLE

a ghost story

a novel by
D.K. STONE

"I wasn't scared; I was just somebody else, some stranger, and my whole life was a haunted life, the life of a ghost."

— Jack Kerouac, *On the Road*

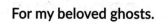
For my beloved ghosts.

PROLOGUE

When Aimee Westerberg opened her eyes, her husband was in the chair next to the bed. George reached out, tugging a wayward auburn curl. "Morning, sunshine."

"Morning yourself," she grumbled.

"Been waiting for you to wake up for an hour."

She groaned. George was backlit by morning sunlight, his grey hair painted gold, transforming him into the earlier version of him she'd never known. Aimee's lashes fluttered closed and she tugged the blankets higher. "Go 'way," she said. "I'm sleeping."

He chuckled at her tone.

Ten years of marriage had proven them opposites in more ways than one, but the differences had only bound them closer. *Except,* Aimee thought in chagrin, *when it's five in the goddamned morning.*

Half a minute passed in silence.

"Sunshine," he called softly. "I *know* you're awake."

"Am not."

George slid the chair closer, the scrape of hardwood like sandpaper over her nerves. "I want to get out to paint," he said. "It's beautiful today. Sky's full of clouds. Mount Rundle's gorgeous." He sighed and Aimee could imagine George smiling the way he did in the studio. *Breathing in the colours* as he called it.

"The sun on the mountain. The light on Lake Vermillion. It's a bright cadmium yellow with just a hint of crimson in the edges. But we need to go." George's voice grew chiding. "It won't last."

She made a non-committal grunt. *George and his damned hikes!* She'd expected he'd outgrow that at some point, but he never had.

When he'd been the teacher, and she the student, George's obsession with painting from life had inspired her. Lately, her amusement had worn thin.

"Come now, Aimee." He pulled the blankets off her shoulders and she shivered. "I finished the underpainting this week, but I need the play of light over the mountains for the highlights."

"I will," she said. "But not yet. It's too early."

"It's never too early." He nudged the bed with his foot, jiggling the mattress. "C'mon now. For me, sunshine."

George's tone was firm, the sound of someone who expected to get his way. *Maybe*, Aimee thought, *if I just lay here he'll leave me be.* But she knew that wasn't likely. Once George Westerberg got something into his mind he could not let go. His determination was downright irritating.

"Ai-*mee*," he sang.

"Another hour."

He chuckled, but the happy sound rankled her. "Ten minutes, and then we go." The blanket slid down another inch. "For me, darling. It's only a half hour walk to where I've been setting up."

"An hour."

"Fifteen minutes." Another tug.

Her jaw clenched. "I said *an hour*."

"Twenty and—"

"Fuck it, George!" she snapped, jerking the duvet back up to her chin. "I'm the one who drove out from Calgary last night, not you!" Her words held a petulant tinge. "I'm *tired*, alright?"

Long seconds of silence passed. Aimee forced her eyes shut and waited for sleep to retake her, but her heart pounded in her temple, any exhaustion burned away in her quick-fire temper. Another minute passed and she opened one eye. George sat at her side as he had before, staring out the window to the mountains beyond. His brow was furrowed. He stood, rolling his shoulders and winced. The tendinitis was bothering him again.

"I'll go downstairs and set up myself up on the porch then," he said, stretching his arm. "You sleep."

He left her side, closing the door behind him, quiet footsteps marking his passage down the stairs. Aimee's guilt rose in time to the sound. A childhood of want had taught Aimee many lessons, and gratitude was foremost among them. They had this cabin, this room, this very *life*, because George was a successful artist, and artists of all kinds needed to follow the whims of their muse. (That she'd once been the source of George's artistic energy—and wasn't any longer—was a twist to her gut.) The worry that had been building since she'd awoken with him at her side grew into a knot of panic, frustration replaced with fear.

If she didn't have George, what *did* she have?

With a groan of defeat, Aimee sat up, pushing the riot of knotted red hair away from her face. "Just hold on, George," she shouted at the closed door. "I'm coming!"

Downstairs, her husband whooped in triumph and Aimee grimaced.

She hated mornings.

—

Aimee was coming down the stairs from the bedroom clad in jeans and a t-shirt when she heard the sound: a whine like a dog's howl, or child's cry, somewhere outside; loud for half a second, then gone. Halfway between floors, she paused. Beyond the window, dawn was gilding the Rockies, the peaked roofs of Banff twinkling in the sunlight. George would be anxious to go. She put her foot down on the next riser.

A deafening crash rocked the kitchen below.

The sound launched her into motion; she sprinted down the stairs two at a time, bare toes gripping the floor as she headed through the kitchen to the half-open doors to the porch. The glass of one panel was a web of cracks held together by the wooden frame. Her husband slumped beside it, forehead bleeding.

"George!"

He lay on his back, legs twisted beneath him, his newest painting

—*Mount Rundle, Dawn* with its half-cured oils—tossed against the wall at his side. She blinked. The carefully articulated light and shadow he'd so proudly shown her when she arrived last night was a muddy smear, lines of dark pigment rising birdlike into a gouged sky, while echoing hatches of colours marred the door frame. Instinctively her fingers went to the canvas—to protect it, *to fix it*—but George's voice dragged her attention back.

"Aimee," he croaked.

Her hand jerked away as if burned. She dropped to her knees. "What's wrong? Did you fall?" She parted his hair, catching sight of blood pouring from a small cut, then ran her hands over his limbs, searching for more damage while George writhed against an unseen force.

"It's only a little cut," she said. "Did you wrench your back? You must've slipped on—"

"M-my chest—" he said haltingly. "Can't breathe."

Aimee's throat caught.

"My god." She pulled her cell phone from her pocket, dialling 911. Random thoughts pulsed like lightning through Aimee's mind: George was fifty-nine; ten years older than Aimee's own father had been when he'd died. Her mother had nearly lost everything that year. The untimely death unsettled their small suburban life with the ferocity that left Aimee aching even decades later.

"911 dispatch," a brusque voice answered. "What is your emergency?"

"My husband's fallen," Aimee said, amazed by the calmness in her voice. "I think it's an angina attack. He's cut his head and—"

George clawed for her arm and she yelped in surprise, her eyes jerking back to him. His face had faded to the colour of raw canvas. "Need the nitro," George said through clenched teeth. "Now!"

A flash of memory superimposed on the scene: George's insistence that he complete an updated will after he'd returned home from New York last fall. The hours he'd spent with their lawyer, arranging for charity contributions and bequeathments. She'd been asked to leave the room not once, but twice, that day, while George had gone through a seemingly endless list of minutiae.

"*What's going on?*" *she'd asked.*

"*Nothing. I'm just getting ready in case.*"

"*In case of what?*"

"*Oh Aimee,*" *he'd laughed.* "*A man my age can't pretend the sun will shine forever...*"

George groaned and his grip on her arm loosened. Aimee searched his pockets one handed, fear turning into sharp-edged panic. "Where is it, George? Where's the bottle?"

"Ma'am?" the dispatcher interrupted. "Ma'am, can you hear me?"

"Yes," Aimee snapped. "I'm still here." She couldn't find the nitro!

"Ma'am, we're sending an ambulance, but I need you to stay on the line. I'm going to talk you through this..."

The dispatcher's words rolled over Aimee, unheard.

"Hurry!" George rasped. "My chest—Get the nitro. I—"

Cradling the phone against her shoulder, Aimee's search redoubled. She tore from one pocket to the other as the first teardrops tumbled over her cheeks. They fell in splotches on George's shirt. A random thought appeared: There were paint flecks across the fabric—colours she recognized from the now-destroyed canvas—and those colours would never be matched again.

"Hurry!" George cried.

"I'm trying!" Aimee's fingers caught on the small shape of a plastic bottle. "Got it!"

"Ma'am?" The woman on the phone was still asking questions but Aimee wasn't listening. She tugged the bottle free, biting the cap to unscrew it. George took a hissing breath as she brought it to his lips. His eyes were half-closed, a line of spittle dripping from the corner of his mouth.

"Open!" she ordered. "Hurry, George! Open your mouth. I have the nitro!"

Another memory floated forward: George's last angiogram had shown a minor blockage; "*Nothing to worry about,*" had been the doctor's words that day, "*just a part of growing old.*" Aimee had wanted George to get a second opinion, but he'd refused. "*Old is old, sunshine. Nothing but the truth."*

"Ma'am, I need you to answer me," the dispatcher said. "Is your husband still breathing?"

"Yes! Yes, he's breathing," Aimee replied. George's mouth fell slack, and she squirted the liquid under his tongue. She counted the seconds, waiting for George to relax, to return to her the way he'd done all the times before. *"Angina's nothing to worry about, Aimee. Just a little blip with the old ticker."* But today, his expression didn't change. Aimee leaned closer, searching for a clue, her heart pounding so loudly she could hear it in her ears.

"George? George, can you hear me? I—"

Without warning, he arched and began to thrash, animal sounds rising from deep inside his chest. His head banged against the floor. George—who never showed pain, who taped up broken fingers so he could paint, who refused aspirin for headaches, and ignored the tendinitis that had plagued him all winter—writhed in agony, the tendons in his neck tightening into ropes.

"George!" Aimee screamed.

"Ma'am," the dispatcher continued. "You need to check if—"

George's pupils were dilated, his gaze glassy.

"Something's wrong! The nitro's not working!" Aimee shrieked. A stream of images danced across her thoughts: Aimee, a student, mixing pigments by hand in George's class; the takeout dinner from Maple Grill they'd shared late last night; George's cabin studio, filled with half-finished works; the last argument she'd had with Jacqueline when Aimee admitted she didn't *really* understand why George was changing his will yet again; her refusal to get out of bed that morning when George had asked her.

"He needs an ambulance!" Aimee cried. "Hurry, please!"

"EMS is on its way. They'll be there in just a few minutes."

Aimee dropped the cell with a clatter and grabbed George's shoulders, pulling until he was half in her arms, loose-limbed and heavy. "Hold on, George. The ambulance is coming."

Another, solitary flash: George Westerberg, feted Canadian artist and playboy, standing at an opening at the Gainsborough

Gallery—the very opening that Aimee thought of as 'theirs'. This was the moment that changed things. She'd attended the gala as his one-time student from the Alberta College of Art and Design (now graduated from and starving). She was supposed to be making the connections that would launch her non-existent career. Partway through the night she'd turned to catch him watching her from across the room. George was old enough to be her father—they argued as much as talked while she toiled in his studio—but there was nothing paternal about his gaze that night. Danger and desire smoldered in his dark eyes, unspoken promise in a hungry smile.

He walked toward her, stopping a half-step too close for a teacher-student chat.

"Aimee, Aimee, Ai-mee," he chuckled, giving her a once over. "Must say, you look all grown up in that dress." His gaze drifted down, caressing her curves before rising.

She lifted her chin, and smirked. "I always was grown up," she said. "You've finally noticed."

On the floor, George gulped for air like a fish out of water, eyes bulging. He fumbled blindly for her hand. "Aimee, listen. If I—If I don't make it, I want you to know—"

"Stop! You're going to be fine."

"But if I—"

"You've had angina before. It's nothing to worry about!"

"Aimee listen!" His fingers tightened into a vise, silencing her. "The will, Aimee. I never explained why I asked you to leave that day." A tinny voice echoed from the forgotten phone, distracting Aimee from his words. "I couldn't tell you then, but—" He took a heaving breath. "But when I was in New York—"

The EMT's voice echoed distantly and Aimee scrambled to grab the phone.

"We can talk about this later, George. Just hold on. Okay?" She put the phone to her ear, catching the last few words.

"—will be there shortly, but you need to put your husband into the recovery position. Lay him on his side. Make sure his mouth is free of obstructions—"

"Aimee, listen." George's grip loosened. "If I don't make it, when I'm d—"

"No!" She couldn't bear to hear him say it, couldn't imagine him—George, her husband, the most celebrated modern painter Canada had seen in a generation—dead and gone. The first, thin wail of an ambulance rose in the distance. "You're not going to die. Stay with me, George. The ambulance is almost here."

She stared out over the bowl of mountains that cupped the town of Banff in its hollow, desperately willing the EMS team to come faster. The sky above the limestone ridge was a bright cornflower blue, crimson clouds fading as dawn passed into day. *A new day*, her mind whispered. Nothing would ever be the same. Not now. Not after this.

"Aimee, listen," George said. "I need you to know that—"

"What?!" Aimee shouted, tears wrenching through her.

"Just listen," he whispered, voice fading. She caught George's gaze and held it. His fingers squeezed once, but it was faint and weak. "W-want you to know that I always loved you," he said. "No matter what happened between us. No matter what I did or—"

"I love you too, but hold on, alright? Just a minute longer."

"Don't think I can." George's lips were blue, his skin ashen, but it was his expression which terrified her. His lids drooped, his body slumping, as if all that had been him—bold, brash, and genius—was leaking away into the morning air.

"Don't go," she whispered. "Stay with me, George. Stay."

The siren had grown into a scream.

He gave her a wavering smile. "I'll try."

CHAPTER ONE

When Aimee Westerberg opened her eyes, her husband was waiting in the chair next to the bed.

"Morning, sunshine."

She pressed her eyes closed, heart pounding in her ears. "Go away," she hissed.

The ghost, of course, ignored her.

It didn't surprise her to discover George in the cabin. She'd come to expect these flickers of pervasive memory in the long year since his death. They appeared when stress or grief overwhelmed her and in the last months, there'd been more than enough of that. She counted to ten, hoping the vision would fade.

"I *know* you're awake," George said.

She opened her eyes to find him smiling and her heart twisted. Unlike the fateful day last year, there was no morning light pouring through the window behind him. Spring storm clouds clogged the mountain valley much as they'd done when she'd arrived. This season matched her mood: day after day of sleet grey rain and darkness.

Aimee had known returning to the cabin would make these episodes sharper. She just hadn't expected George to look so alive. If she looked—*really looked*—she could see through him. She knew she shouldn't allow herself to imagine him like this, but she couldn't seem to stop it. She drew in details like they were water and she was dying of thirst: the fan of wrinkles at the corner of laughing eyes; the shirt splotched with paint; the long, painter's hands; fingernails stained with pigment and nicotine. The ache in her chest blossomed into a pain so sharp she couldn't breathe and she rolled onto her side, breathing in shaking gulps.

"I said g'morning, sunshine."

"Morning yourself," she muttered as she untangled herself from the covers and escaped to the ensuite bathroom. She glanced back at the bed. Stark, crisp sheets marked his side of the bed. Seeing it, her chest released. She wasn't certain why it mattered, but it did.

"Glad you're finally up," George said. "It's beautiful out today. Sky's full of clouds. Mount Rundle's gorgeous."

Aimee slammed the bathroom door and leaned against it. She didn't want to deal with her turbulent memories. Not yet. It was still too painful.

"I want to get out early today so I can catch the play of light over the mountains," he continued through the partition. "It won't last."

Aimee walked shakily to the sink, catching herself against the icy porcelain. She counted to ten, then twenty, then thirty, the way she'd done as a child to force dark thoughts away. On the other side of the door she could hear George humming—*I can imagine him humming*, her mind corrected—the way George had always done when working on a big project. The remembered sound was enough to bring her to tears. Aimee struggled with the faucet, splashing freezing water over her face and neck. The sound of humming faded as she became alert. Calmer, she moved through her morning toilette with numbed repetition. Toilet. Sink. Shower. Her body in the present, mind trapped in the past.

By the time she emerged from the bathroom, the last dregs of the dream had been scoured away with a bitter lather of obligations. The real estate agent would be coming by in less than an hour. The cabin was to be sold, the money divided between the will's many recipients. Another stab of pain. This had been their place—hers and George's escape—but her husband's will had been seeded with land mines. Aimee's heart twisted. She needed to pull herself together, play it calm. Do what needed to be done. This was her life now— hers alone—and every decision mattered.

She put her hand on the doorknob and took a slow breath.

"It's not real," Aimee whispered. "George is dead and gone." She repeated more firmly. "Gone."

Aimee pushed the door wide.

The room was bare, just as she'd known it would be. Murky light filtered through half-parted curtains, rain running down the windows like tears. The unmade side of the bed sat untouched. George's ghost, so painful, so reassuring, had disappeared. One part of her was relieved, the other grief-stricken.

Truth was, she missed him.

—

It was a relief to leave Banff behind.

The movers would take out the furniture and pack up the household items this week; next weekend she'd return to divvy up George's personal items. After six months of lawyers, she was grateful to be at this point: sell it all, send it away, let the law firm deal with the rest.

"I'll have the cabin sold in a month," David Arturo, the real estate agent said. "You rest assured."

Aimee didn't share his excitement, nor certainty, but she nodded all the same. "Good," she said as she handed him the key. "I just want it done."

A bitter smile tightened the edges of her mouth as she imagined the boxes sitting on the wide front stoop of Jacqueline's sprawling New York estate, cluttering the snow white living room that had graced the cover of more than one decorating magazine. *She's the one who contested the will*, Aimee thought. *Let her sort out her father's mess*. Aimee no longer cared.

"Oh, you'll do better than just sold," he said, giving her an oily smile. "This place is prime. It'll get a tidy profit."

Aimee shrugged. "Keep me updated."

"I'll call you as soon as I get an offer," he said, tossing the keys into the air and catching them. "Safe travels back to cow-town."

"Thanks."

Aimee stepped off the porch. Away from the awning, the rain

was a sheet, soaking her. She turned up the collar of her jacket as she trudged through the mud to her car.

"*Aimee...*"

The sound of her name was a whisper, but a shiver ran up her spine. She glanced sideways. David was already inside his black sports car, cell phone in hand. *It sounded like George*, she thought, but shoved the idea away just as fast. She picked up her pace, steps slapping in puddles. The back of her scalp prickled, but she stared steadfastly forward. *I won't check*, she thought grimly. *There's no one there.*

She climbed into her car, and started the engine, waiting while the windows unfogged.

"Aimee!"

She jumped at the sound of her name, everywhere and nowhere at once.

"Fuck this," she hissed, popping the car into drive and tearing away from the empty house and down the waterlogged street. Fans of water sprayed out on either side, tires hissing angrily.

Coming to Banff had been a terrible idea.

—

Back in Calgary, the depression Aimee had been fighting for months resurged. Like the low clouds which wrapped the city, her despair darkened everything in her gaze. She couldn't sleep. Couldn't eat. Only work kept her sane.

Why did you have to die, George?

Days passed. Grey skies became the norm, the patter of rain became the static sound of her life, no longer noticeable. It had always been raining, hadn't it? She climbed out of bed, and followed her routine like a sleepwalker, stumbling the five blocks from her downtown condo to the Glenbow Museum. Hiding in her office. Doing it all again.

God, I miss you so much.

On a Wednesday, Aimee arrived just after six a.m. Sidestepping the cleaning crew, she headed to the staff room. She peered around the small space, relieved to see that her intern hadn't arrived. Knowing Niha, the Glenbow's receptionist/assistant/jack-of-all-trades, there'd be questions—ones Aimee didn't want to answer—but the room was blessedly empty, and the tightness across Aimee's shoulders eased. After eight years as a restorer at the Glenbow, Aimee's workload had grown enough that she needed someone to assist with the paperwork side of her job. She just wasn't prepared for Niha's joyful exuberance at this time of morning.

Aimee hung her dripping coat in her locker, and pulled on the white smock she wore for restorations. She counted the buttons as she did them up—another pattern, another routine—then stepped in front of the wall mirror to inspect the face which greeted her. Blue shadows ringed both eyes. Her cheekbones were angrily sharp, hollows under them. Her freckled skin had grown so pale it was translucent. Aimee frowned and the girl in the mirror did too. "I've aged a decade since you died," she muttered. With a sigh, the reflection ran her fingers through her hair, twisting the curls into a loose bun at the nape of her neck and sliding on a hairnet. Aimee followed the mirror's lead.

"You're in early again."

She squeaked in surprise, turning to discover Steve, the night security guard, waiting in the doorway.

"Yeah, I guess I am," she said with a nod, hoping he'd leave it at that.

"You got a big deadline or something?"

"Not really."

Steve leaned against the door frame and crossed his arms, watching. "Then why all the early mornings?"

"I don't know what you mean," she said evenly. There was another answer, one she couldn't give. It was easier when she came in early, and left late. No knowing looks or well-meaning hugs she didn't want. Nothing like this.

"I always work these hours," Aimee added.

Steve's expression faltered. "Really? I figured you must be working on something important. Seems like you're always here."

She forced a bright smile. "Oh, they're all important," Aimee said. "But no. Nothing rushed."

He nodded, but still didn't leave. Seconds passed.

"Then why?" he asked.

Aimee's smile was rigid, hands clenched. "I just work better alone," she said. "I like the quiet. It lets me focus. Lets my mind drift."

"I don't know about you, but I find the basement creepy as hell." He chuckled nervously.

Aimee shrugged, turning her back to him to look at the mirror instead. Perhaps then he'd take the hint. She smoothed an unruly curl back under the hairnet. Her reflection did too. In the last months, her long hair had lost its lustre. It hung limp and brittle around her pale face.

"I swear I hear footsteps sometimes at night," Steve said. "You don't get lonely down there?"

"Not so much," she said, straightening the hairnet. "And I like the quiet downstairs. Besides, being alone lets me—" She stumbled, realizing she'd almost said *forget*. "—get stuff done without interruptions," she quickly added. "And I should get going, actually."

Steve grinned, stepping out of the doorway. "Well, don't let me stop you," he said with a wave. "Was good talking with you, Aimee. Always nice to see you around."

"Yeah, you too."

"Let me know if you need anything."

"Thanks, Steve. I will."

She kept the smile on her face until he strode down the corridor. The expression felt odd on her mouth, like the clothes she wore that no longer fit. The grimace fell from her lips the moment he disappeared around the corner. Aimee swallowed against the lump in her throat and headed for the stairs.

Pretending drained her.

—

The archives and restorations wing was located in the bowels of the Glenbow. Aimee rushed down the service stairwell, hoping to avoid anyone else.

I just want to be left alone.

Reaching her office, she took a slow breath: the faint vapour of paint and solvent warmed the recycled air, the hidden musk of pigments—stored in a grid of tiny jars—a subtler perfume hidden beneath it. To the untrained eye, the room, with its stark white walls, stainless steel sinks, empty tables and bright lights, appeared antiseptically bare. Even the line of brushes, arranged by hair type, medium, and width, seemed to be more appropriate for a medical display than an artist's studio. But Aimee knew from experience that the barren aesthetic allowed her to dissolve herself into the painting she was repairing. The room was a blank piece of paper, on which she could redraw whatever lines that time (or damage) had erased from the artwork she restored.

A place she was free to dream.

The restorations room was as different from Aimee's one-time studio had been that—if she wasn't the same person who'd inhabited both—she wouldn't have believed it possible. A narrow line appeared between her brows as her long ago studio floated forward from memory. It had been on the third floor of an aging Stephen Avenue building, the high-ceilinged room cluttered with pigment and canvas, its walls hung with scraps of paper and pinned photographs, all of it inspiration for the bold, multi-layered canvases that filled the space. She sighed. These days, the thought of that sort of chaos exhausted her, but a decade earlier, it had been her lifeblood. She'd thrived in that vividness, finding beauty and focus in its disarray. And then George had fallen into her life and every colour in the world had faded besides him. The old pain returned with a jolt.

Why did you have to leave me, George?

Hands shaking, she pressed down her apron, smoothing non-existent wrinkles. These days, the quiet of white on white, the bare walls, the paint whose colours she matched rather than selected fit her better. There was no choosing here. No anything. She could channel the genius of someone else while she, herself, could be nothing at all.

Of the numerous paintings she'd restored over her ten year career, the one she would work on today provided a unique challenge. It was a small study for Delacroix's famous *Raft of the Medusa*. The newly-acquired work of art had required cleaning prior to the cracks being repaired, and Aimee and two assistants had spent three weeks and endless cotton swabs dabbing away two centuries of murkiness from the painting's surface. The newly freshened pigment had revealed an unexpected issue. Sometime in the last century, another repair had been attempted. Whatever restorer had undertaken the task hadn't thought to first remove the earlier decades of grime, and the additional brush strokes stood out in glaring contrast to the remainder of the image. These strokes were two shades darker than they should be, and painted with a novice's sloppy hand. With utmost care, Aimee had slowly undone the previous-restorer's gaffe, peeling off layers of damage with a solvent-soaked fine-tip until only Delacroix's original, and the jarring damage, remained.

Aimee pulled off the drop cloth, the first hint of a smile returning to her lips. This morning she'd begin the restoration.

She laid out a work area on one of the room's many wooden easels, clamping the painting into position before selecting her paints and organizing them based on colour and hue. Each of the raw pigments had been ground with mortar and pestle, based on centuries-old recipes. Everything—from the lapis lazuli in the blue to the original rabbit-skin glue mixed with chalk in the gesso—was as original as she could recreate. No detail too small. As many hours went into the preparation of pigments as the actual process of repair. Sliding her chair up to the easel, Aimee mixed a small dab of colour on the surface, brackish blue tinged with grey, and dabbed it on a test board. There were lines of dried colour tabs along the side of her test canvas, but she still double checked, tilting it one way and the next in position near the original, adjusting the lamp to catch the light.

"Perfect."

She swirled the brush again, lifting a minute amount to the surface with trembling hands. She breathed out and her fingers stilled. She touched the brush to the surface.

The world fell away.

Nearly an hour later, Aimee had inpainted an area the size of a postage stamp. A small step forward, though the heaviest damage, where the cracks went right down to the board, had been painstakingly recovered. With the under-painting reemerging, the work quickened and her mind began to drift. She could imagine Eugène as a young artist living alone in his hovel in Paris, the way she'd read about in his journals. She'd studied his diaries when she was taking art history in university. Aimee smirked as remembered details rose in her mind: Eugène, dark haired and brooding, his sensual mouth downturned in disdain, an image she recognized from his earliest self-portraits. Mind wandering, hands busy, it was easy to imagine the artist standing here. As a child, magical flights of imagination had been her whole life, but nowadays that feeling was hard to rekindle. Today she longed for the escape.

A flicker appeared in the corner of her eye.

Eugène would be wearing an old dressing gown, Aimee decided, paint-flecked and dirty, a stained linen shirt underneath. She smiled to herself, leaning in to place another dab of paint on the canvas. The warm smell of linseed oil and turpentine rose like incense. If Eugène had been here, Aimee thought, there'd be the other odours too: unwashed male and wine, the heady scent of Parisian cologne. Most likely Eugène would be scowling at the painting, unhappy with his work. Poor Eugène, Aimee thought, *so dark, so dismal.* In the corner of the room, the shadow coalesced under the prompting of her thoughts. She added a flicker of light with a twist of her wrist, moving her hand sideways as she dove back into the painting.

Eugène had been young when he'd written his first journal, searching for a way to fit his avant-garde style into the classical system of the times. In Aimee's mind, the vision grew solid, stretching one muscled arm, then the other, as he walked nearer. A line from the young painter's journal came to mind: "*All my days lead to the same conclusion; an infinite longing for something which I can never have, a void which I cannot fill.*" Aimee understood that sentiment better now than she had in her twenties. Eugène Delacroix was more than an artist, he was a revolutionary. He wanted to change the world through his art.

"That stroke is all wrong," the ghost announced.

Aimee peeked up to find a twenty-something Eugène—eyes wild and black hair tangled—watching her in distrust. Like his self-portraits, he was unexpectedly attractive. His skin had a Spaniard's tanned warmth; his thick hair shone the colour of jet. Aimee recognized the expression from an etching she'd once seen of him: young and angry. She turned back to the painting, inspecting the raised smear of paint.

"Go away, Eugène," she said. "I know what I'm doing." She lifted the paintbrush, about to continue.

"You don't," he interrupted, breaking her concentration. "It's wrong."

She lowered the brush, tipping her head to the side. "You think?"

Eugène made a sound of disgust. "Yes, I do! I wouldn't say as much if I didn't."

Aimee bit back a smile. She loved these flights of fancy, imagining people long-dead. The ghost stepped closer. She knew if she looked, he'd be almost fully solid, but she stared at his painting instead. There was something wrong with the patch she'd finished, and she couldn't figure out what.

Eugène's ghost made an angry sound in the back of his throat.

"Go on then," she said. "I'm listening."

"It's the wrong angle," Eugène said tartly. "These strokes? Here and here; they don't match." He gestured at the marks that filled the surface. "See that bit of black? And this swirl of ochre?" His finger, semi-transparent and trembling, hovered just above the original lines that appeared on either side of the crack. "I was rushing when I painted this. The light was gone in my studio, and I'd run out of candles. Money, you see, was always short." He sniffed as if the thought was below him. "I took the canvas to the window, and set it on the table, catching the last of the daylight. This wasn't painted at an easel."

Aimee peered closer. There was something about the angles of the strokes. "Hmm...I don't—"

"It was on a table. Painted from above. Even you should be able to see that."

Aimee nodded, she should have been able to see the evidence, but in her excitement to begin, she'd rushed forward. She unclamped and lifted the canvas down, setting it on a nearby table.

"Fine," she sighed. "I'll fix it."

"As you should," he said, lip curling in disdain. "It's entirely and completely wrong."

Aimee glared at him. "I *said* I'd fix it."

She picked up a clean brush, dabbed away the undried paint, and restarted. The apparition waited at her elbow as she twisted her wrist to match the angle of the original brush work. She imagined the scent of sweat mixing with the odour of spices. *Cloves?* she wondered. There was almost always a reason why she imagined her artists a certain way, but she couldn't remember this particular detail. She expected Eugène to vanish, but he didn't. He waited through her work, pacing. The repainting was slow going, unpleasant, and another half-hour passed. Her neck had begun to throb when the apparition spoke again.

"Yes, yes. Much better, madame," he said, leaning in. "Almost as good as it was." Eugène moved closer, momentarily blocking her view.

That's the difference between artists and restorers, Aimee thought. *The ego.*

"Now if you'll just add a little more light," the ghost advised, "and a bit of shadow here, then—"

"I don't need your help."

He turned, hands rising to his hips. "Everyone needs help, no matter what their trade. Artist," he touched his chest, "or not." His gaze rested accusingly on Aimee. "It's just a matter of playing the game long enough to find it."

"Hmmph," Aimee snorted.

Eugène stood taller, adjusting his painting jacket like a prince's robe. There were burgundy marks, Aimee noticed, on the white shirt-sleeves. And as irritable as he was, he really was attractive.

"An untrained eye might not see what needs to be done," Eugène sniffed.

"I was an artist before I was a restorer," Aimee said. The ghost had the temerity to look surprised. "I know what I need to do. I don't need anyone's help."

"Are you certain of that?" Eugène leaned closer; his cheeks were flushed, breath warm. *Cloves in the wine*, she realized. *That's what I smell.* "Because it seems to me that you're locked in a basement of a museum, talking to yourself, while you rush through your work." His gaze dropped to her hand. "Careful now, madame, or you'll smudge my work and have to restart."

Aimee opened her mouth to argue with him, but began to giggle. She *was* talking to herself, as she often did when lost in a painting. She set the brush carefully to the side, unexpected laughter breaking from her chest like a breath of fresh air. Eugène—like any of her other ghosts—wasn't actually there. He was her own thoughts reflected back to her; Aimee's own mind, wandering and lost.

Mirth faded into giggles and she wiped at teary eyes. "Well, Eugène," she said dryly, "when you put it that way…"

Her words faded. The ghostly form of Eugène Delacroix was long gone. It was only Aimee and her paint, and a tiny, repaired section of an artist's work; the artist himself, long since turned to ashes. She glanced around the empty room. Her smile disappeared.

Imagined or not, Eugène was right. She did need help, but not the kind he could give.

CHAPTER TWO

May melted into June. The rain stayed. Aimee felt the cold draw inward, wearing away at the brittle shell which had protected her since George's death and forcing its way inside. Even the places she'd once loved—like the tiny coffee house where she and her mother sat on Friday afternoons—felt cold. Empty. Only work gave her reprieve.

Did life change? she wondered. *Or just me?*

The waitress stopped at the small table, unloading a teapot and filling two cups. Aimee's mother, Claudine, carried on the conversation without Aimee's participation, her narrow hands fluttering like birds as she chattered.

"Haven't had a spring this bad in years," Claudine said with a dramatic sigh. "Snow in April. Snow in May. Snow all spring and now the endless rain! *Incroyable!*"

Aimee nodded, a conditioned response. She held her cup with icy hands, but didn't drink.

"And I can't very well start gardening if it's freezing each night," her mother continued. "I'm still wearing my winter boots, for goodness' sake."

"Terrible." Aimee knew she *should* be concerned about this—about life—but she couldn't feel anything.

"June!" Claudine scoffed. "You'd hardly believe it if you looked outside. Not with all the rain. The tulips in the garden are barely up, for goodness' sake. A month late."

Aimee made another sound of feigned interest, but like everything else, the effort wearied her. She was stuck in limbo, frozen.

Damnit, George. Why did you have to leave me? At the thought, her gaze flicked up, fearful, but the coffee house was blessedly empty. This place was one of Aimee's haunts, not his; no shadow of his memory filled it.

"Hasn't felt like this since we first came to Calgary," Claudine said. "I can remember how cold it was the year we moved. There was snow that June too, but not the deep, heavy kind. Just cold, bitter cold and dry heaps of snow. Ah! Such a time."

"Mm-hmm."

"And I wanted to go back to Montreal, but your father had a job here, and I didn't. Mon Dieu, what a mess! I remember how terrible it was for you: No friends. All alone. New school, new house. Oh Aimee, you were such a sad little girl in those days. Barely talking or eating. Lost in your own world. Talking to imaginary friends rather than other children."

Aimee stared down into her cup. It felt like she was stuck, like the spring weather that wouldn't change, and the cabin that wouldn't sell. "*It's the time of year,*" the real estate agent assured her. "*Come summer, I won't be able to keep the buyers away.*" But it felt like something worse. An omen of all that had gone wrong since that morning.

Why, George? a voice inside her cried. *Why did you have to leave?*

"Aimee?" her mother said sharply. "Are you even listening?"

She dragged herself back to the surface. "Sorry, Mom, I have a lot on my mind."

"Like?"

"Like the cabin. The will."

Her mother's expression darkened. "Jacqueline still being a bitch about it?"

Aimee winced, remembering the last weeks of disagreements. The primary settlements had been agreed upon, but George's daughter, Jacqueline, was fighting tooth and nail for the details. "Mom," Aimee groaned. "Please don't start."

"Well, she is!" her mother said.

"Jacqueline's just Jacqueline. She's always been like that. Always will be." That the two women—daughter and widow—were nearly the same age had been a thorn between them since the start. In the beginning, Aimee had fought for her share of George's estate, but now—months into litigation—she didn't care anymore. Her dead husband's will was a tangled mess, just like his life. And Aimee was drowning in it.

"Well, I don't like how she's treating you," Claudine said. "It's not right. George loved you. He wanted you to be taken care of."

Aimee nodded. "I know he did."

Her mother blew over her tea. "I just wish he'd cleared up his affairs before, well, you know."

"He didn't know he was going to die."

"Yes, but it could have been done!"

"Mom, please just let it go," Aimee sighed. She pinched the bridge of her nose. "This isn't helping."

Claudine watched her for several long seconds. Aimee could feel her mother measuring her, testing the way she'd done when Aimee had been a child, claiming illness.

"You're not eating again," she announced. "I can tell."

"I'm fine."

"You're not. You're skin and bones. Your clothes are hanging off you."

"I had a touch of the flu, that's all," she lied. The fake smile was beginning to hurt her cheeks. "I'll be back to normal in no time."

Her mother reached out, pressing Aimee's hand between her two warm palms. She dropped her voice. "Have you been back to the doctor again?"

Aimee jerked her hand back, annoyed. The mask dropped. "I don't need more pills."

Her mother frowned. "I know you want to do this on your own, cherie, but sometimes the pressure is too much for one person."

"I told you I'm fine."

"You're not."

"I am. And I wish you'd believe that."

"Believe?" Claudine coughed, throwing her hands into the air. "I believe what I see."

Aimee scowled. "I'm fine. I just need time."

"You've had a year, and if anything, it's gotten worse," her mother said.

Aimee shook her head, fighting the urge to scream. Her mother had forged her way through her husband's death with stolid determination, rebuilding a solo life in no time, something Aimee had—even as a teenager—never truly understood. Claudine expected her daughter to do the same.

"You don't go out. You don't call," she continued. "Honestly, Aimee, you haven't been the same since that day. You can't go on like this. You're too young. You can't—"

"But George *died!*" Aimee shouted. Around the coffee shop, people turned in surprise. An uneasy silence followed her explosion.

"Aimee!" her mother gasped.

She closed her eyes, fighting unwanted tears. Her mother's hand returned, patting her arm. "I'm doing the best I can," Aimee said haltingly. "I'm trying, Mom. I am. But your pestering doesn't help."

"I'm just worried. It's been over a year. You're young, Aimee." She smiled sadly. "You could meet someone else, you know. I did, after your father passed."

Aimee jerked her hand back. That too, had been something Aimee hadn't understood. "But I don't want someone else." She couldn't keep the venom from her voice. "I told you that."

"How can you know that, unless you go out on a few dates, eh?"

"I don't want to date."

Her mother's lips pursed in an irritated moue. "Fine, then don't. But at least stop shutting yourself away."

Aimee took a swallow of tea, scalding her mouth. The heat burned her throat before settling like a coal in her chest. "I'm here, aren't I?"

"Tell me this: where are your friends? Do you talk to anyone?"

Aimee took a long time before answering. She wanted to run, but that would make it worse. "I talk to lots of people," she said in a saccharine voice.

"Anyone you *don't* work with?"

"Well, I'm very busy trying to sell the cabin," she said, fiddling with her teacup. It was burning her fingers, but she needed something to hold. "I've had a lot of restoration work on my plate."

"A-ha! I knew it," her mother said, waggling her finger under Aimee's nose. "Locking yourself away in the Glenbow. Working all the time. Not answering my calls. My only child and I don't even see her."

Aimee sank lower in her chair. "Don't start with the guilt, please."

"I'm worried, and I love you. Please, cherie. I just want you to get out once in a while."

"I *do* get out," she lied. "In fact I'm going to George's retrospective on Friday."

Her mother's expression softened. "Oh? I didn't think you would. I mean, I think it's good, I just thought after what you'd said about avoiding the art crowd, you wouldn't."

Aimee took another sip of tea. She couldn't taste anything, but burning her mouth was better than discussing that.

"Anyhow, it's good to hear," Claudine said with a smile. "And if you're getting out again, you should think about dating too."

"Mom, *please*." Claudine had been widowed at forty-eight, but she'd bounced back into the dating scene within six months. Teenaged Aimee had carried her father's death like a personal badge of grief, raging at her mother's pragmatic: "*C'est la vie.*" With each date, Aimee had felt her mother's betrayal on her father's behalf, and today it felt like her mother wanted *her* to do the same to George.

"I'm not saying run off and get married, but a *friend* might be nice. George is gone, after all. Get out, do things, don't just—" The sound of ringing interrupted Claudine's words. Aimee jumped for her purse in relief.

"Hello?"

"Aimee, hey girl! Where you at?" The voice on the other end was muffled by the sound of the other patrons in the coffee shop, but Aimee recognized it at once: Niha, the intern. Her ebullient chatter was unmistakable.

"I'm at lunch with my mother," Aimee said. "It's Friday, remember?"

"Right! Right, yeah. Sorry!" Niha laughed. "You hardly ever go out, so I didn't even think of phoning you until I'd paged you, like, three times." Aimee winced, imagining how the other staff would feel about that.

"Well, you found me," Aimee said. "What's happening?" She crossed her fingers beneath the tabletop, hoping for an emergency that would give her an excuse to leave.

"There was a man here about twenty minutes ago," Niha said cheerily. "He said he needed to talk to you."

"A man?"

"Yes, a man," Niha said. "And a good-looking one too! He seemed disappointed when we couldn't find you."

Aimee glared at her mother who was refilling their cups. It was on her tongue to ask if she'd set this all up, but subterfuge wasn't Claudine's strength. All the same, it didn't make sense. Who would be looking for her? When Aimee had disappeared from the art scene, she'd lost touch with many of the acquaintances who'd done the rounds when she and George were a couple. And Aimee's closest friends from art school lived in Toronto and Vancouver. Who else was there?

"Was he there for a restoration?" Aimee asked. "I told Luis I couldn't finish the Delacroix for at least another week."

"That was my thought too, but he told me he wasn't. Just said he needed to talk to you. Seemed really peeved you weren't here."

"Why?"

Claudine turned, her thin brows rising in interest.

"He didn't give me details," Niha said. "But he told me it was very important." She dropped her voice conspiratorially. "I think he might've been a reporter or something."

Aimee's hand tightened on the phone. She'd been fielding all the reporters to George's agent: Hal Mortinson. It worried her that one had made it through her barriers. "Did he leave a number for me to contact him with?" she asked.

Across from her, Claudine's brows were almost in her hairline. *Who is it?* she mouthed.

"No number," Niha said. "But he promised he'd call back. Like I said, Aimee: he seemed really determined to talk." She paused dramatically. "And he only would talk to you."

—

The retrospective for George Beecher Westerberg was held at Calgary's Gainsborough Gallery, the oldest of the city's many art galleries, and the same one which had represented George for the last three decades of his career. Aimee had left all the arrangements for the affair in the hands of Hal Mortinson, George's agent and dealer, refusing—under the threat of not attending—any part in the ceremonies. Hal had begrudgingly agreed, though he'd given her dark looks all evening. Aimee fought the urge to flip him the finger, but knowing Hal, he would have taken that as an invitation to chat. A piece of conversation Aimee and Hal had once shared in this very room, years earlier, floated to mind.

"You don't mind travelling out from New York for George's openings?" Aimee asked him. "Seems an awful long way to fly."

"Not at all," Hal said. "Besides, it's worth my while. George is a blue chip artist."

"Blue chip?"

Hal slung his arm over Aimee's shoulders, gesturing to the milling crowd. "There's two types of artists in the world. Blue chip and white chip." He winked. "George is one of the blue chips. That makes all the difference."

Aimee pulled away, forcing a smile she didn't feel. Even then, Hal made her uneasy. "What do you mean?"

"Oh, white chips are fine, important even. They're artists, and talented ones at that. But they don't make what sells." He snorted in laughter. "Can't very well put an installation with rotting fruit, or a photograph of dying children in the front entrance of a bank,

but a Westerberg painting, on the other hand. Now that'll bring the money in."

"Money."

Hal grinned, sharklike, at the crowd that circled them. "Blue chip is big money. And George is one of the best."

Aimee frowned as the memory faded. For all George's earnings, he hadn't saved her from money troubles. From her position at the back of the room, Aimee's gaze lingered on the press of people. *Vultures,* her mind whispered. It wasn't easy to make small talk with George's friends and colleagues, but it was endlessly easier than being centre stage. She'd left that to Jacqueline Westerberg-Kinney. George's daughter had done a long, touching speech about her father's life and his importance to the Canadian art scene. It would have been perfect except for one glaring omission: George's widow hadn't been mentioned once.

Eyes smarting, Aimee turned to peer up to the front of the gallery. There near the podium, Jacqueline held court. She laughed and smiled, greeting the throngs of friends and neighbours who had come to pay homage. A New York socialite, her status was embossed on every detail of her attire: she wore a narrow-legged black suit, and a single string of pearls. Her long blonde hair hung in a sheet down her back.

Aimee turned away and lifted her wine glass to her lips, taking another sip. *"Liquid courage"* was what George had called it. Aimee called it coping. There was an open bar, but the thought of bourbon—George's favourite drink—made her stomach roil. Tonight felt more like a celebration than a retrospective. The room was sickeningly hot from the swell of people that filled the downtown gallery, laughing and talking, toasting George's memory.

George would have loved it, she thought, draining her glass for the third time. *Everyone who's anyone is here.*

She scanned the room with a critical eye. Journalists jostled for photographs of George's last works. Artists talked animatedly about the loss to the Canadian art scene. Rich and wealthy patrons spoke in hushed tones about investments. These people she could easily avoid, as they barely acknowledged her existence, however the bevy of acquaintances who patted Aimee's arm as they passed were another matter.

"So sorry to hear about your loss, dear."

"Better it was quick, Aimee. He wouldn't have wanted to linger."

"It gets easier with time. I promise you that."

"Call me if you need anything…anything at all."

Their empty words made her want to scream.

When the final speeches were over, Aimee focused on escape. She had done her duty by attending, but she refused to do more. She set the empty glass on a passing tray. The door to the front was blocked with a who's-who of Calgary high society, but there was an access door at the side. With that in mind, Aimee stepped back, bumping headlong into a man standing behind her.

"Sorry," Aimee said, backing away. "I didn't see you standing there." The room was so full it was impossible to get more than two steps of space.

The stranger turned to glare down at her, and Aimee's voice was lost.

He was in his early thirties, with short black hair, and dark, hooded eyes that spoke of First Nations' heritage. That wasn't what caught Aimee's attention.

Barring the leather jacket and blue jeans, he looked almost *exactly* like the ghost of Eugène Delacroix.

CHAPTER THREE

The woman stared at him for a long moment.

"Sorry, I wasn't watching where I was going." She stepped back, bumping directly into the person behind her. "Sorry!" she squeaked.

Bear smirked. The gallery was filled with people from many countries—a variety of languages buzzed in the air—but you could always tell a true Canadian in a crowd. "It's fine," he said. "No damage done, right?"

"Still, I should watch where I'm walking." She looked around nervously.

"Or don't." Bear shrugged. "Fine by me. I've had worse."

"Right, thanks."

She swiveled in place, seeking escape, but the crowd had them caught in its current and dragged them along.

Bear hated events like this, but research was part of the job. While his unexpected companion glanced right and left, he drew in details: thrift-store clothes, wary eyes, wavy red hair atop a lean frame. There was something familiar about her that he couldn't quite place. The feeling was like a word trapped on his tongue. For a moment an image appeared: her face tipped backward, hair tumbling over her shoulders, but the moment he tried to follow the thought, the picture was gone.

"Have I met you before?" he asked.

"I don't think so."

Bear narrowed his gaze. "You seem familiar. Are you certain we haven't met?"

She blanched. "Just one of those faces I guess."

But he was sure that wasn't it. *Work?* he wondered. But a woman like her—with wide, solemn eyes and pouting lips—he'd definitely remember if he'd interviewed her. It had to be something else. A smile curled up the edges of his mouth, and he offered his hand. "Then let me remedy that," he said. "I'm Bear."

Her gaze dropped to his fingers, then back up. "Bear?" she repeated, not taking his hand.

"Barrett Cardinal," he said, hand outstretched, "but my friends call me Bear."

She frowned as if weighing his words. "Any relation to the *writer* Barrett Cardinal?"

"So you've heard of me." He laughed. "That's surprising."

She took his hand and shook it quickly, then pulled her hand back and crossed her arms. "Of course I have. You won the Giller prize," she said. "I remember that. Calgary pride and all." The first hint of a smile crossed her lips. "I just didn't think you were so young."

The swirl of people shifted like running water. Someone passed nearby, and the two of them stepped closer. Bear nodded to the crowded room. "So what are you doing here?" he asked. While everyone else wore black tie outfits and looked like they were attending a red carpet event, this woman, with her wrinkled jeans and black turtleneck, looked like someone he'd run into in a coffee shop. Someone he'd talk to if he did.

The tentative smile faded into pain. "I came for a friend," she said, dropping his eyes. "I was just leaving, actually. This is all a bit tiresome."

"Art crowd not for you?"

She bit her lip. "No, the art crowd is fine. This many people all together are just too much. You know?"

He nodded. "I do." He pointed to the paintings at the side. "And you're right. The fawning *is* a bit much."

"I suppose I should have expected that," she said glumly. "It's a retrospective after all. That's kind of the point."

"Guess so." He chuckled. "But this sort of send off is a little bit funny, given who the guy was."

The woman's throat bobbed, colour draining from her face. "What?"

"You know, Westerberg," Bear laughed. "Tonight's retrospective. The whole song and dance about him. The guy was beyond talented. I'll give him that! But I've researched his life. Not all of it was as perfect as everyone here is making it out to be. He was so intense he was almost a caricature. And I say this as someone who actually *likes* his art."

"I don't know what you mean."

"Oh come on. Look at his paintings. Beautiful, yes, but overdone. A little pretentious."

"Pretentious."

"Even the themes are overdone," he said dryly. "Nudes and mountain lakes and the like. Christ. His paintings are like the love-child of Tom Thompson and a Leonard Cohen song."

His companion had gone utterly still and she stared at him with doe-like eyes. Long seconds drew out.

"What?" Bear asked warily. "I mean, everyone here loves his work. Heck, I do too! George Westerberg's *the* Canadian artist—I'd kill to own one of his pieces—but everyone takes the guy with a grain of salt, right?"

She tipped her head to the side, birdlike. He remembered that afterwards—how she'd settled near him for a minute—before she'd flown.

"Why would you say that?" she asked.

"I don't know. I suppose because Westerberg was bigger than life. The whole tortured artist routine, troubles with alcohol, tax evasion, a parade of women. And then the whole scandal with his will. He's not—" Bear gestured to the room with the bevvy of fans. "—as perfect as the speeches tonight would suggest."

The woman's expression was brittle, a mask of tight control. It seemed like she was going to do something, say something. Her lips trembled. For a moment he couldn't tell if she was going to burst into tears, or scream at him, and Bear had no idea what he'd do if she did either. Then suddenly she was giggling. She clasped her hand over her mouth, but the laughter broke through her words.

"Tortured artist," she choked. "Oh god, if you only knew!"

He cleared his throat. "I'm sorry, I never meant—"

Her cheeks were flushed. "But you *did* mean it," she gasped. "You did."

"Yeah, but I never would have said anything, if I thought—"

She cackled, the sound sharper than Bear expected. "And you're right," she said. "George was completely pretentious. Totally, utterly focused on his art. Ignorant, even. Everyone else took second place. He didn't love anyone like his artwork. Not friends or family!" Another chortle bubbled up from her chest, but it was high pitched, unnerving. "I never thought about it, but you're right. Totally right!"

The sound of laughter grew into the shrill gasps of hysteria. People around them turned, staring at her as she began to wipe at her eyes. It struck Bear that she was crying—sobbing actually—and he had no idea *why*.

"Look, I'm sorry if I offended you. I didn't mean anything by it."

"It's true!"

"Are you alright? You seem—"

"I'm fine!" she shouted, backing away from him.

"I never meant—"

"I've got to go." She bumped into people as she headed into the crowd, dodging elbows and feet, wiping at her tear-streaked face. "I can't stay."

Bear followed, concern growing as she wove her way into the crowd. "Wait," he called.

The woman's sobs grew louder, the room that had been buzzing seconds before dropped into uneasy silence as everyone turned to watch. A path appeared before her, closing as she passed. An aging man waved a silk handkerchief in a strange pantomime of formal manners. She tore it from him, pressing it to her eyes but not slowing. In seconds she reached a side exit and stepped through. The door was marked 'staff only'. *Someone who works here?* Bear wondered.

Around him, voices returned to conversation, faint murmurs reaching his ears.

"Such a shame..."

"Lovely girl."

"So young to bear such a loss."

Bear glanced up. The entire group was staring at the exit door as if still following the woman's passage. Their whispers rose.

"She was the love of his life, from what I heard."

"One of many," another sneered. "George was hardly a saint!"

"Still, it's so sad. I've heard she's not quite right in the head anymore."

"Anymore? I heard she's always been a bit off."

"Broken by his death."

"Touched. Always has been."

The déjà vu that Bear had felt when he'd first met the woman returned, bringing with it a hint of uneasiness. He tore his gaze from the onlookers, searching through the images that surrounded him. In the alcove where he stood, a group of George Westerberg's smaller works were on display. Bear had passed through this way an hour before, but hadn't spent much time investigating them. Now one came into focus. He staggered toward it.

"Oh shit."

The hair rose on his arms as he read the gallery tag: *Nude portrait; graphite on rag paper, 2002. Aimee en déshabillé, George Westerberg.*

It was the same red-headed woman he'd just spoken with, though her image was softer, less broken, and naked. "A model," Bear murmured, just as another voice—someone deep in conversation—spoke.

"Just tragic, to lose him and then everything else too," a woman said. "Absolutely terrible."

"Very sad, indeed," a man answered.

"And his daughter's been completely awful about it," she added. "Dragged poor Aimee through the courts. Heard the lawyer's fees alone will take whatever she inherits. A total mess."

"Oh dear."

"But that's not the worst—"

Bear stepped between them, interrupting.

"That red-haired woman who just left," he said, gesturing to the now-closed door. "Do you know her?"

The woman nodded, but offered nothing. Her companion lifted his nose in disgust and turned away. "Come along, darling," he said. "I think I'm ready for another drink."

Bear put a gentle hand on the woman's arm before she could follow. "Who is she?" Bear asked, a feeling of dread rising up his chest and choking him. "That woman who ran out of here a moment ago. The woman you were talking about: What's her name?"

The woman gave a sad smile. "That was Aimee Westerberg, dear," she said. "George's young widow."

The words were a blow. A hundred details from Bear's research fell into place and he stumbled back, ears ringing. The woman with the red hair, the woman in the drawing, and the widow he'd been trying to contact for weeks were all one and the same.

—

Aimee left for Banff at dawn.

Attending the retrospective had been a terrible idea. Distraught after the meeting with Barrett Cardinal, she'd stumbled out of the gallery in tears, waving frantically for a cab. Finding none, she'd walked. Reaching home half an hour later, things had grown worse. There was a message from David Arturo about the cabin. The furniture was gone, but the remaining boxes needed to be removed. Would she be coming to do that sometime this weekend? Aimee ran her hands into her hair, fighting the urge to scream. Why was this *her* job, when she didn't even want to sell it?

After David's message, there were three separate voicemails from Hal Mortinson, begging her, in increasingly frantic tones, to call him when she got home. On the third message, he'd mentioned that he'd run into a "very prominent Canadian writer" at George's retrospective. This writer wanted to interview some of Westerberg's friends and family. Would Aimee mind if Hal gave the writer Aimee's contact information?

"Oh Jesus, no," she gasped, deleting the messages. If Bear had talked to Hal, it was only a matter of time before she'd have to deal with him again. But where to go? She needed time to think.

The cabin had always been George's escape. It could be hers too. Drunk and irrational, she briefly considered getting the car from the parking garage and driving to Banff that night, but the thought of sleeping in the cabin and dreaming of George...or perhaps *seeing him* again, terrified her. Instead, she waited out a restless night, sober and angry by the time the sun rose. Aimee was almost certain she could keep her thoughts in order under the glare of daylight. Besides, she needed to check in with David and load up the last of the boxes. One of them included the marred painting George had been working on the day he'd died.

The real estate agent was delighted when she showed up in his office a little after ten. His assistant fed Aimee stale cookies and bitter coffee while David cleared his schedule for the day. From there it was another hour of updates before he dragged her back to the cabin. *I'll be fine*, Aimee told herself as they carried boxes down the driveway to her car. *Just fine. George is gone. I've been to the cabin before.*

"Now that you're here," David said, shifting a box to the other hip, "I thought we might talk about wiggle room."

Aimee popped open the trunk and looked up. "Wiggle room?"

"To get the cabin moving." He set the box inside. "Don't want it sitting on the market too long, and things haven't been going as smoothly as I'd hoped."

"Oh?"

"Drop the price ten percent and we'll definitely see some movement."

"Ten percent of asking?"

"Uh-huh. I've had a potential buyer waiting for a bit. I think that wiggle room would make all the difference to getting an offer."

She frowned. "If you think so."

"I do." He gave a too-wide grin. "You finish up here. Let me make a call."

The movers had taken out the last of the furniture, and the cabin looked bigger than she remembered it. Barring the pile of small boxes near the front door, it could have been anyone's home; there were no pictures on the walls, no clutter to remind her of her husband. Even George's studio had changed. The faint scent of linseed oil lingered in the air, but there was no hint that he'd ever inhabited the place. Sensing that, Aimee relaxed.

Aimee was packing the car with the last boxes of knickknacks when a phone call interrupted. The real estate agent stepped aside, hastily answering.

"David Arturo. How can I help you?"

Maybe it's a buyer for the place, she thought hopefully. There'd been several people interested, but no one had followed through.

"No problem at all," David said. "I'm up at the Westerberg place right now, actually. Did you get my message about the price drop?"

Aimee's chin bobbed up and David gave her a thumbs up, heading back into the house. She tucked the last few items into the car's hatchback, and came back to find him deep in conversation. David was pacing the floor—another good sign, Aimee hoped. She waited in the doorway, uneasy at entering what had once been her favourite spot in the world.

David stopped walking as he saw her. "Alright, Bill," he said. "Well, you just call me back when you're ready." He ran his fingers into his hair, leaving it a spiky mess. "Nope. Not a problem. Any time." David gave Aimee a tight smile. "Not at all. I understand. Bye."

He dropped the phone back into his coat pocket and shrugged.

"An offer?" she asked hopefully. Money would be so much easier if they had that.

"Sorry. No go."

"Even when you told them about the ten percent?"

"Yup. That's why they called back." He rocked on his heels. "It's odd. They'd been sure before, but today they backed out."

Aimee's breath caught. "But why?"

"I can't explain it," David said, gesturing to floor-to-ceiling windows. "I've had more people through this place than any other property this year, but it just doesn't seem to want to sell."

Aimee took a tentative step into the room, glancing warily one direction and the next. It looked like any other high-end house. George had been fastidious about keeping it up to date.

"Any idea what's holding it back?"

David smiled. "Oh, I'm sure it's nothing," he said. "Just a little slump in the market. But now that we've dropped the price to give a little wiggle room, we should be good again."

Upstairs something bumped. Aimee's eyes jerked up to the ceiling, but the real estate agent didn't seem to notice. "Anyhow, I'm certain it'll go as soon as the weather improves," David said. "It's been a really wet spring."

"Are there any other cabins in Banff on the market?" Aimee asked.

"A few."

"And are they selling?"

"Now, Aimee, that's not the same thing at all," David said. "Comparing apples and oranges, practically. This cabin, with the location and all, is well over four million, but the others I've represented have been more reasonably priced and that—"

"Did they sell or not?" she interrupted.

David smiled nervously. "Er…yes."

Upstairs, there was another thud. Aimee looked back up. "What was that?"

"What was what?"

"That sound," Aimee said. "Didn't you hear it?"

David frowned. "No."

Aimee took a hesitant step past the foyer, the wood creaking beneath her feet.

"You have to think about the market," David continued. "It's not like buying a car or something. The weather—as frustrating as it seems—has a hell of a lot to do with pushing through a deal. We had snow last Monday."

There was another bump—a clear footfall—and then another.

"Seriously, David. You heard that one, right?"

"Heard what?"

"The bump," Aimee snapped. "There's someone here."

David shook his head. "I didn't hear a thing."

Aimee crossed her arms, hugging herself tightly. "I'm sure I did."

"Hold on," he said. "I'll run up and take a look." He'd just started to mount the stairs when a figure appeared. Aimee gasped. It was George, smiling down at her as David trudged toward him.

"Might need to think about staging the house," David called over his shoulder.

Aimee stared in mingled fear and pain at George's ghost.

"Put some decorative accents in," David added. "Maybe repaint a few rooms. The trim is getting a little worn in places. Maybe lighten up the kitchen..." The agent's litany of requests continued, but she barely heard them.

"Good to see you, sunshine," George said, his deep baritone echoing down to her. "I was wondering where you'd gotten to. I want to get out to paint today. The sky's full of clouds. Mount Rundle is beautiful right now."

"No!" she cried.

David turned in surprise. "You don't have to repaint it," he said as George reached his side. Aimee wanted to scream, but couldn't. With a bemused smile, George stepped *through* the real estate agent and carried on down the stairs. "But you should do something," David continued, "if you want to move it faster. Freshening up the place is usually all it takes to get it moving. And now that we've dropped a price point like we talked about, there'll be new viewers coming through—"

"The sun's already on the mountain," George said. "A bright cadmium yellow with just a hint of crimson in the edges. But we need to go."

"No," she gasped. David didn't notice; he was still walking up the risers.

George's voice turned chiding. "But it won't last, Aimee," he said, offering his hand. "Come now, love. It's time to go."

She bolted from the cabin with a shriek.

"Aimee? Aimee, you alright?" David shouted from the landing at the top, but she didn't stop until she reached the end of the drive and the car, full of boxes.

"Not real," she whispered. "George isn't real."

But when the curtains moved in the upstairs window, she was too frightened to check if it was David or George looking out at her.

—

Nightfall came early in the mountains, the road from Banff a silver ribbon in the moonlight by the time David locked up the cabin and walked to the end of the driveway to where Aimee waited.

"Call me if you change your mind about staging the cabin," he said.

"Do it," Aimee snapped.

"But I thought you said—"

"Stage it. Repaint it. Drop the price. Do whatever you need," Aimee said, "just get the fucking thing sold."

David stared at her for a long moment, then nodded. "You got it." This time there were no smiles.

The long drive back to Calgary was on mostly empty roads, the mountains disappearing into a wall of black clouds. It was raining again: cold, hard sheets that slashed down against the windows, blurring the road. Aimee gripped the wheel tightly, but didn't slow.

"Nothing to worry about," she muttered under her breath. "I'm fine. Just tired. Overworked. Imagining things." If she repeated it enough, it was true. Wasn't it? For a moment, she could imagine George laughing at her words, but she flicked on the radio, drowning out the sound.

She'd done her duty. The cabin was completely empty. Everything else would be sold or given away. Aimee didn't care. She was beyond that. A new song began and memories rose to displace it. She didn't want to think of George, but the return to Banff had uncovered a festering wound. The hypnotic thrum of the wipers blended with the music and a decade peeled away…

She'd been a student in his Advanced Painting Studio class when she and George had first met. George Westerberg. He was everything she'd wanted to be at that moment in her life: rough, brash, brilliant. That he was a hard drinker, a womanizer, and a tortured artist with a chip on his shoulder, never bothered her.

Alone in the car, Aimee smiled. George Westerberg was bigger than life. Her smile faded. *Or at least he had been.* She wasn't used to thinking of him in past tense.

Under his tutelage, Aimee's skills had grown. George argued with her about everything she'd painted, urging her to improve. In her last semester, he'd invited her to work in his downtown studio, a two-storey walk-up full of students who—like Aimee—wanted the connections and apprenticeship he offered. With floor-to-ceiling windows, air-conditioning and modernist stylings, George's studio was *nothing* like the single room Aimee rented on Stephen Avenue. By summer, she had passed his course and was one of three interns working alongside him. She stretched canvases that George painted, cleaned brushes that George dirtied, and ran errands George was too tired (or too drunk) to manage on his own.

"You're perfect, sunshine," he slurred, as he dumped a pile of used brushes into her waiting hands. "Couldn't manage without you."

She blushed and turned away. Her infatuation with George's talent grew until it spread itself into an infatuation with his very being. Even his fury held glimpses of genius. The near-constant affairs with a parade of women written off as 'passion' and 'artistic temperament' rather than lechery.

Nearing Calgary, the drizzle shifted into a squall. The rain rose in intensity until it was a roar on the car roof. The tires slid and shuddered on the highway's surface, the wipers blurring. George, as he'd been a decade ago, appeared again in Aimee's mind.

She'd been twenty-three that summer, George more than twice that, but they'd 'fit' in a way she didn't understand. (If some part of her knew that he'd been a replacement father for her own dead one, Aimee ignored the thought.) She remembered watching George scrape a painting down, and rebuild it layer after layer. The process amazed her, and at some point she realized she would never be as good as he was. *It was impossible.* But she was drawn to him anyhow. Even the unsettled side of him—George's obsession with painting and drinking and the rages that alarmed her and the other interns—didn't scare her away.

Aimee loved him.

The sudden insight terrified her at the time. She worried he might discover her burgeoning feelings. George was unhappily married—yet married all the same—but he'd never noticed the change. George had his turbulent life, and she had hers. The studio where they spent their days together was neutral ground.

Aimee tapped the brakes as traffic slowed, her memories of George and their studio days fading as she focused on the growing number of vehicles on Calgary's edge. Reaching the city centre, traffic thickened to a crawl. Aimee peered through the windshield to the river as traffic finally came to a standstill. The water in the Bow river was dangerously high, banks crumbling with wet mud. A man and a shivering dog walked passed. Aimee watched the two of them skirt the high water, moving from the sodden grass to more solid ground. Cars inched through the river-bottom, leaving her thoughts to roam.

She'd graduated from ACAD in May. By the time September rolled around, George hired her full time. He had an opening coming up in December, and needed the help. She "*knew his work*" and could put up with his tantrums. Either way, their closeness grew. They were more than friends, on the brink of *something* until that night.

The opening had changed everything.

A car's horn blared, bringing her back to the present, and Aimee reflexively hit the brakes, her hands white-knuckled on the wheel. The traffic moved another car length forward, and she turned on the defrost, waiting as the glass cleared, showing the dismal spring weather. Beside her, the rain-swollen river raged.

The night of George's opening, they'd left arm and arm, and never let go. George and Aimee had fallen together, fucking in her apartment, in his studio, in the back rooms of galleries. Everywhere. There was no end to their needs. No way to stop it.

The traffic light outside the window changed and someone honked. Aimee tapped the gas, her thoughts pulled back to the present. Driving toward the condo in the growing dark, a new thought intruded in Aimee's mind: If George's demon had been drink, then her demon had been George.

—

Bear lifted the phone and set it down again.

On the couch, Leo, an aging Husky with a grizzled muzzle and a coat like a molting camel, snored quietly, oblivious to his owner's discomfort. Bear had always been a "dog person." Growing up on the Tsuut'ina reserve outside Calgary, a never ending list of mutts had wheedled into his heart through the years. When he moved to cow-town, as his rural cousins called it, he'd found himself lost. The only unbreakable requirement on his first apartment had been that it allow pets. Leo had been sprung from the local animal shelter two days later.

A minute crawled by, then another. Bear glared at the sheet of grey sky beyond the windows.

"Goddamnit," he muttered. The dog's ears perked up at Bear's words, but he didn't move.

For the fourth time in an hour Bear had started to call, and changed his mind. *You have her number*, a voice inside him murmured. He flexed his fingers, fighting the tension that had been mounting for the last twenty-four hours. *Just call.* He lifted the receiver again, glancing at the details he'd collected. Her name was written in his own, scratching hand, a shorthand of a grief-filled life next to it.

Aimee Tessier Westerberg. Age: 35. Born: Montreal, Quebec.

Mother, living. Father, deceased. Attended the Alberta College of Art and Design for her undergraduate degree. Completed a Master of art conservation degree at Queens University. Second wife to George Westerberg. Restorations expert by trade.

His eyes dropped to the next line.

Widowed.

Beneath it was her private number, unearthed by the old standby of schmoozing George's agent, Hal Mortinson. Bear scowled. He hating having to do that—it made him feel dirty—but Aimee had been purposefully avoiding him and the book wasn't going to write itself.

With a sigh, he dialled for the fifth time, lifting the receiver to his ear before he could change his mind. The phone rang twice before being interrupted by the booming growl of a man's voice.

"*You've reached the Westerberg residence,*" the recording announced. "*If this is regarding a commission, please contact Hal Mortinson. New purchases can be made through The Gainsborough Gallery...*"

The voice had a deep rumble—arrogance in the rolled r's—but it was warm too. Bear had heard it on the many interviews he'd watched in the last weeks, as he prepared for what should have been an easy biography to write. But George Westerberg wasn't an easy person to look up, and it seemed his wife wasn't either.

"*If you're looking for me, just stay on the line and leave a message.*" There was a chuckle. "*If I like you, I'll get back to you. If not...well, you know what that means.*" Hearty laughter followed.

Bear frowned. There was no mention of Aimee at all.

The phone began beeping down the seconds and Bear cleared his throat, ready for a brief spiel. Suddenly there was a crackle and a woman's voice interrupted.

"Hello?"

"Aimee, hi," he said, his calm unexpectedly shattered. "It's Barrett Cardinal. We met the other night." Bear closed his eyes, praying. "I was wondering if we could talk."

—

Aimee couldn't breathe, couldn't think.

"Aimee?" the voice repeated. "You there?"

She took a choking breath. It was the man from George's retrospective. *Barrett Cardinal*, a voice inside her chattered. *The writer from Calgary. Winner of the Giller prize.* It was the same man who'd been trying to contact her at work. She'd left for Banff to avoid him and now he'd found her.

She opened her mouth, but no sound came out.

"Mrs. Westerberg. Are you okay, ma'am?"

Somehow that word—*ma'am*—so strangely out of place, unblocked her throat. Aimee took a wheezing gasp, chest releasing. "Yes, I'm here. Sorry. I was just…" She couldn't even come up with a lie.

There was the sound of papers rustling. "I'm sincerely sorry to bother you, ma'am," Bear said formally—so different from the person she'd talked to that if he hadn't introduced himself she wouldn't have recognized his voice. "But I really need to talk to you."

"How did you get this number?"

His voice lost the steady tone. "I called the Glenbow first. I did. But when I couldn't get in contact with you, Hal Mortinson gave me your number. I hope that's alright. This is strictly professional."

Aimee's fingers tightened into a claw around the handset. "Hal did, huh?"

"Yes, and I'm sorry for intruding," Bear continued, "but I'm working on a project about your husband—a book project, to be precise, about his life and impact on Canadian art. And while most of it can be done with items I can access from public archives, my publisher has decided that the book needs to include some insights into your husband's personal life."

The room swam, and Aimee caught herself against the edge of the kitchen counter. Her fingers tightened around the phone. "Personal? What do you mean?"

"Friendships mainly, relationships with people he knew, family members and the like," Bear said, his tone easing. "The initial research regarding Mr. Westerberg's painting is done. The facts, I mean, but now I'm looking into the human aspect of his life."

Outside, the wind rose, thunder growling over the river valley which sheltered the downtown in its centre. The noise of the storm came alongside Aimee's panic, bellowing gusts shuddering the windows. Amid the wave of vertigo, a single thought grabbed her, held her still. The slanderous gossip about her relationship with George. She'd been half his age when they met, and George had been married. Though his marriage to Margot had been close to breakdown for years—George entangled in a string of affairs—he'd ended things permanently at the same time Aimee became his muse. People still judged her for that transgression.

"I'm not sure if I can," she choked. "I mean, I'm sure George's daughter, Jacqueline, would talk to you but—"

"Please," he pleaded. "It wouldn't take long. A couple interviews at most."

"I don't know." Aimee's hand was sweaty where she held the handset, heart thudding. She hadn't felt this blinding terror since the day George had died. The rain outside the windows was a roar against the glass. A white claw of lightning slashed the sky followed a heartbeat later by a clap of thunder. The phone line crackled.

"Hello, Aimee? You still there?"

"Yes. I'm here."

Another rumble of thunder matched by static.

"Please," Bear said, his voice so low she almost missed it in the clamour. "Just give me a chance to explain this all in person." His voice dropped by half. "And to apologize for being so rude regarding Mr. Westerberg at the gallery. And then decide if you—" The last of his words were lost as another flash lit up the room, chased by a deafening peal of thunder. The lights flickered and went out.

Aimee glanced up, heart in throat. The condo was silent, the steady hum of motors, gone. The darkness drew closer, pressing down on all sides. Only the faint sound of Bear's breathing on the other end of the telephone remained.

"Aimee? Can you hear me? I think the phone's—"

Lightning flashed the room like a camera, burning her retinas, followed almost immediately by a resounding boom. Aimee screamed, and dropped the handset.

In that moment between the flash and the thunder, she'd seen George in the shadows.

CHAPTER FOUR

Night passed. More rain fell.

The phone rang twice, but Aimee didn't answer.

In the morning there was a short message from Bear—who assumed he'd been cut off by the storm—but she didn't return the call. What could she say? The lightning had faded, but the rain was stubbornly settled onto the city. *God, I just need the sun for day... an hour*, Aimee thought as she struggled through the Monday doldrums. By mid-week, there was a rainfall warning.

"Morning, sunshine," George whispered as she woke each morning. "It's beautiful out today."

Aimee's memories of George had become a physical thing, pooling in the condo they'd decorated together, a flood of pain—held back for too many months of ice—rising inch by inch. She could imagine him everywhere—the study, the kitchen, the bedroom—and the more Aimee looked, the more she could sense him there. Feel him. She couldn't keep him away without effort.

"Aimee," he whispered in the darkness. "I know you can hear me."

What if I stop trying to keep the thoughts away? her mind asked. It was the same thing she'd felt as an intern, working in George's studio, thinking about all the things that could go wrong if she gave in to her desires. Then, like now, the idea excited and terrified her.

Can't do this. Can't keep imagining he's here. He's dead... dead... DEAD.

Late at night, when sleep wouldn't come, she could hear George moving through the condo, rustling through drawers and pulling items out of his desk. *Stop it. He's not real!* Aimee squeezed her eyes shut, focusing on the sound of the never-ending rain instead. She counted raindrops and tiles and even sheep, the coping mechanisms she'd built as a child.

Still the ghost tormented her.

She filled her hours with as many tasks as she could manage, fearful of what she'd see if she didn't. She arrived at the Glenbow at dawn each day, working through lunch in an effort to be free of George. Work let her imagination go free, while keeping George at bay. It was easier to imagine Eugène Delacroix with his arrogant, snipped comments about her work, rather than her late husband.

"You're rushing," Delacroix grumbled. "The strokes are too long. Too flashy. Patience, girl. *Écoute-moi!*"

"I'm no girl!" she snapped. "And those strokes are exactly like yours."

He threw his hands in the air with a snort of exasperation. "Hardly! They're a mess. Look at them! A child could do better. Garbage!"

"They're not," she said through clenched teeth. "They're just—"

"*Sacre bleu!* Why bother, if you're doing it wrong? They are awful!"

"Damnit, Bear. Give me a second and I'll—"

Her eyes flicked up as she realized what she'd said. Cheeks flushed with annoyance, her imagined Delacroix really *did* look like the wayward author, petulant full lips, broad jaw, wildly passionate eyes. She remembered Bear's words from the gallery: "*Oh come on. Look at his paintings. Beautiful, yes, but overdone. A little pretentious.*" It felt like a betrayal to admit she agreed with much of that. Guilt rose as she blotted away the last few strokes and started again.

Each day another phone message from Barrett Cardinal accumulated. Another thing she wouldn't deal with. She closed her eyes, focusing her attention on the painting and the flicked lines on the unmarred canvas. She took a slow breath and restarted the patch.

"Better," Eugène said after a moment. "I knew if you slowed down, you'd see that I'd—"

"Oh fuck off," Aimee snapped. "No one wants you here anyhow."

The ghost let out a shocked gasp. Aimee ignored him. In twenty minutes, she'd finished the revised brush strokes and she sat peering from one side and the other. They really *were* better.

"There," she sighed. "It's fixed now, Eugène. You happy?"

The ghost unfolded his long legs from where he'd been lounging atop a cabinet. He jumped down from his perch with the grace of an alley cat, and joined her at the table.

His lips pursed as he inspected her work. "I suppose it'll do," he said sourly.

Aimee smirked. *Artists*. They were all the same.

—

By Thursday, the damaged Delacroix painting was completely repaired, and Aimee was working on reframing a faded Frida Kahlo painting which had been donated by a wealthy patron. She wanted to imagine Frida here, wanted to talk to her, and hear *her* imagined voice, but Aimee's ghosts could be a stubborn lot and Frida had yet to appear. Sometimes it took weeks to call them to her.

Delacroix sulked in the corner, picking his dirty fingernails with a paring knife while she took the frame apart.

"So are you going to see him again?" the ghost asked.

Aimee's gaze flicked up, and back to the rusty frame. "See who?"

"The writer. Bear." Delacroix rolled his eyes. "You've been thinking about making the call for a week."

"Have not," she grumbled, working at the edge of the frame with a chisel.

"Liar. You think no one knows what goes on in your head," the artist taunted. He tossed the silver blade in the air and caught it again. "But I *do*."

Aimee let out a weary sigh. "Go away, Eugène. Your painting is finished. I don't need you anymore," she grunted, pressing down into the edge. With a snap, the metal plate was unbound, and the first corner released. The others followed in quick succession.

"You should talk to the man," he said. "Find out what he wants."

"Shut up! You're distracting me."

Delacroix let out a loud snort. "*Impossible!* You're the one imagining *me*. Not the other way around."

Frustrated, she glared at him over the top of the frame. "Fine. Then be quiet."

He hovered at the edge of her perception, distracting her with his inspection. Sometimes it took days to be done with someone she'd imagined into being. She knew how to *bring* them, just not how to let them go. Eugène was fading, but not fast enough.

She lifted the backing off. "Oh for Christ's sake!"

"What is it?" Delacroix asked.

She shoved the frame aside with a grunt. "Some fool taped up the back. Look at the mess."

"Awful," he tutted. "That's going to be a challenge for your—" His brow rose. "—skills."

He turned away, strolling off and melting into the shadows. The ghost wasn't quite as clear as he'd been earlier, the light sifting through him, dust motes appearing where he passed. These days his resemblance to Bear was less clear. Eugène had faded, whereas the writer was all too real.

"Nothing to it but to do it," Aimee muttered, heading to the cabinet for supplies.

She covered the age-brittle tape with purified water and cotton wool. It would take at least a day for the tape to soak it up and loosen, so there was nothing else she could do.

Half an hour later, the studio was unexpectedly quiet. Noticing, Aimee lifted her gaze, peering through the room: Eugène Delacroix was finally gone.

"About time," she sighed, though there was a pang of disappointment at the silence that greeted her.

She pulled on her jacket. "Goodbye, Eugène," she whispered, "and hello Frida."

There was no answer.

It was near seven when Aimee headed home in the rain. The answering machine's light was flashing as she walked into the condo, a beacon in the darkness.

The first was from George's agent: "*Hello, Aimee. It's Hal calling. I was wondering if you could give me a shout when you have a minute. I've an idea about George's last series I'd like to run by you. There's a gallery in Prague which would like to do its own retrospective. I can give you details later, but I need your okay. I have a few other things, too…*" His voice rose the way it did when he was lying. Aimee's jaw clenched. What was he pulling now? "*But nothing too pressing. I'll just wait for your call and we can talk. Later then!*"

The second message was from David Arturo, the real estate agent: "*Aimee, hi! David here. I contacted the guys about staging the cabin and touching up the paint, but the rain's put a real damper—*" He laughed at his own joke. "*—on anyone coming or going. Water's kind of high in the river. So just be patient, alright? I'll get it set up. No worries.*"

There were two more empty messages where someone had called, but had not stayed on the line long enough to answer. She scrolled through the sender list; the number was private. *Barrett Cardinal*, she thought in exasperation. At some point she'd have to deal with him.

Not tonight.

Aimee cleared all the messages and dropped her sodden clothes in a pile. She'd deal with them later. Ignoring the growls of her stomach, she headed to the living room, flopping down on the couch and turning on the television. A riot of images, and flashing red warnings along the bottom of the screen, greeted her. The news was full of images of rising water and flood watches.

"Shit," she grumbled, flicking it off, and closing her eyes.

Around her, the apartment was full of sound: slashes of rain splashed against the window frames, the clock ticked on the mantle, people in the hallway laughed, a door a floor above closed. *Somewhere, George was laughing at her.* She winced, as another memory rose, to join the patter of raindrops against the window, buzzing in the room.

She knew that sound.

—

Heart racing, Aimee stood in the crowded room, watching George Westerberg, her once-professor, *watching her*. People stepped between them, chattering, but it felt like a line of tension had been drawn between their two gazes. Seconds passed, but Aimee didn't step forward or back. There was power in her choice. She wasn't *just* his assistant. There was something else boiling under the surface.

Tonight she'd wait for *him* to make a move.

"Aimee, Aimee, Ai-mee..." George murmured as he sauntered closer. She was trapped by his eyes; couldn't move. "Must say, you look all grown up in that dress."

The smile Aimee gave him was coy. "I always was grown up. You've finally noticed." George's eyes widened and he grinned. He moved a half-step closer, and Aimee's throat caught. She wanted to run—which made no sense at all—but she wanted to stay more. She'd been half-in-love with him forever, and now she had his attention.

All of it.

George leaned in, his mouth almost against her ear. It could be two friends chatting in a crowded gallery, Aimee thought, but she knew that wasn't true. "What say we move along?" George murmured. "Grab a drink or something." He smelled of bourbon and cologne, his stubbled jaw scratching her cheek.

Aimee shook her head, tossing her curls. "I think everything's closed by now," she laughed. "Your best bet for a drink is probably here."

"Ah," he said with a wink, "but I know where we can find our own bottle."

She swallowed hard, forcing her voice to be steady. He couldn't *seriously* be thinking of taking her back to his house. Perhaps, she thought, he meant the studio downtown. Yes, she decided, that made sense. George always had a bottle on hand while he painted.

"Do you have a car?" she asked warily. "I could drive us."

"Nah," he chuckled. "I walked here."

"Walked?" George lived in the bedroom community of Chestermere.

"Margot kicked me out a few weeks ago," he said with a mischievous grin, like he was admitting to stealing candy, not the end of a decades-old marriage. "My new apartment's just up the street."

"I'm sorry, George," she stammered. "I didn't know. You never said."

His eyes moved down her frame, lingering. "Don't be sorry, sunshine. I'm not." George let that sit for a few seconds, then held out his hand, nodding to the door. "Let's walk." It wasn't a question.

Aimee slid her fingers into his, letting him lead her away. The pounding of her heart was so loud she could hear it in her ears.

It was barely raining when they left the opening, but by the time they were halfway to George's apartment, it had begun to pour. The moisture, pent up in the heat of the day, released in torrents, soaking them as they navigated the slick streets. Everything had darkened to a deep shining black, the snap of fat, wet drops onto the asphalt around them lifting a grey layer of mist into the air by their feet. The two of them—red and grey-haired—ran side by side through the rain, clinging together, George holding his wet jacket over their heads.

"Oh Lord!" he cackled. "We're going to get soaked."

"Who cares!" Aimee shouted, buoyed by the sheer joy of being alive. Danger and excitement mingling.

There was a sudden flash of lightning and for a split second, everything around them was lit like a camera's flash. George's hair had flattened to his head like a cap, his wet shirt clinging to his body, making him look more like a carved sculpture than a man. He had a boxer's broad-shouldered build. Wet, his hair looked dark, peeling back the years, dragging him from his middle years, and leaving him closer to her age. That made her bold. Aimee's fingers tightened within his just as a deafening boom of thunder almost directly overhead, broke the bowl of the sky.

George shouted something Aimee couldn't hear—her ears were ringing—and then he tugged on her arm, leading her off the street, and into an alley where he pulled her into the shallow overhang of an old brick building. He slid his jacket back onto his shoulders, urging her closer to the wall where the overhang offered the most protection. George leaned in, his body tight against hers as they struggled to stay dry. He was close, *too close*. Again, the urge to run fluttered to life, but Aimee stayed. Heat came off of him in waves, contrasting with the icy rush of rain.

Another crack of lightning lit the sky, crackling her ears and burning her eyes. The sound of thunder shattered against the buildings, bouncing in the narrow alley where they stood.

The ridiculousness of the situation—trapped two blocks from George's apartment, five from the studio—left her giggling. Hearing the sound, George moved closer still, his mouth suddenly against her neck, sucking his way down from her jaw. His hands slipped around Aimee's waist, encircling her hips. The sensations of his hot mouth against her cold skin sent frissons of electricity through her.

"Oh god," she gasped. She'd imagined this exact moment too many times to count. But now it had arrived…

George's teeth nipped hard. Aimee yelped as his fingers rucked up the bottom of her skirt, pulling the soaked fabric up over her hips until bare brick brushed the back of her legs. His other hand tugged roughly at her sheer top, sliding it over one shoulder, exposing her breast. Aimee gasped, tasting rain, as George's thumbs caught on the edge of her bra and pulled it aside, the pads of his rough fingers moving against the sensitive skin of her breasts.

"Beautiful," he murmured against her skin. "Perfect…fucking perfect." His teeth caught against the edge of her collarbone as he spoke again. "Like marble."

"George," she gasped. "I think we should get inside."

Another flash of lightning lit the sky, and his answer was lost in the thunder.

George's motions grew harder and less controlled, fingers pinching sharply for a moment, then releasing. Aimee writhed as pain and passion mixed. He looked up for a split second, slanting his mouth down against hers before she'd caught her breath. There was another crack of lightning, lighting the two of them where they stood, clinging together against the rough wall. Aimee's mind, reeling from the kiss, counted out the seconds as George's tongue invaded her mouth, sliding against her teeth and tongue, his lips crushed against hers in bruising intensity. *One Mississippi... Two Mississippi... Three Mississippi... Four Miss—*

The boom caught her off guard and she jumped, her hands tightening against his neck.

"I want you, Aimee," George growled against her mouth.

Her dress was a tangle, the skirt wadded up around her waist, the top hanging open, bra undone. Everything Aimee'd imagined in the months she'd worked in George Westerberg's studio was happening—*happening now!*—and she had no idea how to keep up with him. This was what she wanted, wasn't it?

She wrapped her arms over his shoulders as he leaned against her—the thin layers of fabric doing nothing to dispel the growing desire between them. George's knee pushed her thighs apart, his hardness grinding against her, a sharp point of tension increasing with each passing second. The rain came down in pounding waves, the sound of it like static. The building's overhang only provided meagre cover and Aimee was drenched, her body growing colder by the second. The rain came off the roof in a solid sheet, blocking them off from the rest of the city. George's mouth explored the skin of her neck, then moved downward, seeking out one nipple and then the other, sucking hard. The cold fingers of his hands ran over her body, caressing in time to the lathing of his tongue. Overwhelmed by sensation, Aimee's head thudded back against the brick and she moaned. A sudden flash of lightning crossed the sky in a great, pink arc, leaving a blue afterimage burned across her vision for seconds afterwards.

George's fingers dropped down to her waist, tugging impatiently at the rain-soaked fabric of her panties. Her fingers were trapped in his hair, lost in the feel of his mouth against her breasts. But without his heat against her, Aimee's neck and arms rose in gooseflesh, shivers racking her body as much in reaction to George's touch as to the chill air. He was fire, but she'd turned to ice.

He glanced up at her, his ruddy face contorting in worry. "Christ, Aimee," he said, pulling her skirt back down into place and standing. "You're freezing!"

"N-nah," she lied through chattering. "I'm j-just fine."

She gave him a wide smile, reaching out for him again, but her shivers gave her away.

George pulled his soaked jacket off and guided her into it. "I'm so sorry," he said, the frown of concern making him look older than he'd seemed minutes before. *Fatherly.* This was the serious side to George Westerberg she knew from his time as her professor. *The adult again.* She smiled seeing it, and the worry in the centre of her chest began to ease.

"How f-far?" she asked through chattering teeth.

"What?"

"How far to your apartment?"

He stared at her for the count of three heartbeats. He too was deciding this. Weighing his choice.

"Two blocks," he finally answered, his voice almost lost in the din of the rain. "Ready to make a run for it?"

Aimee nodded, her fingers slipping into George's hand. She kissed him once, almost chastely, a promise of more to come.

"Then let's get going!" Aimee said.

And they stepped out past the edge of the overhang back into a world of water.

—

The phone on the table next to her rang and Aimee jerked her eyes open, gasping for air. The memory had been so bright— so real—she'd almost forgotten where she was. Tears pooled on her lower lashes.

God, I miss you, George.

The rain against the windows had grown to a malevolent growl. Somewhere in the condo, she could hear the sound of dripping. A window? The roof? She knew she needed to contact the Super to repair it, but she couldn't seem to make herself move these days. Couldn't do anything other than think.

The phone rang again, and Aimee jumped. She turned, checking the number before answering, but it wasn't an outside call at all. It was the front door. Frowning, she picked up the handset.

"Hello?" she said warily.

"Aimee? Goodness, cherie! What took you so long!" Claudine said. "I've been standing down here for ages!"

Not Bear after all. Aimee sighed, wondering whether it was disappointment or relief that she was feeling.

"Hey, Mom. Give me a sec and I'll let you in."

—

Claudine stood in the doorway, a pile of packages in one hand, a steaming casserole in the other.

"What took you so long to answer your buzzer?" her mother asked.

"I couldn't find the phone," Aimee lied. "But you should really call before you come over, Mom. What if I was at work?"

Her mother bustled past her, uninvited. "Oh, I called Niha before I left," she said, dropping items onto the kitchen counter. "I knew you left on time today." Her mother peered over her shoulder. "She said you looked tired."

Aimee sighed. So Niha was in on the *keep Aimee together* plot too.

At the counter, Claudine was pulling down plates from the cupboard. The smell was rich and homey, but to Aimee's empty stomach it was unappealing.

"You don't need to do this, Mom," she sighed. "I can take care of myself."

"I'm your mother. I need to do everything." She pulled out one of the chairs, pointing to it. "Come on, come on. Sit down and eat," she ordered. "Maintenant, ma fille."

"I'm fine."

"Far from it," her mother snorted. She pointed at the chair. "Come now. Eat."

Aimee plodded forward, slumping down. "I'm not hungry," she said tiredly. "I'm grieving."

"And I'm worried about it."

"It's normal, Mom. I can't just pretend to be okay."

Her mother scooped food onto plates, then dropped the spoon into the sink and frowned. Aimee knew she was going to say something stupid right before she spoke.

"Why don't you come to Mass with me this Sunday?" Claudine asked.

"Mom, please," Aimee groaned. "I can't."

Her mother pulled out a chair, sliding in beside her. "Aimee, if you could just put your faith in God, He'd help you."

Aimee shook her head. They'd had *this* fight when she'd been a teenager too: Claudine's insistence that the death of Aimee's father had been 'God's will' had driven a wedge between them that lingered to this day. Divine planning was something Aimee had never believed in. The death of George had only solidified this.

"No, Mom. God wouldn't."

"But if you only had faith—"

"You *know* I don't believe in a God."

"Aimee!" Claudine gasped.

"I don't." Aimee let out an angry laugh. "I never have."

"That's not true. You used to believe in—"

"How, Mom?" Aimee retorted, her voice rising. "How could there be a God?"

Claudine's face was rapt in horror. "Oh now, you don't mean that."

Aimee's hands clenched into fists next to her plate. She hadn't felt like this since she was a child, fighting about going to church. "I do, actually. You just aren't listening." Aimee's jaw clenched. "You never did."

Claudine's chest rose and fell in rapid gasps, her cheeks bright circles of colour. "I can't believe you're saying this," she said. "I raised you to respect the Church, to—"

"Enough!"

Here, again, was the same argument. *God has his reasons.* Aimee was fifteen again, railing against her mother's constant optimism in the face of widowhood.

Claudine stood, the chair screeching out behind her. "You're upset," she said, going to the cupboard, looking for something, though Aimee had no idea what. "You're saying things you don't mean." Her voice wavered.

"I do mean it," Aimee said, deflated.

Claudine pulled out a drawer, and found a serving spoon. She carried another covered dish to the table, ladling more onto Aimee's already-full plate. "Here. I made a tourtière. Have some; it's your favourite." She smiled down at Aimee.

"Mom, I'm not hungry."

"You don't *know* you're hungry," Claudine insisted. "But eat, ma petite. Eat."

Aimee's shoulders rolled forward, the weight of her mother's love pressing down onto her like the night, the rain, even the apartment and the memory of George which wouldn't let her be. She knew she *should* appreciate the help, but she couldn't. Claudine didn't understand. She never had. Never would.

"If I eat, will you go away?" Aimee asked quietly.

Her mother's smile faltered. She leaned in and kissed Aimee's cheek. Her eyes, Aimee saw, glittered with tears. That, too, was a weight. *I always let her down.*

"I love you, Aimee. And yes, I'll go."

Aimee took a bite, burning her tongue. She chewed the tasteless bite, and swallowed it down. *Just like being a teen again.* Pretending she was okay. Living a life that wasn't real. She fought the urge to open her mouth to show her mother it was gone. She couldn't taste anything.

"Mmm," Aimee said, trying to force some life into her voice. "It's good, Mom. Delicious."

The pain in Claudine's face faded. "It's your grandmother's recipe. I knew you'd like it." She reached into her bag, pulling out a bottle. "Now, what you need is a nice glass of wine to go with it," she said, surveying the kitchen. "Where do you keep your wine glasses?"

Aimee nodded to the cupboard above the stove. "George keeps them—" Her words stumbled to an uneasy stop. "They're over there."

—

Bear balanced the phone's handset on his shoulder as he scrolled down the computer screen.

"I think that's about it then," Bear said. "I appreciate your time, Mrs. Westerberg-Kinney."

"My pleasure," Jacqueline said, her cultured voice ringing through the headset. "And if there is anything else I can help you with, you just let me know."

"I will, and thank you."

"No problem, at all. I just want to make sure this book is done right."

Bear's smile tightened. He was glad this had been a conference call rather than a face to face meeting. There he had to be careful with more than just his words. "And I'm sure this goes without saying," Bear said smoothly, "but I want the entire truth."

"Absolutely," she sniffed. "What else would there be?"

Bear's mouth turned down at the edges. He'd met her only once, but he knew Jacqueline wasn't telling him everything. "Nothing," Bear said. "You've given me plenty to start with. But if you think of something more, please call."

"I will."

In seconds, they'd said their goodbyes and the interview was over. As he hung up the phone, Leo sat up on the couch, shaking himself awake. Bits of fur twirled in the air before settling like snow on the cushion. Bear shook his head with a weary chuckle. No matter how many times he brushed him, the dog shed year-round. Sensing Bear's attention, the Husky jumped off the couch and padded over to him.

"I know, I know," Bear said. "She was a talker."

Leo bumped his hand under Bear's palm and whined. "Yes, buddy. Just about done." He rubbed the loose skin on the dog's head. "You ready for a walk?"

Leo barked happily, then bounded to the back door.

"I said just about," Bear laughed. "Hold on a sec. I want to check my notes first."

There was the sound of scratching.

"Leo..." Bear warned.

The dog padded back into the room, giving him a baleful look before laying down at Bear's feet. "I'm not lying," he chuckled. "Just a minute though."

The dog let out a snort of disbelief before putting his head atop Bear's foot.

"Promise."

Bear leaned closer to the screen and began to scroll. The notes were a mish-mash of details, gleaned during the conversation, other bits added from previous research: George Westerberg, deceased, age 59. Nearest living relatives: daughter Jacqueline Westerberg-Kinney, 34; ex-wife Margot Westerberg, 57; and widow, Aimee Westerberg (née Tessier), age 35.

She was the odd one out; the clue that not everything was as rosy as Jacqueline seemed determined to present. *Mentally ill or grieving?* Bear wondered. The accounts varied.

Though he'd researched for months, there were items which made no sense. Why, for instance, was Westerberg's will so complex? What had spurred him to change it months before his death? There were enough loopholes that several recipients—including his daughter Jacqueline—had contested the document. Everyone, it seemed, wanted part of the pie. Only George's widow, Aimee, had refused to fight. *At first*, Bear amended. She'd ignored the situation until the last minute, when the gravity had become clear. Her belated attempts to deal with the will's havoc had resulted in her own minimal compensation. Even that was no longer assured.

The latest interviews had given Bear a sketch of George's final years, but there were still more questions than answers. A cursor hovered next to a growing list.

Why didn't Westerberg inform either his wife or his daughter that he'd altered his will?

Why was Aimee Westerberg getting so little from a supposedly large estate? And what exactly did Jacqueline think Aimee was hiding?

Who or what was the unnamed "charity" recipient Westerberg had set up? And why were the details of the charity kept so cloak and dagger? Did Aimee know about it?

He drummed his fingers on the desk. One name kept reappearing. One person who could answer what others couldn't.

"Aimee Westerberg," Bear murmured. "Why won't you sit down and talk to me?" He knew the answer, of course. The retrospective had been a disaster, but he had tracked her down afterwards. Trouble was, when the storm had cut off their phone conversation, she'd never answered for him again. He'd nudged Hal Mortinson over it, but even he couldn't get Aimee to take his calls.

Bear grimaced. There was no use denying it. He'd had a chance and he'd lost it.

"Screwed that one up good, didn't I?" he said, addressing the dog at his feet.

Leo whined, lifting his head and looking longingly at the door, his tail thumping on the floor. Bear patted the dog's head and looked back to the screen. "Jacqueline's interview is good enough for a start," he said quietly, "but she's not objective. Too worried about how Daddy dear is going to look in print." He scrolled past her clearly-rehearsed answers. There was little discussion of her father's last years and no mention of George's last wife whatsoever. "Wonder if those answers will mesh with everyone else's."

Bear had been through the list of George Westerberg's friends, family and acquaintances more than once. He had enough—more than enough—to write the last chapters of the man's life. Aimee Westerberg's absence wasn't impossible to write around, but it felt wrong.

"If I can just get Aimee to—"

Leo barked, louder this time, jarring Bear from his thoughts. With a sigh, Bear hit save and stood from the desk. The dog's barking grew more insistent, his toenails tapping on the floor in an excited dance.

"Yes, Leo," he laughed. "No more research. It's time for a walk." He slapped his pantleg and a dust storm of dog hair rose from the fabric. "And maybe a little bit of grooming too."

The dog bounded away, leaving Bear to follow. He paused as he picked up the leash, a sudden thought appearing like a flame in the dark recesses of his mind. His fingers tightened.

If Aimee Westerberg hadn't contested the will, perhaps she was the recipient of the charity fund.

—

Alone, Aimee traded the wine glass for a tumbler, filling it to the top. She wasn't tired enough to sleep—not yet—she needed something to dull the pain. Even the television was a layer of grit against frayed nerves. Pictures of flooded waterways and rivers at the top of their banks filled every local channel. It reminded her too much of her first night with George. After a few minutes of channel surfing she flicked to a movie she'd already seen, and lay on the couch, shivering.

It was an old black and white film. She and George had seen it years before at some retro film festival held in Banff. She hadn't thought of it since she and George had sat in the mostly-empty theatre, groping as much as watching the actors on the screen. Watching the film now was like walking into a movie of what their life had once been, but was no longer. She took another swallow of wine, remembering how easy it had been…how happy.

The chill in the air had invaded the condo, but she was too exhausted to fight with the auto settings on the furnace. She tucked her feet under herself, wrapping her arms around her knees as she finished one tumbler and started another. The alcohol didn't warm her, but it softened the sounds. The movie seemed slower, the edges of the images blurring like the ghosts she so often imagined. Today, Frida had finally appeared after weeks of coaxing. The ghost hadn't spoken, but had sat, silently leaning on her cane as she watched Aimee work on the damaged artwork. Aimee didn't know if she was there because Aimee'd thought her up—she didn't recall trying to bring her into being—and if Aimee had done it unintentionally, why Frida wasn't speaking. Almost all Aimee's ghosts had a reason for arriving, but not her. Frida just watched. Having her there was a comfort, however, no matter how silent she remained.

Laughter echoed distantly and Aimee blinked blurry eyes. The building beyond her quiet apartment was busy tonight, people moving around downstairs, the rain against the windows, the laughter in the condo next door, but most of all was the sense of presence. *His.* She couldn't see him yet, but she could tell George was there, waiting for her. Tonight, Aimee was too weary and lonely to keep him at bay. The faint scent of cologne rose in the air.

"I hate being alone, you know. That's the worst part," Aimee said, emptying the second glass, and setting it with a clatter on the table. "Being alone all the time."

Footsteps intruded. She was almost certain it was from the couple next door, or that she had imagined it, but seconds passed and they didn't fade. The room was deathly cold and a bout of shivering overtook Aimee. She reached for the glass. It was empty. Annoyed, she fumbled for the bottle and brought it to her lips, half-inhaling as she did. She choked on the first gulp. Coughs wracked her body.

When they faded, George's ghost stood in the doorway, watching her.

"Christ, it's as cold as a polar bear's tit in here," he grumbled.

Aimee giggled.

"Furnace not working?" he asked.

"Dunno," Aimee mumbled. "Don't care." She took a long pull on the bottle, not even tasting it. "Doesn't bother me."

"You could turn on the fireplace, you know."

Aimee set the bottle down onto the floor with overt care, surprised when it didn't topple. "Guess so," she said. "Didn't think of that."

She searched the couch and coffee table for the fireplace's remote. She couldn't remember the last time she'd used it.

"It's on the mantle," George said.

"No, it's—" She blinked in surprise. "Oh, I guess it is."

She wove her way past the end of the couch and around the coffee table, pointedly avoiding the ghost. She picked up the remote and pressed the button. The fireplace whooshed as gas flowed in through the valves, a dancing fire appearing in seconds.

George ambled over, warming semi-transparent hands. "Pity it's not a wood fire," he said with a sigh. "That's the best kind."

"Beggars can't be choosers," she said.

He smirked. "Then I suppose it'll have to do."

Aimee watched him warily, but she was drunk and sad, and it was hard to fear him when he looked exactly the same. Outside the window, lightning crossed the sky and the dream-memory of that first night pushed forward: the two of them, kissing in the rain. Another night, another year, much like this.

George looked over at her, catching her gaze. He smiled. "Better now, don't you think?"

"Yes, the fire's nice."

"The only thing that's missing is the smell of woodsmoke," he said.

"Always loved that about the cabin's fireplace," Aimee said wistfully. "But at least it's warm."

George stepped closer, and she stepped back, maintaining the distance. His smile faded. "What's wrong? You look sad, Aimee."

She didn't answer, just watched him, and for a long time they were quiet. There was no sound but the rain. Static. Unchanging. *He's not really here,* Aimee's mind warned. *Playing this game will only make it worse.*

Chest aching, she turned away, staggering back to the couch. With the room filling with heat, sleep drew closer. She tried to force George from her memory, but he was stubbornly here tonight. Her lashes had just fluttered closed when he spoke.

"Do you remember that opening in New York?"

She opened her eyes, struggling to focus. George shimmered like a flame, light passing through him. "What opening?" she mumbled.

"At the MOMA. It was Warhol's."

"That was long before us, George. I wasn't even—"

"Now Andy was a true artist," George said. "God, I miss him."

Aimee snorted with mirth. "I see him all the time."

George pursed his lips in disdain, the sight of it so lifelike—so perfectly pulled from memory—it was a blade to her heart. "Don't start on this nonsense again."

"It's true," she said, snuggling deeper into the nest of the couch.

"I wish you wouldn't say things like that. It sounds crazy."

Another giggle burst from her chest. "But it's true," she said. "I imagine all of them. All the artists. All my ghosts." Her voice broke. "Even you."

George's expression darkened. "You shouldn't say that."

"Why? I told you that ages ago. You just didn't want to hear it."

He took a step closer. "Stop it. This isn't funny."

"But it is."

George's hands rose to his hips. "Christ, Aimee, even Margot knew when she'd had enough to drink!"

The phone rang beside her and Aimee turned, the room spinning as she did. She fumbled to find the receiver. Near the fireplace, George droned on. "There was this opening and all of Andy's friends were there. Margot and I'd had a fight and I left a bit late. Sped all the way from Connecticut, but when I got there it was just getting started…"

"Hello?"

Static crackled in her ear, overlaid with George's voice.

"Edie was there too," the ghost continued. "She was the muse of the moment, and Andy brought her everywhere. Could barely talk to him without having her lecturing you about art and fashion and…"

Aimee shushed George, but he continued on, the night and the story and the voice on the phone blurring.

"Hello?" she repeated.

"Aimee? That you?"

"Yes. Yes, it's me."

"It's Hal. I'm calling about George."

Aimee glanced up in confusion. "For George?" The room rippled. For a moment, her dead husband looked solid, but then the edges faded out again, like a camera struggling for focus.

"Yes, about George," Hal said. "Been trying to get hold of you since the retrospective. It's about that writer doing a piece on him. Looks like Penguin is ready to pick up his book. I gave the guy your number. Hope you don't mind. Not sure you've heard of him. The name's Barrett Cardinal. Bit of an up and comer."

"Oh, right," she said glumly. "The Giller prize winner. Yes, we met at the gallery."

"Have you set up a time to talk to him yet? He emailed me about it again today. Wanted to know if there was an issue with you talking to him."

Aimee struggled to sit up. George was still telling his story about Edie Sedgewick and a cast of other characters and their long-ago antics. She could barely follow Hal's words.

"Aimee, are you still there?" Hal asked.

George's voice came in waves, drowning everything else out. "There was this agent there. A friend of Rothko's, I think. Bit of an ass, but Andy'd invited him along, and he started badgering me about my artwork. Told me I was painting in the wrong century…"

She shook her head. "Could you speak up, Hal? There's something wrong with the connection."

"I said it's about the writer who is doing a book on George," Hal said. "The one who called you after the opening. You need to take his calls. Do an interview or two. Get on board with this."

"On board with *what*, exactly?"

"With the book," Hal said, exasperated. "It's the perfect opportunity for the next phase of George's legacy. Not just a retrospective, but a complete biography and summary of his life and all that. When I spoke to Barrett today, he said he was having trouble setting up a time with you."

"We talked, but the phone disconnected."

"Then why haven't you called him back? This is an important step for George's legacy. His post-career, career, if you will. You know what I mean. I'm still working on the angles from my end."

Aimee struggled to follow Hal's words, but George's voice wouldn't let her be. He strode from the fireplace to the couch, swinging his arms as the story grew animated. "And Andy was standing there, watching the whole goddamned thing," he said with a bellowing laugh. "Totally indifferent to my busted knuckles and the blood on the floor. I was scared as hell—just some dumbass college prick trying to get my big break who'd picked a fight with an agent—but Andy now—Andy didn't give a good goddamn about any of that!"

Aimee plugged her free ear, pressing her eyes closed and focusing on the wavering thread of Hal's voice. "Sorry, Hal. Why do I have to do an interview? Why can't he just research the details he needs?"

"It's important, Aimee. *Really* important that you have a voice in this. So will you meet with him or not?"

"I don't know. I haven't decided."

There was a slight pause. George's words had begun to fade into the buzz of the rain.

"This Cardinal fellow is a big deal," Hal said. "And it would likely make a difference to your chapters."

"My chapters?"

"The ones that have to do with your part in George's life, after he divorced Margot and—" George laughed, drowning out whatever else Hal was saying.

Aimee shushed the ghost and sat up, pinching her eyes closed. Drunk, none of this made sense. "Sorry, Hal, I don't understand.

What's going on with the book? Why does he need to talk to *me*, exactly? And why now? What's the big rush?"

"Well, uh." Hal laughed nervously. "You see, Jacqueline and the rest of the family have already given their interviews and I've heard the spin they gave is a little bit off when it came to you, so I'm asking you more as a courtesy. A way of ensuring, should any of what they said about you and George be a bit skewed." He cleared his throat. "That you have time to rectify it."

She sat straighter. "Rectify *what*, exactly? What did Jacqueline say?"

"I'm not sure, but I know her and, well, so do you. I just want to make sure you have your say too. She's said her part."

"Jacqueline's part, huh?" She spat the name like a curse. "Of course she has."

"She cares about George's legacy, Aimee," Hal said, his tone chiding. "She arranged her interview as soon as he called. I hope you'll do the same."

"I will. I just haven't had time."

"Then *make* time. Not next week. Not next month. Now, Aimee. Call him back."

"Okay."

She opened her eyes, finding the ghost waiting beside the fire, his story over. George was barely present. A charcoal smudge on an aging page, nothing more. Tongues of flame danced behind him, shimmering through his legs.

"Talk to this Cardinal guy," Hal said. "Give him your side of the story. Spin it however you need to, but get your side out."

"Hal…" Aimee sighed.

"It's what George would have wanted," he added.

She dropped her gaze to the table and the empty bottle sitting on the floor. It had fallen over, but she couldn't remember when. Her chest heaved with the ache she'd carried for months. She swallowed convulsively, struggling to free herself from the pain.

"So? What do you think?" Hal asked. "Can I call this Cardinal fellow back and tell him that you'll do the interview this week?"

"Don't call him." She stood, walking wobbly out of the room and leaving the ghost behind. "I'll call."

"Just make sure that you do. It matters, Aimee. George would want you to tell your side of things. You know that he would."

"I know." Throat aching, she wiped away tears. Hal was right, of course. George would have wanted this and that meant her decision was already made.

CHAPTER FIVE

In the early hours of morning, Aimee awoke with the inexplicable certainty that something was wrong. Her chest was tight, heart pounding. She listened carefully, but all she could hear was the incessant rain. Aimee blinked gritty eyes, the memory of Eugène Delacroix leaning in to whisper something in her ear, floating from the murky recess of her mind. She'd been dreaming of him—*or was it Barrett Cardinal?* She couldn't remember which it had been, only that the figure had a message for her.

She rolled over and swung her legs from beneath the sheets, shivering in the icy bedroom. The rain, which had been so heavy last night, was still falling, the light beyond the window completely blocked by the dismal day. "When will it stop?" she groaned.

"Morning, sunshine."

Aimee jumped at the sound of George's voice. She turned to discover him waiting in the open doorway. In the dimness of the bedroom, he looked different than he'd appeared last night, or in the cabin in Banff. There was a slightly otherworldly colour to him, as if she remembered him brightly lit, and the room was too dark for that to make sense. He appeared *more* than real. Aimee swallowed hard, dropping her eyes to the floor as she stood and headed to the bathroom without answering.

"I been waiting for you to wake up for an hour," George said cheerfully.

"Go away," Aimee said. "You're not real!"

George followed her down the hallway. "I want to get out to paint," he said. "The sky's full of clouds, love. It's beautiful."

"Go away!" She swung the bathroom door closed with a bang, and started up the shower.

When she climbed out, George was gone, but the phone was ringing. She jogged into the kitchen, frowning at the clutter that littered the table. She hadn't put anything away, and now she'd have to throw all the food out. Another thing she didn't want to deal with.

The shrill bell on the phone rang again, pounding on her nerves. "Hello?"

"Aimee!" Niha squealed, "is that you?"

Aimee winced. She loved the girl, but Niha's excitement at this time of morning was akin to torture. "Yes, Niha," she said wearily. "You called *me*. Who else would it be?"

"Sorry, right! I just wanted— Oh, god, Aimee. Have you turned on the news yet?"

The hand of dread tightened around Aimee's neck. The dream of Barrett/Eugène flashed again in her mind. She turned, glancing to the dim living room. The television remote lay on the couch where she'd tossed it last night. George, thankfully, was nowhere to be seen.

"No, not this morning."

"The Bow River broke its banks. They're evacuating the downtown. Your area too!"

"What? How?" The words didn't make sense. How could they? Aimee stared out the windows—steel grey with great sheets of rain coming down in torrents, the side of the building a waterfall. "I don't know what you—"

"The Glenbow is flooding!"

Aimee slumped against the counter. She couldn't breathe. The unease that had chased her all morning was here. Random thoughts intruded: the unfinished restoration work, the carefully organized pigments, her office. All of that would need to be moved!

"Aimee? Aimee, you there?"

"Yes. I'm here." A surge of adrenaline pulsed through her, and she took a deep breath, like a diver resurfacing. "I'll be downtown in a couple minutes. Just let me get dressed and—"

"They're not letting anyone downtown," Niha interrupted. "That's why I called. They're evacuating the entire area. Your condo is in the flood zone. Hasn't anyone called you yet?"

"Not yet. But I was showering. I might have missed the call." The light on the machine pulsed again, but Aimee could barely understand. Images from years past—New Orleans, in the aftermath of Hurricane Katrina—flashed like lightning in her mind.

"The police have been escorting people to higher ground. You've been coming into work early so I thought—"

"But there are paintings in the subfloors," Aimee said in a panicked rush. "I have to get them!" She could imagine the paintings with their nervous ghosts beside them, waiting and watching as the flood waters rose. *Poor Frida!*

"You can't. The police said—"

"I can't just leave them there!" she cried, uncertain whether she meant the artists or their works.

"The night crew started sandbagging at midnight," Niha explained. "I was down a few minutes ago. Downtown feels like a warzone, Aimee. Do what you're supposed to: Pack a bag and leave."

"But I…" The words faded, her head swimming.

"Get out," Niha warned. "Go stay at your mom's. You can't come downtown."

"Right. Of course."

A sound interrupted her thoughts and she turned, seeing George come out of the bedroom. He wasn't smiling as he'd been before. This time he had a bottle of bourbon in hand. He took a long swig before pointing out the window.

"Fucking rain," he snarled. "Can't paint a bloody thing in this downpour. Jesus Christ! What I'd do to be back in Connecticut!"

Aimee giggled, though it had an edge of panic.

"The hell?" snarled George. "That funny to you?"

"Aimee?" Niha's voice echoed on the phone. "Are you crying?"

"No, Niha, I—" Aimee's laughter grew louder and more shrill. *They'd had this fight before.* She'd always hated George when he was angry or drunk (or both) and this memory was seething.

"Are you okay?" Niha asked.

Aimee took a sobbing breath, rubbing away tears. "No," she gasped. "No, I haven't been okay in a long time." She cleared her throat, hoping she sounded calm. "I should go."

"Aimee, if you need me to come get you, I will."

"No. It's fine. I've got to pack a couple things, and head to my mom's," Aimee said. "I'll be okay. Promise."

"Call me when you get there," Niha insisted.

"I will," Aimee sniffled. "Thanks for calling. Seriously. Thank you, Niha."

"Call," she ordered.

"Alright. Bye."

Aimee dropped the receiver down onto the table with a clatter, a broken sob tearing from her chest. The sound seemed to change something. George turned, his form growing more solid as he moved nearer. He reached out, but she pulled away before he could touch her.

"You're not REAL!" she screamed, and ran to the bedroom.

Outside, lightning split the sky.

—

Ignoring Niha's warning, Aimee headed directly to the Glenbow.

The street around the museum was unrecognizable: sandbags covered the doors, water flowing ankle deep in the streets, a river of brown slurry liquid and garbage covering the sidewalks...and the water was still rising. A line of police cars blocked off the downtown and an officer with a megaphone guided traffic away from the buildings. As she arrived, Luis Santos, the museum director, along with several other staff members, came out the museum's main entrance carrying boxes.

Aimee sloshed forward, clambering past a barricade amid shouts of "move on!" and "clear the streets!" She reached Luis' side just as a siren pierced the air.

"What's going on?" she shouted over the din.

"Bottom levels are flooding," he replied grimly. "Moved as much as we could upstairs." His jaw clenched. "But not all."

"And the items in storage?" she gasped. "The ones set aside for repair?"

Half a block away, an ambulance passed, the sound momentarily blocking his words.

"I'm sorry." Luis gestured to the milling streets, the emergency vehicles passing by. "There's a mandatory evacuation." Another siren joined the first, further off, fading. Aimee shivered. It was a sound she'd learned to hate.

"We got some of it, Aimee," Luis added, "but we had to stop when the basement level started to fill. Things are bad; just, bad. Police are worried people could get caught in this and drown."

"Oh god."

A car squealed past, wings of water spraying over the rim of Aimee's gum boots, leaving her feet soaked. The officer turned. He shouted orders at the passing cars. Seeing Aimee and Luis waiting by the doors, he pointed to the street.

"You there, Mr. Santos!" he bellowed, red-faced. "It's time to GO!"

"Sorry!" Luis called. He turned to Aimee. "We've got to move." He tightened his grip on the boxes and trudged forward, Aimee at his side.

"So what now?"

"We get to higher ground," Luis said, shifting the boxes yet again. "Wait for things to get settled down, then see what we're dealing with."

"Right. Of course."

Aimee stepped down from the submerged edge of a curb, nearly falling as she followed Luis into the flooding street. She could feel the current tug at her boots, the weight of water threatening to drag her away. One false move and she'd drown.

"It's going to be okay. We'll get through this." He gave her a weary smile. "Just water."

She nodded, wishing she believed him. It felt like her entire life was caught in the deluge.

"Meant to tell you," Luis said. "Someone called for you this morning. Called twice, actually."

Aimee flinched. *Barrett Cardinal.*

"Seemed very concerned that he find you," Luis said, reaching his car and balancing the boxes on one hip so he could open the door. Aimee waited uncertainly at his side. She should get her car out of the parking garage, but what then? She couldn't bear the thought of staying with her mother. Not right now.

"Did you get a name?" she asked, hoping against hope that it might be David Arturo, and the cabin had sold. Another thought chased the first: She needed to check on the cabin too. If it was flooding in Calgary, Banff couldn't be much better.

"It was a writer," Luis said, jarring her from her thoughts. "Name was Bear something-er-other."

"Barrett Cardinal."

"Yeah, that's right," he said. "Said he'd been trying to arrange a time for an interview for weeks, but you hadn't called back."

Aimee did up the button of her coat, refusing to hold Luis' eyes. "I've been...busy."

"Busy or not, you should return that call," Luis said. "The guy mentioned something about a book about an artist of some kind. Contemporary Canadian, I think. It's important that the Glenbow cooperate regarding our artists."

"It's about George," she whispered, but Luis didn't seem to hear.

"In any case, you should do the interview," Luis said, putting the last box inside, and slamming the trunk, "Might look bad if he runs an article saying the Glenbow staff wasn't willing to help."

Guilt rose inside her. George had been an expert at self-promotion. She could imagine his reaction. She looked up, suddenly nervous that she'd see him, but the street was full of evacuees and police.

"I'll set up a time. I will."

"Good." Luis reached for the door handle. "You got a place to stay?" he asked, keys jingling. "Anywhere I can drop you off?"

Aimee blinked. With her worries about the artwork, she'd almost forgotten she needed to leave. "You can stay with me and Marc if you need," Luis said. "We have a couch in the living room."

"Thanks, but no," she said, glancing up at the sky. "I've actually got someplace to go."

Luis pulled her into a quick hug. "Good to hear," he said. "I'll be in touch when we're let back in to deal with the mess." Another car passed by and they both jumped out of the way of the splashing water. "Keep dry, my friend!" Luis laughed, before climbing into the vehicle and driving away.

Aimee stood for a long time, staring one way and then the other. She had to get back to the apartment for a change of clothes, but after that, she was free.

"Free to do what?" she wondered aloud.

The image of Eugène Delacroix—dark haired and brooding—popped into her mind, shifting like smoke into Barrett Cardinal, in his leather jacket and jeans. She wasn't certain she'd ever met someone who reminded her so much of her muses. *Maybe it's because Barrett Cardinal has the attitude to go with the look,* Aimee thought.

"Might as well get this over with."

Decision made, she gritted her teeth and headed back into the rain.

—

Bear waited outside the coffee shop, watching the people pass on the street through the blurry windshield of his truck. Figures moved through the veil of rain—appearing and disappearing in the haze—the sound of static a hum below the twang of the radio.

He checked his watch: 11:53 a.m.

She wasn't late. Not yet. But it was going to be close. With a sigh, Bear's gaze went back to the glass, fingers drumming on the scratched paint of the door. The question was: Would she cut and run?

Bear had grown up on the Tsuut'ina reservation. His family held with many of the traditional ways, including a flexible sense of time. As a little boy, he woke when the sun rose him, slept when exhaustion pulled away the day, and those who surrounded him had a sense of seasons, but not chronology. Bear's great-grandmother, who'd lived with the family when Bear was a child, hadn't even known her age. "I was born in the summer," was what she'd always say. In Bear's memory, the time from birth to five years old felt like an eternity, but all that disappeared when school began, and schedules began to rule Bear's life.

Bear squinted up the street at the dreary passersby. "Don't disappear on me again," he muttered.

The words were a prayer. After the faux pas at the gallery, he'd gotten her on the phone exactly once. That discussion had been cut off by the thunderstorm, and she'd dodged his messages ever since. Even with Hal Mortinson's insistence that Mrs. Westerberg was "*definitely on board with the project*" and "*just tied up with the will*", Bear hadn't really expected to talk to Aimee face to face again. Then this morning, she'd abruptly called *him*.

"I'll do one interview," she'd announced. No discussion, no negotiation. Just the offer.

"You will?" Bear had stammered. "That's...well, that's great! When do you want to meet?"

"Noon."

"Like noon today?"

"Yes, today." Her voice had been tight, as if she'd been crying and was trying to control it. "Glenbow's been evacuated and I have nowhere to be right now."

"Where do you want to meet?"

"There's a little tea shop I go to," Aimee had said. "How about there?"

"Sure. Whereabouts?"

"It's in Kenzington. Past 14th Street."

She had given him directions while Bear scribbled notes. "Thank you. I really appreciate you taking the time to do this."

She'd laughed, but it had been hard edged. "I just want to be done with this," she'd said and hung up before he could reply.

Inside the truck, the radio station changed songs, a mellow love song taking the place of the honkey-tonk ditty. Bear checked his watch again: *11:57 a.m.*

"C'mon, c'mon," he chanted.

With the run-around he'd been getting from Aimee Westerberg over the last few weeks, he half-expected her to be a no-show. He'd had troubles getting interviews before, but Aimee's involvement with the project would make or break it. She was the controversial topic of so many other people's interviews. The widow who, it was rumoured, had possible mental issues. Leaving her without a say would make the chapter about her seem biased.

Bear knew how one-sided stories could change. He and his sister, Margaret, had spent three months in foster care when he was in first grade. Half the story was that his mother had lost her job and couldn't put food on the table or get her children to school in the morning. That was true, but no more true than the fact that she'd been forced to quit her job to care for her dying grandmother. And as soon as Bear's great-grandmother passed away—*in the winter,* Bear's mind whispered—then life for the growing family had returned to normal. Bear had returned home, and things had almost been the same.

That was why Bear *needed* Aimee's side of the story.

The radio chimed the hour with the CBC chord and the news began. Outside the window, a city bus passed, stopping at the curb half a block away. Bear's gaze caught on the passengers departing. *Please,* his mind begged. *Just be here. Don't run.*

A bright flash of red hair drew his attention to the second door of the bus. Umbrella in hand, Aimee dodged puddles as she walked up the street toward the cafe, oblivious to the swirl of traffic around her. Bear put his hand on the door, catching details he'd missed the first time they'd met. Aimee Westerberg was in her thirties, but looked younger. Long auburn curls hung halfway down her back, cork-screwing around her shoulders like a cape. Her face was fine-featured, gaunt, a more fragile version of the woman in the drawing he'd seen. Narrow shoulders rolled inward as she walked, her coat buttoned up to her neck. As she reached the door of the cafe, she peered behind her, lips moving as if mid-conversation. From this distance, he couldn't hear her words, nor see who she was talking to.

He opened the truck door, heading out into the rain. "Mrs. Westerberg!" he called.

She jerked in surprise, her expression schooling itself into wariness as he neared.

"I wasn't sure you'd come," he said with a lop-sided grin.

A smile ghosted over her lips then faded. "I wasn't either."

"I'm glad you did."

She nodded, pushing open the door of the cafe and stepping back so he could walk in. "Come on," she said tiredly. "We should grab a table if we can get one."

—

An hour, and two pots of tea later, they were still talking, rain still falling. Barrett Cardinal wasn't as invasive as she'd expected, nor was he hounding her for insidious details of the illicit affair that had led to her marriage. Instead, he was unexpectedly gentle. That side of him surprised her. The writer seemed content to stick to facts about George, things that she could answer with little or no guilt. Barrett wasn't at all like the paparazzi who'd hounded her in the wake of George's death. Yes, he had questions—hundreds of them—and he scribbled notes as she talked, but he was polite. Kind. There was no tape recorder, no camera, just the two of them drinking tea in a cozy booth.

Civilized, Aimee thought. *And genuinely nice.*

She took another sip of lukewarm Darjeeling and sighed. For the first time in ages, she wasn't in a rush to go somewhere, do something to avoid thinking of George. Here, she could let him be a part of the conversation without worrying about losing her mind. She was content.

Barrett finished writing the last note, and looked up. "Your husband had started a new series in the months before his death," he said. "Mountains, wasn't it?"

Aimee nodded, setting her cup aside. It clattered on the saucer. "Yes. Mountains and lakes. He spent most of his last winter at our cabin in Banff. Some of those paintings were on display at the Gainsborough."

"No portraits though," Barrett prodded. "Just landscapes."

I wasn't his muse anymore, a dark voice inside her whispered. Aimee winced, looking out the window. There was a featureless man behind the blurry glass, and he seemed to be staring right at her. She frowned, turning back to Barrett.

"Yes. George had been working with the human form for years, but in the last few years he'd reconsidered his process. He was interested in mountains and light. He was doing an exploration of Canadian art. A return to the Group of Seven and Carr and the like." She shook her head, remembering George's bombastic rants about the simplified beauty of the landscape, and the love of the vast untouched Canadian panorama. That stereotypical screen of trees, blocking viewer and vista. She rolled her eyes. "God! George was so determined to live up to them."

Barrett smiled. "And did he?"

Aimee's chest tightened. "I think he did—or would have—but he never finished the series." Her throat caught, remembering the last unfinished painting which sat in her bedroom even now. It was smeared across one side, with a gouged mark near the centre. She hadn't been able to bring herself to repair it. Some part of her didn't want to! She couldn't imagine George appearing in her studio, pestering her about pigments like her other ghosts did. It was a toothache she couldn't ignore, nor bear to deal with.

"I've never seen his last series," Barrett said, flipping back to his notes. There were photocopied images on the pages; Aimee's gaze caught on one in particular: the frontspiece from the show where she and George had embarked on their relationship. "I should check into that." He turned the page, revealing colour copies of George's early works, and began scribbling notes. Aimee recognized them at once. They were from the mid-sixties, when George had been in college in Connecticut, spending evenings at parties with Warhol and Lichtenstein and—

Aimee blinked in the realization. He'd painted these before she was even born.

Barrett turned another page, interrupting the thought. "You won't be able to find his new paintings," she said quietly.

Barrett looked up, pen pausing. "Oh?"

"He never had a show. Hal has a couple pieces in New York, but most of them are with—" her words stumbled. "—with Jacqueline, George's daughter. I only kept the one, you see."

"I'd like to see it, if I could."

"Maybe sometime, but it needs repairs. It's damaged." She swallowed against a painful throat. "I have pictures of the group I could send you."

"Thank you, I'd like that." Barrett smiled, the expression transforming his otherwise stern features. Though he shared the same dark looks as Delacroix, the brooding young artist, he was, Aimee decided, much less irritating than her imagined ghost and much more attractive. A wave of heat rose up her neck at the thought.

Barrett flipped his notebook closed. He stared at her for a long moment; attentive, probing. It felt the way it had when George used to draw her, except the writer wasn't lost in his art the way her husband had been. His attention was entirely, sharply, engaged with her. A minute passed, the silence drawing out until Aimee's nerves began to tingle with anxiety.

"Well, if you're done, I should probably go," she said, dropping his gaze.

Barrett rapped the table with his knuckles. "Yes. Sorry for keeping you so long. Jesus! Where'd the time go?"

Aimee laughed nervously. "Who knows. Time flies when you're playing twenty questions." She peeked up at him through flutter of lashes, finding him smiling.

"I appreciate you meeting with me, Mrs. Westerberg," Barrett said. "I know talking about your late husband is hard for you, but I want you to know I'll do my very best to represent him fairly. George Westerberg's contributions to the art world are incomparable and I—"

"Don't do that," she said tightly. The use of her married name had startled her, but it was his sycophantic tone that prickled under her skin. Fawning wasn't *like* him, and she didn't know why that even mattered.

Barret's smile faded. "Do what?"

"Don't treat me like I'm part of him," she snapped. "George was George, and we were married—yes!—but I was never his keeper." She began doing up the buttons on her coat, looking down at her shaking fingers instead of at him. "If we're going to talk, then at least be truthful about him. Alright?"

"I don't know what you mean."

"Say what you mean when you talk about George. Be honest. Be blunt." Her eyes darted up at him, sharp and angry. "Like you were at the opening."

"I—Okay?"

His confusion lit another flare under her irritation. Aimee shook her head, glaring away from him. The man still waited behind the grey haze of glass. Was he waiting for the bus or prying? Suddenly Aimee didn't trust him. His long fingers rose to the murky pane and the silhouette—broad athletic shoulders, and long painter's hands—became an echo of her late husband's physique. *Is that George's ghost?* Aimee jerked her gaze away, heart pounding.

"Everyone's so bloody certain that I knew everything about George, but the truth is he could be awful, and he *didn't* tell me everything." She laughed sharply. "God, just look at the will! He made me fetch him coffee twice the day he changed it. I was there with him at the lawyer's office, but he never told me the truth about what he was doing. He was talented—yes!—but judgemental too. He looked down on my artwork. Called it 'playing'. George figured he could do no wrong and it drove me crazy sometimes."

The realization of what she'd just said hit her and she lifted her

eyes to find Barrett staring. He wasn't writing anything, just waiting. Listening.

"I'm sorry," she said. "It's just Hal—George's agent—he treats
George like he's a fucking saint." She cringed. "Like he was a saint.
And he certainly wasn't."

Barrett's brow crinkled in concern, his fingers motionless on the
table. "Mrs. Westerberg," he said evenly. "I apologize for upsetting
you. I never meant to."

"No, it's fine," Aimee said. "And the other night, it was fine too.
I just wasn't ready to hear it then." When Barrett didn't answer, she
pressed on. "The things you said at his retrospective: they were true.
George was pretentious, and overblown, but he was also brilliant!
He was bigger than life. So talented, so driven. He had a spark of
genius in him that's a rarity in an artist."

"Or a person," Barrett said quietly.

"Yes." Aimee nodded, the room blurring before her eyes. She
turned away so he couldn't see the tears. The man standing outside on the street was inexplicably gone, and that bothered her even
more than his prying. *Where is he now?* She rubbed at her eyes and
took a slow breath before she looked back to the table.

"Mrs. Wes—"

"I'd rather you just called me Aimee," she said, offering her hand.
"Like my friends do." The words surprised her even though she'd
been the one to say them. During their marriage, George had been
the outgoing one. After his death, Aimee had become even more
withdrawn, but there was something about this man, with his con-
flicted confidence and unease, that she recognized. She *wanted* to
help him.

"Alright," he said, shaking her hand. Not timidly as she expected, but with strength, his fingers enveloping hers, warm and tight.
Aimee smiled, her heart thudding a little faster as he squeezed her
hand and let go. "It's Aimee then, but only if you agree to call me
Bear." He chuckled. "My mother and editor are the only ones who
call me Barrett."

She nodded. "Bear."

"Yes. And I'm glad we talked today," he said. "For real this time."

"I am too."

A heartbeat passed. "Did you want to do this again sometime?" Bear asked. He nodded to the now empty cafe. "Talk, I mean."

"What for?" Her lips quivered, the smile fading. "I told you everything."

"You told me about George today. You didn't say *anything* about you. You've got a part in the story too."

"I don't know," she murmured, her fear returning. This was the part she wasn't good at. Because when it came to her, she'd never really felt like there was anything to share.

He leaned forward, dark eyes imploring. "Please, Aimee."

She scanned the curling mop of dark hair, the warm eyes, and faded leather jacket. Bear was a stranger and yet his face had an unnerving familiarity. With the sensation of jumping off the edge of a cliff, she forced herself to answer him.

"If you want to," she said.

Bear grinned, the expression so bright she felt her cheeks warm. "I definitely do."

—

Leaving the tea house, Aimee's phone—which had been at the bottom of her purse during lunch—began to buzz. She pulled it from her pocket, staring in shock at the screen.

"Good lord, Mom," she groaned.

Twelve separate texts and two frantic voice messages awaited Aimee's reply. Her jaw clenched as she walked up 14th Street to the bus stop, tapping out a message:

I told you I had a mtg.

I'll be at the house by 5.

Relax.

She hit send before she could change her mind, watching the transfer bar stretch across the top of the phone in anxiety. Less than a minute later, the phone buzzed in answer. Aimee cringed.

Good. You'll be home in time for supper! <3 Mom

With a sigh, Aimee dropped her phone back into her pocket. Her mother didn't get it, and never would. For Claudine, Aimee was a project. Something to fix.

And she wasn't the only one who felt like that. The thought was so unexpected, Aimee's breath caught.

It was true, of course, George had seen her as his muse—a piece of clay to shape into what he wanted—but she hadn't thought about that aspect of their relationship and its repercussions for years. Its reappearance left her aching. Unsettled ripples of arguments resurged and Aimee's gaze dropped to the sidewalk, watching the water swirl down the drain. The past was a force, tapping at her shell, but George was a key.

Why'd you have to leave me, she thought. *It was all so easy before.* Aimee blinked, and the watery world disappeared…

In the memory, George leaned against the bedroom doorway of her cluttered apartment: the one she'd hated at the time, but now longed for with a desperate fury. The trio of rooms was dimly lit, an icebox in the winter and a deathtrap in the summer, but it was hers. He stood, arms crossed, glaring at her. His cheeks were flushed, the broad lines of his chest, with its fuzz of greying hair, rising and falling in rapid succession.

"I don't know why you're so against it," he snapped.

Aimee stretched her naked legs over the rumpled sheets of the bed. She didn't bother to look up from her magazine. "Because I don't want to."

"It makes no sense," George argued. "My apartment's twice the size, and far more convenient. Jesus! The bus ride alone eats up an hour each day."

"Maybe," Aimee said tightly. "But this place is *mine*."

He took a quick swallow of his drink, baring his teeth at the burn before he answered. "It's a hovel!"

"Hardly," she said with forced calm. She flicked to the next page. "More like a work in progress."

"Why are you being so goddamned stubborn about this? What?

Why *this*, Aimee?"

Her gaze flicked up from the page she wasn't reading. It felt like a storm was about to break: Aimee's body was warm, the scent of sex and bourbon lingering in the air.

"Why are you having such a hard time with me saying 'no'?"

George coughed angrily, swallowing the last of his drink and slamming it down on the top of the dresser. Aimee flinched, but didn't move. George's temper wasn't something she understood. *Not yet.*

"Well, if you don't want to move in," he growled. "What the hell *do* you want?"

She shrugged.

"Come on then," he snarled. "You're the one who refused. I deserve to know—"

She slapped the magazine down on the bed, her temper flaring to life. "You deserve?!"

"Yes!" George spat. "I deserve to know why you won't!"

"Because this isn't all about YOU!"

He leaned over her, putting a hand on either side of her legs. They'd been fucking minutes earlier, the embers of passion igniting into something else, something dark and violent. "What do you want, sunshine?" he sneered. "Power? Money?"

"No!"

He loomed nearer. "A step up the art crowd ladder? A little push to get your shitty, non-existent career off the ground?"

"No, I never—"

"So what? Are you fucking me to get through the door?"

"Stop!" she cried, tears glittering along her lower lids. "It's not like that!" But his words drowned her out.

"Because you're gonna have to do a little better than your second-rate knock-offs if you want to make it in that world! You're a little girl trying to play with the big boys, and you haven't got the balls for it!"

"It's not like that!"

George grabbed her chin, forcing her to look at him. "Is that all I am to you?" he sneered. "Someone to use? Someone to screw around with, to fake your way to success?"

"No!"

His fingers tightened painfully on her jaw. "'Cause I've got better things to do that waste my time with users."

A tear rolled over Aimee's cheek. "Please, George," she choked. "It's not like that at all."

"Then what the hell do you want?!"

She jerked her chin away, rolling to the other side of the bed, presenting her naked back to him. She grabbed tissues, wiping away her tears. Aimee hated when George was like this.

"I don't know," she sniffled. "A life, I guess." She winced, waiting for his taunting reply—more accusations of her ineptitude and failings as an artist—things she'd already started to believe.

Long seconds passed. Aimee had just began to wonder if he'd left the room when he spoke.

"What kind of life?" he said gruffly.

She gave a teary laugh, shoulders slumping in defeat. "I don't know. Traveling, work, the restoration program I told you about at Queens." Her voice dropped. "Marriage, maybe."

George made a sound of disgust. She turned in surprise to see he'd come around to the side of the bed where she sat. She watched him warily, but his eyes held no anger, just weariness.

"Not marriage," he said tiredly. "I've tried it. Doesn't work."

He slid his arm over her shoulder. Aimee tensed for a heartbeat, but she felt raw, and George was here. The tears welled up again, threatening to fall, and she leaned into him rather than show him her ravaged face. "You and Margot didn't work," Aimee said thickly. "But that doesn't mean that we couldn't."

His hand played over the skin of her bare arm as if considering her words. "Perhaps."

"Perhaps?"

His fingers stilled. "It's too hard to be trapped together. Two artists, I mean." He spoke in slow even tones, as if explaining a complicated subject to a dull student. "It'd never work."

"But it could."

"Oh, sunshine. Sometimes you seem so very young."

She pulled from his embrace, wiping the last hint of tears away. "But I get you, George. I understand your work; you always say that! We could work it out."

He lifted an eyebrow. "Name two artists."

"Two artists who what?"

He reached out, tracing her lips with the pad of his thumb. "Two artists. Two wild, impetuous souls, two who made it work, in all the years since time began."

Aimee's heart clenched. Her mind ran through the many artists she'd read of in her studies. Those who'd married and stayed together.

"Who's done it?" George prodded.

"Married?" Aimee said, playing for time. "Why, there are lots of them. I mean—"

"Not just married. But were happy. Name me two artists, equally famous, who made it work."

A smile tugged at her lips. "That's not fair. Female artists have never been seen as equal."

George rolled his eyes. "Maybe not equals, but they were still artists. Good ones."

Aimee felt his unspoken words: *not like you.* She didn't have time to consider it; George had already started a running tally.

"'Cause the screw-ups are paramount. Think about it," he said. "Artemesia Ghentilesci and Pierantonio Stiattesi. Lee Krasner and Jackson Pollock. Vigée Le Brun and—"

"Kahlo and Rivera!" Aimee interrupted.

George snorted. "Hardly say they were happy. They ended up divorced for Chrissake!"

"And remarried."

George let out a harsh laugh.

"Frida loved him," Aimee insisted. "And he loved her."

"That wasn't love. It was obsession."

Aimee chewed her lower lip, uncertain how to reply. A painting of Kahlo's floated to mind: Rivera, huge and looming, brush and easel in hand, while Kahlo stood next to him, so tiny she looked like a child. She held his hand, a bird carrying ribbons and script flying above her head. They stood side by side, but Rivera dwarfed her.

Aimee knew that feeling.

She stood from the bed and began to dress. She pulled on her panties, then bra. George sat for a moment, watching, his brows pulling together when she didn't return to him.

"Aimee?"

She searched the floor for discarded clothes, nudging aside George's pants and shirt.

"Come on now," he sighed. "Don't be like that."

She pulled on her jeans. They were torn across one knee, and needed mending, but she didn't have money for a new pair. Not with all her student debt—debt that would surely grow if she was accepted into the Queens University graduate program. She swore she wouldn't burden her mother, after all Claudine had gone through, raising Aimee alone, but that meant borrowing money she didn't have.

"Aimee?"

She couldn't see her t-shirt, so she went to the dresser, digging for a new one. The empty glass sitting on top rattled when she slid the drawer closed.

"What's going on here?" George asked.

Her eyes flicked over to him as she pulled it over her head. He looked genuinely perplexed.

"What?" he repeated.

She squeezed her eyes shut, breathing slowly to hold back tears. "I get it," she said, surprised at the strength in her own voice. "You have your life. I have mine. You made that clear."

George stood. "Now, I don't think—"

"No. It's fine," Aimee said, slipping her feet into her sandals. "I understand."

She went to step past him, but George caught her wrist. His grip was tighter than it needed to be. "Understand what?" he asked. His tone was sharp, a hint of his earlier anger returning.

She glared at him through tear-brightened eyes. "I get that you want different things than me. I get that I'm not the same type of artist as you."

"That's hardly the issue!"

"Then what is?"

His grip loosened but he didn't let go. For a long moment they stood this way, caught together, unmoving.

"I don't want children," George said. "I've done that. That's not an option."

"I never said anything about children."

He opened his mouth, then closed it again. His thumb began to move circles on her wrist, as if he was caressing her, not preventing her from leaving. Aimee knew better.

"No," he said. "I suppose you didn't." His words were slow, careful.

Aimee pulled back. "Let me go."

George tugged her forward and she bumped against his hips. The room was swimming, her heart breaking. His hands wrapped her back, and she flashed to the painting of Rivera and Kahlo. *Bigger than life*. That described both Diego Rivera and George, didn't it?

"I can't let you go," he said darkly. "I won't!"

Aimee set her cheek against his shoulder, fighting the tremors that had begun to shake her from the inside out. Sobs internalized.

"Shh," he whispered, patting her back. "If it's so important to you, then we'll do it."

She tried to answer, but her throat was blocked, the pain in her throat choking her.

"Marriage. No kids," George said with a laugh. "An old rutting bastard and his pretty little muse. That's not such a bad place to begin, right?"

In the same city, a decade later, the same muse jumped as a horn blared, real life returning. The faded apartment of Aimee's memory had been demolished years before, making way for a high-rise of million dollar condos. Aimee's memory disappeared with the same, sudden force as the wrecking ball that had brought the building down. Confused, she looked up, discovering a beat-up truck with Bear Cardinal leaning out the window, waving at her.

"You need a ride somewhere, Aimee?" he shouted over the mingled roar of traffic and rain. Behind him, a car honked, someone's commute being blocked by his offer.

"I'm fine," she called. "You go on."

Another truck blared its horn, holding for several seconds. Bear winced.

"Well, I'll catch you later then," he shouted. "Round two interview: *Your* perspective next time."

With a wave, he pulled away from the curb and drove away. The traffic streamed past but Aimee's gaze followed the faded vehicle down the street. The rain poured down in sheets blocking her from where the truck trundled up the hill, fading into the mist. She bet Barrett Cardinal—*Bear*, her mind corrected—wouldn't compromise on what he really wanted. He wouldn't let himself be goaded into putting aside his hopes and desires for lukewarm compromise and the barest comfort.

"He'd fight for what he wanted," she whispered. "He'd find his joy."

And at that, Aimee finally smiled.

CHAPTER SIX

The entire city held its breath as it waited for the waters to recede. There were first floor condos underwater, million dollar properties swallowed by river sludge. Unable to go back to the condo, Aimee moved back home, staying in her childhood bedroom at her mother's insistence. Subjected to Claudine's smothering attentions, Aimee soon regretted the decision. She fought down her fear of George's ghost to go to Banff.

"But there's flooding in Canmore," her mother warned.

"I need to check on the cabin," Aimee lied. "I need to know it's okay."

"Be careful, cherie. It's not safe."

Aimee ignored her mother's worries and left, more intent on escape than ever.

She got as far as the outskirts of the Park before she had to stop. There was a line of police vehicles crossing the flooded highway. Aimee rolled down the window, already knowing what she'd hear.

"You can't get any further," a weary officer explained. "It's flooded out. Don't you watch the news?"

"No," Aimee fibbed. "But I have a cabin in Banff. I need to get home."

"Not going to happen. Nobody's getting in or out."

"But I—"

"The highway's completely gone in some areas," he interrupted. "River tore right through it, so unless you've got a helicopter, you ain't going anywhere."

Furious, Aimee banged her hand against the steering wheel.

Tears of frustration filled her eyes and she blinked them angrily away. *Just want to get away!* her mind screamed.

"Miss?" the officer said. "You okay?"

"I'm fine," she said. "Just frustrated."

"We all are," he said with a grimace. "But it's better safe than sorry."

"Of course."

In minutes, Aimee was following the police cruiser across the highway and back away from the barricade. The car passed a sign which read: Dead Man's Flats.

"Don't even think about showing up, George," she snarled. But the car was empty save for the drumming of raindrops and as the miles passed, her mind roamed through the early years of their relationship.

She blinked, and a new memory appeared: Banff, eight years before.

Aimee stood in the doorway of the cabin's studio, a box of art supplies cradled in her arms. She'd brought them home when she'd returned from Queens University upon graduation. During the first two years of their marriage, she'd never really used the space, but now that she was finished with her studies, she planned to work on her own artwork. Aimee expected there'd be room for her supplies in the studio at the cabin.

George had other ideas.

"But if I can't leave my things here," Aimee said, "where do you expect me to work?"

"At the Glenbow, I'd presume." A massive canvas covered the entire south wall and George moved down the canvas a step at a time, leaving her to watch him paint. He might be twenty-five years her senior, but the bold lines of his brushwork were smoother than hers had ever been. Swathes of pigment spread outward across the massive stretch of canvas: a roughly blocked out image of a nude sitting on the edge of a bed. Riotous colour bloomed into broad shapes of a woman's curving back, her pale nakedness and face half-turned toward the viewer.

George glanced back at her. "You've got an office there. Right?" he asked. "I thought you said that when you took the job."

Her husband's work had changed in the years since she'd started her graduate degree, spending weeks at a time away from him. Aimee no longer worked as his studio assistant, though she remained his muse. Coming home after the final semester, she was surprised by the intensity of the colours he was using. Bombastic images filled the arena of his work. The naked woman was her, yes, but she'd grown larger than life in Aimee's time away.

"Yes," she said, distracted, "and Luis is fine for me to use it as I need."

"Great."

"But the office at the Glenbow is meant for restorations. That's *why* I have it."

Her words faded as she followed the motion of George's hands as he added another layer of colour on top of the first, the glazing catching the faint coolness of bluish shadow against warm alabaster skin. Bit by bit, the woman's hip and stomach morphed from Gauguin's warm, blurry colours to the subtly shifting underwater tones of Lucian Freud's nudes. The approach was so simple, yet impossibly right. An ache, somewhere between jealousy and admiration, bloomed in the center of Aimee's chest. George really was an incredible painter. Even his underpainting was heartbreakingly beautiful!

"Then you can use that studio for your own painting too," he said, drawing her from her thoughts. "No need to work here."

"You're not listening. My office is only for work, George, not artwork."

"There's a difference?" Another stroke, this time the hollow under the figure's jaw. He switched colours—dark brown rather than auburn—and began to block in shadows in the hair. Aimee stared at the brush and the thinned brown paint. Was this nude actually her? With the darkness of the hair, she couldn't tell.

"Well, yes, of course there's a difference." Aimee took two steps towards the canvas and stopped again. She tried to find the familiarity in the shape of the cheek, but found she couldn't. "I always assumed when I finished at Queens I could move my paints in here. I just need a place to work."

"As do I. That's the issue." George's brushstrokes grew faster, the curve of a jaw reaching up to meet the shell of an ear, all exposed through negative space, the face emerging from the darkness of the blocking. "Why don't you rent a place for yourself?"

"A second studio?"

"Yes. Here in Banff, or maybe in Calgary. Wherever you want. I'll pay, of course."

"But why?" She frowned as the muse's neck appeared, hair tumbling down her back. It was curly, but not curly enough. Her frown deepened. "The cabin studio is huge. It'd be no trouble for me to move in here and—"

"Goddamnit!" George erupted into a string of epithets as a drip of dark brown splashed down the canvas, marring the bare shoulder below. "Paint's too thin by half!" He grabbed a rag from the table, swiping the wayward pigment away, his lips pulled back in a grimace. A smear of brown—like a bruise—spread over the nude's arm.

Aimee cleared her throat, forcing herself to stay calm. They were still getting used to one another, after all. They'd only been married for a couple years and for much of their time together she'd been in Kingston. "I'll just take the far corner of the room," she said. "Over by the window would be fine. I work smaller than you do, so I wouldn't take up much—"

"I need my space!" George barked. "You know that." He scrubbed away for a few seconds. The bruise grew until even the underpainted skin tone began to lift. George made an angry animal sound, smearing once more, the paint spreading further, the wet hair and dried jawline blurring. "Fuck! Now look at this mess!"

Aimee's hands clutched reflexively at the box in her hands. She didn't come any closer. They'd lived together long enough to know that most of George's anger was bluster. *Most.*

"The acrylic's still wet and you're rubbing too hard," she said quietly. "If you keep scrubbing at it, the cloth will lift the under-painting."

He swiped at the canvas again. Another punch of darkness, the beauty marred.

"Motherfucker! Now look at it!" he roared. "Destroyed!" He slammed the brush into the canvas, a line of darkness slicing across the muse's grieving face.

Aimee flinched. "Stop!" She stepped forward and her free hand lifted. "*Please*. You're making it so much worse."

George's lip curled. "You're distracting me by being here!" He whipped the rag to the side and picked the paintbrush off the floor, giving her his back. "This is why I can't have you underfoot all the time. THIS!"

"But it's a big space." She set down her box on the floor and picked up a fresh cotton towel from the side table, wetting it at the sink before she returned to the canvas. "I assumed now that I was back home I'd be able to—"

"I told you already: I need a place to focus!" He stepped up to the canvas and reached out to add to the contour again, but she blocked his arm.

"Please wait, George." She sighed. "I can fix this for you."

He glared at her.

Aimee leaned in, bringing the soaked cotton to the smeared mess and dabbing away as she'd been trained. The bruise slowly faded from the figure's cheek, the muddy colours shifting into clean hues. "I'll give you space when you need it," she said quietly. "We've worked together before, after all."

"No," he sneered. "You worked for me."

His words stung, but she refused to rise to the bait. "Maybe so, but I helped you. I was there in the studio at your side."

"There's a world of difference between colleagues and their assistants."

Hands shaking, Aimee tossed the paint soaked cotton into the sink and crossed her arms. "There. The smear is fixed."

George grunted and went back to painting, his turned back dismissing her. She watched for a minute, then two, waiting for him to turn around. Aimee's temper flickered under her calm facade. *Not even a thank you for the help.* For the first time in months, she felt the long-simmering anger rekindle. They were married, weren't they? She wasn't just an assistant anymore. She was his wife. His equal. She deserved better than this.

"It's a big studio," she said, forcing her words to be gentle but firm.

"So what?"

"So there's room for me here." She gestured to the massive studio with its floor to ceiling windows. "There's plenty of space."

"But what would be the point?!" He spun back around, and then she could really see how angry he was. How frustrated he was that she didn't just nod and agree to his terms.

Aimee's temper flared hotter still. "Why are you so against this? Why are you being so…so…*selfish*, George?"

"You're the selfish one! I'm the artist in this house!"

"I have my own art!" she cried. "My own vision. You're not the only one who can paint. My art—"

"Your art?!" He stepped closer but she dodged him, putting the table between them. "You play with paints like a child, Aimee! Your 'work' is to restore. The rest is just craft, not real art at all."

Her throat bobbed. "That's not fair. I have a Master's degree."

"In restorations!"

"And an undergrad in Fine Arts. For goodness sake, George, you taught me how to paint! You said I could make a career out of—"

"I said lots of things to you, half of them to get you on your back!"

The words were a slap and she stepped backwards, bumping into an easel. It's legs screeched across the floor, and she spun around to catch it—protect his painting!—before it fell.

"Don't be like that."

"It's true!" he barked. "You're naïve to think otherwise. You used me as much as I used you."

"It wasn't like that for me!"

"Like hell it wasn't." George's mouth hardened into a line. "We both knew what we were after."

"Why are you being like this? I just want to use a space in our house. Our house! That hardly seems like an unreasonable—"

"You make noise when you paint! Mutter and talk to yourself. It's goddamned distracting!"

"I talk aloud. So what? You do the same sometimes. But I still need a place to create art."

"You're NOT an artist!" he bellowed. "You're a restorer!"

Her mouth dropped open, shocked into silence.

"It's a trade," George snapped. "The world needs it. Hell, even I need it once in a while." He nodded to the cleaned section of paint, his impatient mess gone. "I appreciate you, Aimee. I do! But your art—" He made air quotes. "—isn't the same as mine and it never will be. You need to understand that. I'm not going to bolster your nonexistent career. Stop fooling yourself about that! You AREN'T an artist!"

Somewhere deep inside her, something broke. Her anger shifted to pain. Half a minute passed before the first quiet sobs broke free of her chest. There it was, the thing she'd always feared, but never said aloud: That she really wasn't good at what she loved.

"Fuck you, George," she choked. "You're such an asshole some-times." She headed for the door, but he blocked her way. "Move," she said. "I'm going for a walk."

"Enough of this foolishness. I'll rent you a goddamned studio if you really want one. The biggest studio you ever saw."

"I don't want a separate studio. I want to work here!"

"This is nonsense!"

"Let me out, George!"

"Out?" He smiled down at her, but his flushed cheeks and nar-rowed eyes showed no kindness. "And here I thought you were try-ing to get in here the whole—"

"I'm not playing games here! Get out of my WAY!"

She lunged for the door, but George caught her by both arms. His hands were smeared with paint and dark circles smudged her skin like manacles.

"You're acting like a spoiled child. Stop it!"

She pulled and jerked, trying desperately to get away from him. The painted bruises grew into real ones. The truth was there, waiting just under the surface, like this unfinished painting of the nude. She loved George but she'd never ever be good enough for him. The canvas with the woman who was clearly *not* Aimee stared back over her shoulder with sad, knowing eyes.

Who did he bring in to model for him while I was away?

"Let me GO, George!"

"No!"

Aimee fought against him then, but every move she made seemed to bring them closer rather than further apart. Older though he might be, George was stronger and bigger. He soon had her wedged against the painting table. An easel to one side of her pinned her in position like a butterfly. George's hip pinned the other. Rough hands moved over her shoulders and back, holding her still as she fought him.

"Let me GO!" she said through clenched teeth.

"You're fucking beautiful when you're angry, you know," he growled. "Gets me harder than a rock, seeing you scream at me."

"I hate you!"

"No, you don't," he said with an angry laugh. "You love me." She smacked her forehead against his chin, but it didn't stop him. His lips moved against her ear, stubble grating against the soft skin of her face. "You've *always* loved me, Aimee!" One hand slid up to cup the back of her head, the other holding her still. "You want me more than you even know."

"Let me GO!"

"Tell me you want me."

"I don't!"

"Tell me!" George kissed her hard, leaving her head spinning when he broke away. "Say you love me!" he ordered.

"I hate you!"

"You're a bad fucking liar!" He kissed her again. She pounded against his chest with her hands, but George was a whirlpool in the ocean and she was drowning in him. He let go of her mouth, but his hands held tight.

Aimee's sobs grew in intensity.

"Tell me!" he repeated. "Tell me you love me!"

"NO!"

"Tell me you want me to fuck you, right here. Right now!"

"I don't!" she shouted.

"Lies!" George kissed her again. The embrace was punishing in its intensity, but it warmed her to her core. She could feel the moment things tipped for her. The heat that always seemed to pour off George had expanded to fill the room. Somewhere, she heard a distant crash. The easel fell, some abstract part of her noted, but she couldn't focus on it, not with the taste of him, the feel of him. He was right, of course, she did want him with an intensity that terrified her and always had. Aimee's struggles slowed as the kiss deepened, George's hands roving over her body. Her fists stopped pounding and she clung to him.

"You want me!" he grunted, as his hands slid over her breasts. "You love me!" Breathless, she writhed in his grip, her rebellious body igniting against her will. "You need me exactly the same way I need you."

The admission broke through the pain and her tear-ravaged eyes widened. "Y-you need me?"

"Aimee," he murmured between breaths. "My beautiful Aimee. Sweet, dangerous, wicked, Aimee. God, how I hate how much I love you!" He nipped his way down her neck, ripping open her shirt, sending buttons flying. He slanted his mouth down on hers again, bruising her lips. Aimee's heart pounded through her chest. *George loved her*. He needed her and that's why she had the upper hand. "You're mine!" he growled. "All mine!"

He abruptly reached down, grabbing her under her knees and pulling her into his arms. Gravity tilted.

"George don't!" she squeaked as he carried her from the studio to the bedroom. "You'll hurt your back."

Five steps took them down the hall. He kicked open the door and it banged against the wall.

"Tell me!" he said fiercely. "Tell me you love me."

"Put me down or you'll pull something! You won't be able to paint tomorrow."

"Tell me!"

He tossed her onto the bed and rolled on top of her a second later, pinning her beneath him. He was panting hard, his age coming through in the flushed colour of his wrinkled cheeks, the lines of purple veins that webbed his temple. Aimee's heart ached to see it. He looked older than he'd looked when she'd left for Kingston, but she loved each and every detail.

George cupped her chin, staring down into her eyes and soul. "You need me and I need you," he growled. "Tell me you love me like I love you!"

He leaned in until he filled her vision, the entire world becoming George Westerberg, the way it had always been since the moment she met him. Aimee's heart twisted in pain and grief and all the love for him that she couldn't bear to carry. He loved her. True. *But I love him more.* The pain of that certainty tore through the walls she kept trying to rebuild.

"Of course I love you," she whispered brokenly, new tears rolling down her cheeks and disappearing into her red hair. "How could you think otherwise?"

George leaned in and the entire world disappeared.

With a shaky breath, Aimee fought her way back to the present. She blinked. The water-clogged highway and the slashing wipers reappeared.

"That's how it is, to be a man's muse."

Aimee yelped in surprise and the vehicle swerved. She turned to discover a woman sitting in the car next to her.

"Frida," she breathed.

The artist wore a floor length red skirt and heavily embroidered white blouse. Long dark hair wove around her head in braids, a crown of flowers perched on top.

"Your husband," Kahlo said. "He was an artist too?"

"Yes," Aimee said. Her gaze flicked to the windshield splattered with rain, the highway teaming with cars, then back again. She couldn't remember thinking of the artist at *all* and yet here she was, talking with her for the first time!

"Was he a good artist?" the ghost asked.

"Very good."

"I wonder that I didn't know him then."

"Oh, George wouldn't have painted in your time. He's one of the best contemporary Canadian artists. Was, I mean. George was one of the best." Aimee winced. "He died last year. But he was genius when he was alive."

The ghost nodded. "Ah…That's the hardest type to manage."

Aimee gave a bitter laugh. "If you only knew."

For a long moment, the ghost sat quietly. Aimee took surreptitious glances to her side, but Kahlo remained. Vibrant and detailed, she looked even more real than Delacroix had.

"Can I ask you something?" Aimee asked.

"Of course."

Aimee's hands tightened on the wheel. "Why did you leave Diego, if you loved him?"

The ghost frowned, her lipsticked mouth tilting downward into a slash of crimson. "He'd taken up with my sister, Cristina. I could forgive the other affairs—it was Diego, after all, and I was no saint— but that particular one—" She sighed. "That betrayal, I could not."

"Then why did you come back to him?"

"Because I loved him more than my own skin and even though he didn't love me back the same way, Diego loved me in *his own way*. I learned to be satisfied with that." She smiled, the pain fading into deep sadness. "Besides, he believed in my art when others didn't. He told me I 'must continue to paint' and so I did. His certainty in my success became my own."

Aimee's eyes blurred with tears. "George never believed in my art. Never." She swallowed against the pain in her throat. "I wonder if that's why I stopped painting."

"Only you'd be able to answer that."

Several long seconds passed, marred by the sound of the windshield wipers. "Do you think I could start again, now? Could I find my own muse again?"

There was a long silence, and when Aimee glanced over at the passenger seat, she found it empty. Frida's ghost was no longer there to answer.

—

Days passed. Rivers broke their banks, tore houses off their foundations like children's toys and dashed them to pieces. Calgary's downtown core was still off limits and the damage tally growing. When the news announced that the water had finally crested, Aimee let out a sob of relief, but the troubles weren't over. A week later she was allowed to return to her apartment. Everything above the first floor of the high-rise was fine, but the Glenbow hadn't been so lucky. The lower levels had partially flooded, and the floor of Aimee's office was covered in an ankle deep layer of mud. While the custodial team shovelled the floors clean, Aimee had the insurmountable task of restoring the damage.

"You've got to be kidding," she said to Mr. Santos when he carried the last painting into her newly-cleaned office.

"I'm not kidding at all."

"But there are more than fifty of them, Luis!" she said, scanning the pile of canvases that filled the room. She'd never had more than two at a time. Today she had enough work for a year.

"There's more than that, but the least damaged ones are being cleaned by volunteers."

"Volunteers?" Aimee stepped between Luis and the paintings, hands rising. "They won't know how to—"

"They know enough," he said wearily.

"But what if they make it worse?"

"They won't. I'm supervising the clean-up myself." He gave her a weak smile. "These are the ones I'm most worried about, and that's why I'm leaving them to you."

She ran her hands through her hair in frustration. "There are so many of them."

Luis headed to the door. "I know that," he said. "But we've got to salvage what we can." He pushed open the door and a wave of moisture flooded the room. In the distance, the sound of high-powered fans, drying out the building, could be heard. "You're the best, Aimee. Everyone knows that."

"Thanks."

He rapped his knuckles against the door frame. "You need me to find you an assistant?"

"No. They'd just be in the way. Besides, I like working alone."

"That's what I thought," Luis chuckled. "Give me a shout if you change your mind."

—

Aimee spent the morning separating the work into categories of damage. Some of the oil paintings looked far worse than they were. She set them in the deep sinks to soak. The remaining ones she prioritized by damage and value. By noon, the works of several artists awaited her attention. The first was a small painting by Georgia O'Keefe.

Aimee set about organizing her tools after clearing the mud from the bottom of the frame. With the worst of it cleaned, she began to remove the final layers of silt with a fine tip brush. Stroke by stroke she peeled back the damage, until only a mostly clean painting remained. There were a few cracks and peeling areas, likely there prior to the flooding, but Aimee took her time matching colours as afternoon stretched out into evening.

"That's very good," a woman said quietly.

Aimee didn't jiggle the brush she was holding, just smiled. She'd been thinking about Georgia for some time, but the artist hadn't appeared. Aimee wondered if she'd been waiting behind her for long.

"I'm not actually doing much," Aimee said, "just touching up a bit of wear. The mud took the finish off."

"Ah, but the colours are right," the ghost said, coming around the other side of the table. "That's difficult to do."

O'Keefe's ghost was dressed in a floppy-brimmed hat and long dress, a man's jacket atop the ensemble. Aimee smiled. This wasn't the young version of Georgia, but a woman at the end of her life, her long grey hair a rope that twisted down her back.

"Your colours are very pure," Aimee said, adding another layer of glaze and blending away the edges. "They aren't muddy." She smirked. "Or at least not any longer."

"Not muddy, that's true," said the ghost, "but hardly pure."

Aimee stopped painting and looked up. "They're not?"

"Oh no. They have layers and layers of variation to them. A tint of blue in the red, a tint of red in the yellow. Nothing real is pure. At least not that I've found."

"I suppose."

"People are more comfortable thinking of things in extremes," O'Keefe said. "We like the clarity of black and white. Not just in painting, but in life. We think of everything this way."

"People too?"

"Of course. We're at our worst when we consider the failings and successes of others."

Aimee's expression dimmed. "I used to think George was perfect. As an artist, he certainly was."

"But?"

"But as a person, he could be difficult." She laughed tiredly. "I loved him with my entire being. I was his—body and soul—but there were parts of him that I ended up having to overlook."

"The tints in the colour," the ghost said.

"Yes, exactly."

"Was it jealousy?"

Aimee frowned. "A bit, I suppose, back when George was my teacher and I thought that—with enough time—I could learn to paint like him."

"Oh, not *your* jealousy, dear." O'Keefe laughed. "I meant his.

Weak men are always threatened by strong women."

It was Aimee's turn to laugh. "I'm not strong."

The ghost tapped her cane on the floor. "That's what he wanted you to believe."

"But George was never jealous of me," Aimee said. "He thought himself far superior as an artist. He was the one who suggested I move into restorations work. I was very skilled at mixing colours when I worked in his studio, you see."

"And he advised you to put aside your artwork?"

"Well, yes," Aimee said with reluctance. "But I'd already been thinking of going back to university. I was struggling to paint, to find a style that felt right."

"Hmm," O'Keefe said. "I wonder at that."

"At my style?"

"No. That he told you to set aside your art." She frowned. "Perhaps that's the tint you couldn't see in him."

"Perhaps." Aimee's expression tightened. "I've been thinking a lot about George lately. How many things could have been different for us if he wasn't so stubborn." She laughed and turned back to the painting, reloading the brush with pigment. "Difficult doesn't mean I didn't love him. George was my everything."

"You're just getting better at seeing the entire picture of him, now."

"Yes, I think I might be."

She leaned in, adding another shade beside the first. Another twenty minutes passed. When she lifted her head again, the vision of the artist had moved to her other side. The ghost held her hat in wrinkled hands, peering forward in interest.

"You understand it," O'Keefe murmured. "The beauty in the details. You've caught what I wanted to show perfectly."

Aimee squinted at the wash of colours. "I suppose."

The ghost laughed. "Don't suppose. You should be sure. You're the one restoring the painting."

"I just try to follow the path," Aimee said, adding another small spot of glaze. "Trying to find the exact spot where your brush went down, and came up again." She sighed. "It's very calming."

"The details," the ghost agreed. "That's where you can find the centre point in the storm. Details are the joy, the heart of all things."

"Details," Aimee repeated.

"Look too far and the world is utter chaos," the ghost said. "Happiness lies in the minutia of life." She nodded. "That's the secret no one knows. That's where your joy is hidden."

Aimee finished spreading the last spot of glaze and looked up. She could see through the ghost, but details were visible if she didn't look too hard: the freckled age spots on the back of O'Keefe's sinewy hands clutching the hat; the wrinkles spreading away from faded eyes; the soft wave of her hair.

"I'm not sure I know how to be happy anymore," Aimee whispered. "I haven't been happy since…" Aimee frowned. She knew she *should* say 'since George' but she had been *almost* happy the other day when she and Bear had sat and drunk tea. A flush rose up her neck at the thought. "In a long time," she finished lamely.

The ghost nodded. "Then you'll have to look closer," she said. "It's always there, under all the mess and muck. Joy. Waiting to be found."

Someone knocked and Aimee turned to find Niha standing in the doorway, phone in hand. She wore a full length painter's jumpsuit and gum boots, her long hair in ponytails on either side of her head.

"You were talking to yourself again," Niha said with a grin. She pointed at Aimee with the phone. "Just then, a second ago. I told you that you do that."

Aimee's cheeks burned; she turned away, pretending to finish a final stroke. "Side effect of working alone."

"Doesn't bother me any," Niha said. "I talk to my cats all the time. Some people think that's weird."

She laughed, and Aimee tried to join her, but failed.

"You have another message," Niha said, coming forward and setting the yellow sticky note on the desk beside Georgia's painting. "From that Barrett Cardinal guy again. Something about a second interview you agreed to do?" Niha gave her a mischievous grin. "Something you want to tell me, Aimee? Something personal, maybe?"

"There's nothing between us, Niha. He just wants to get my perspective this time. He has more questions."

She giggled. "Still, it's a start. Luis told me he's the same 'Barrett Cardinal' that won the Giller prize last year." Niha pulled a stool over from the side, and settled down next to Aimee. "He's a big celebrity, you know. You could find worse people to date. Luis said as much."

Aimee ignored the not-so-subtle dating hint. "Luis said that, hmm?"

"Uh-huh." Niha grinned. "Seemed really worried you were going to insult the guy or something. Don't worry, I told him you already did an interview."

"Thanks."

Aimee turned back to the painting, hoping Niha would leave her alone.

"He's determined, isn't he?" Niha said.

Aimee glanced up. "Luis?"

"No, this Bear guy," she laughed. "So are you going to call him back, or what? Second interview might be the pretext, but I'm thinking there's more to it."

"More, like what?"

Niha leaned in as if sharing a covert piece of information. "If you ask me, I think the guy likes you."

Aimee fought the urge to smile. "Doubt it."

"He keeps calling. Following up on things."

"He's researching," Aimee said dryly. "It's literally his job."

"But he *already* talked to you. And now he wants to talk to you again."

"Doesn't matter," Aimee said. "I'm not going to see him again."

Niha's expression fell. "But why not? He told me you'd already agreed to the second interview."

"I did, but I've changed my mind." Aimee set her brush aside, pushing back from the canvas. There was no use pretending; Niha wasn't leaving. "He's not interested in me. He's interested in George. It's a book he's writing, not a single's ad."

"Pfft! You're blind," Niha laughed.

"And you're young."

Niha clucked her tongue. "I'm right. You're just too stubborn to see it."

"Not even going there."

Niha opened her mouth to argue, but the phone in her hand rang. Aimee smiled in relief. She liked Niha, but the prying was exhausting. Some days it felt like managing her mother's good intentions.

"You've reached the Glenbow," Niha chirped. "How may I direct your call?" She paused, glancing over at Aimee. "Uh-huh. Yes, I *did* give her your message, Mr. Cardinal." Niha smirked. "Actually, she's sitting right here."

Don't! Aimee mouthed, her eyes widening in horror.

"No problem," Niha said with a victorious smile. She held out the phone. "Aimee, there's a Mr. Barrett Cardinal on the phone for you," she said in a slightly-too-loud voice.

Scowling, Aimee picked up the phone. *I hate you*, she mouthed at Niha.

"Blind, huh?" the assistant whispered, dodging Aimee's swat as she headed to the door. "And I want my phone back when you're done."

Aimee sighed, and lifted the handset. Her heart was pounding.

"Aimee Tessi—" she stumbled on the words. She no longer used her maiden name. "Aimee speaking," she said, fighting down the urge to scream.

"Aimee, so glad I caught you," Bear said. "Everything okay?"

"Yes…no." She sighed. "No worse than usual."

"You have time to chat? I know how busy you are, but I'd really like to do this second interview sooner rather than later."

Aimee glared at the pile of damaged paintings. Several were soaking, but none were ready for repairs. Georgia O'Keefe was back over at the side, watching her with a knowing smile.

"Yeah, I suppose we could find a time to talk."

—

Bear watched Aimee as she sat at the table, her hair a rippling curtain that hid half her face. Through the first half hour, she'd struggled to pull the words, answering him in fits and starts, but as they started another pot of tea, something changed. She didn't look at him, just stared into her empty teacup, her lips curled in wistful smile. Bear didn't know what had caused the change—that he'd asked the right question, or that she was just tired of hiding the truth—but either way, he was relieved that it had.

Aimee's voice rose and fell in waves as her fingers played with the edge of the tablecloth. "The first thing I fell in love with was George's passion," she said. "The way a brush in his hand could transform him, the way a painting drew out the best and worst from him."

"The worst?"

She smiled sadly down at the table, not holding his gaze. "All the things you said about him at the gallery were true. He was driven, but sometimes—"

"Sometimes?" Bear prompted.

"Sometimes when he was in the middle of a painting, he could be—" She abruptly sat taller, crossing her arms. "I mean, he always drank but there were times when—" Her gaze jerked up. Bear could feel her fear, palpable between them as if she'd suddenly realized that he was going to write about this. "I'm sorry," she said. "I shouldn't have said that. I didn't mean—"

Bear leaned closer. "Tell me about his painting," he said quietly. "Tell me about the process."

Aimee's arms uncrossed and she reached out for her tea, taking a sip and watching him over the rim. "George painting, hmm?"

Bear nodded. "You worked in his studio," he said. "Ms. Westerberg-Kinney—George's daughter, that is—she told me she was never allowed in his studio at home. But you," Bear said gently. "You were."

A flush rose up Aimee's neck. "Well, I had to be there," she said with a nervous laugh. "I was his muse for many years. And then…" Her voice drained away.

"You were telling me about George's painting," Bear said.

Aimee set her cup on the table, nodding.

"It was exhilarating to watch George paint. He'd be consumed by the need to create; not eating or drinking, not sleeping for days. His hands moving in a blur, barely aware of me in the shadows watching." She sighed. "Or posing."

"Consumed by his painting," Bear said, scribbling a note. "I like that."

"Watching him paint was amazing. A little crazy. Scary even," Aimee said. "That's what I thought a true artist was supposed to be. And to see him like that, it made me want more." She reached out tracing the handle of the cup, eyes unfocused. Bear was hesitant to break the truce between them, but knew that this was the time to ask it. The tea pot was dry, the cups half-empty. There was no more time.

"Is that why you fell in love with him? Seeing him paint?"

Aimee giggled, the sound surprisingly light. "Oh god, no," she laughed. "I didn't think of him like that at *all* in the beginning. He was much older than I was and I was in love with his talent. Jealous of him, I suppose. I wanted to learn everything from him." She looked up at Bear, grinning mischievously. He had the sudden, irrational urge to touch her, but he tightened his fingers around his pen instead. "My infatuation with George came much, much later," Aimee said. Her expression had changed and her gaze flitted away, warmth colouring her cheeks.

Bear wanted to know why. "But you *did* fall in love."

"Yes," she said. "And then I knew I was entirely lost. I couldn't compete with his real passion. Couldn't be the lover that art was for him. But I could be his muse, and like that, even my dullness could be transformed into—"

"But you aren't dull," Bear interrupted.

"You don't see the world like George did."

Bear frowned. "You're an artist too."

"Was," she said. "I'm a restorer now."

"You don't paint for yourself anymore?"

Aimee took another sip of tea, setting the empty cup carefully down in the saucer. "Not in a long time."

Around them the noise of the coffee shop had faded into a buzz. Bear placed his hands on the tabletop on either side of his cup. He watched her for a long moment, waiting for her to continue. Aimee's gaze skittered nervously to him, and then away.

"Did he ask you to put your art aside?"

Aimee's lashes flared wide, white appearing around the green. "Oh god, no! No. At least not directly."

Bear frowned. "Then why?"

"I was his muse at first, and his painting, his process, took priority." She went back to tracing the cup handle as she spoke. "I could have painted on my own time, or after George was done his own paintings, but we couldn't paint in the same room."

"Why not?"

"He found my process distracting."

Bear frowned. "I don't understand."

She laughed, but it was high-pitched. More like the woman he'd met at the opening, not the woman he'd spoken with all afternoon. "I can't, Bear." She swallowed hard. "You'll think I'm crazy."

He winked. "Try me."

Aimee peered behind her as if searching for onlookers. "I don't just paint," she said warily. "I sort of…channel my artwork."

"Channel?"

"It sounds nuts, but I think of things before I create them. I can imagine them—imagine them so perfectly!—and if I'm in the moment, really in flow, sometimes I can even—" She dropped her voice to a whisper. "See them."

Bear nodded. "And?"

She squinted at him. "And that's crazy, right?"

Bear grinned. "Depends what you mean by crazy," he said. "I mean, when I was sixteen, I went on my first vision quest. I saw things when I was fasting—real things—that had meaning for me. Things that changed who I became."

Aimee stared at him. "A vision quest?"

Bear nodded. "A spirit journey. It's an altered state where you get guidance from the Creator and the spirit world. It's a rite of passage—at least it is with the Tsuut'ina—that signifies your transition into adulthood."

"Messages from the spirit world. How does that work?"

"Well, there are different rites for different tribes, but in almost all of them you fast, you pray, and—hopefully—you see things during the journey."

"Do you mean see them physically?"

"My great-grandmother used to describe it this way: We all have two eyes. One lets you see what's there. The other lets you see what you feel."

"The artist, Paul Klee, said that too."

"He did?"

Aimee nodded. "One eye sees, the other feels." She reached out, laying her hand open on the table next to his. "Thank you for telling me," she said. "It means a lot to me."

Bear slid his fingers into hers, his body reacting to the connection. Two palms together, warm and cool, nothing more; but something changed in that moment.

He nodded. "Same."

—

Aimee slid the key into the lock, a faint smile lingering on the curve of her lips. Lunch with Bear had been unexpectedly good. If he called her again to get a third interview—and there was a secret voice inside her that kept shouting that he would—she knew she'd say 'yes' without delay. Today had been a turning point. A step forward. Aimee had wanted Bear's company, and he wanted hers too.

Aimee pushed the door of the condo open and stepped inside, the smile widening into a grin. She'd felt alive while she and Bear had talked. *Real*. It felt like she'd been sleeping, and today, for the first time in months, she'd finally awoken. She looked up, and her expression froze.

George's ghost waited in the foyer, foot tapping.

"You're late," he growled, the raw scent of alcohol wafting forward.

Aimee looked away, chest tightening. She hadn't thought about George in the last half hour or so, but here he was.

"Go away," she said. "You're not really here." Aimee tugged off her coat and reached for a hanger.

"I bloody well am here," George snapped. "And you're late."

Aimee hung up her coat, and lifted her gaze. "Go away," she repeated firmly.

The apparition stepped nearer.

"No."

Aimee's hands curled into fists, heart pounding. "Go away, George. You're not—"

"Why are you late?!" he barked.

Aimee took a step backward. "I had a meeting."

"What kind of meeting?"

He swirled the glass he carried, ice cubes clinking.

"I was meeting with a writer," she said evenly. "Someone doing a book about you."

That stopped him, but not for long.

"A man?" he snarled.

"Yes, a man," Aimee said, lifting her chin. "What of it?"

Aimee stepped past George and headed to the kitchen. She could walk through him—she'd seen David Arturo do it—but something held her back.

A second later, George followed. "Who was he?" he taunted. "Someone I know? Someone you've been chasing around with while I'm here at home?"

She knew those words. Their intonation was so close to the fights they'd had before George had taken off to New York that long-ago winter. Aimee's throat closed and she fought to breathe. She hadn't believed he'd return to her that time, but he had.

"He's a writer. A very good one, actually."

George's mouth twisted into the semblance of a smile. "You fucked him yet?"

"No!"

"But you want to."

"He's an author," she said. "He's writing a book about you. That's all." She turned her back to the apparition, breathing hard. Her ears were ringing, body tense. "This isn't real," she said shakily. "This is all in my mind. When I turn around, the room is going to be empty. George will be gone, and I'm—"

George stepped in front of her, and she yelped.

"You always knew how to turn heads," he sneered. "Did it with me too. You've lowered your standards!"

"Stop it!"

George's lips twisted angrily. She could smell the alcohol, could feel the warmth of his breath when he shouted: "He's talented, huh? That must get you nice and wet!"

Aimee took a step back and George followed. "It's nothing like that. Nothing like that at all."

"You think?"

"Yes," she said hoarsely. "Yes, I do. I'm doing this—" Her voice broke. "I'm doing this for you, George. For your legacy. You've got to believe me."

"Guilt has a face, sunshine." He lifted the drink in silent toast. "And you're the one wearing it."

Aimee opened her mouth and closed it again, her attempted calm crumbling under the weight of his accusation. The trembling of her hands had grown in intensity; the room around her was inexplicably icy cold.

"Not true."

"You're fucking him, aren't you?!"

"I'm not," she said. "But even if I was, it wouldn't be wrong.

You're dead, George. Dead."

George smiled darkly, baring even white teeth. "Might be," he said, looming nearer. "But I'm not going anywhere."

He lunged.

With a scream, Aimee bolted past him, heading out of the condo.

CHAPTER SEVEN

Aimee walked the downtown streets, too upset to return. *He's not real,* her mind screamed. *George is dead. He can't be back!* But there was another part of her mind which wasn't so certain. The part that remembered another conversation that had taken place on the floor of the kitchen in the cabin in Banff:

"Don't go. Stay with me, George. Stay."

"I'll try."

If he was real—*If!* her mind shouted, he was a poltergeist, and not just a figment of her imagination—then she was the cause. The two voices went round and round in her mind until she was weak and weary. *If George wasn't real,* then she was creating this, the way she imagined the artists whose works she repaired. *If George WAS real,* then she was cheating, or would be, if things progressed with Bear. Aimee had no idea which option was true, but long after her tears had dried, the threat of George's temper kept her away.

Walking without direction, her feet fell into a well-worn path and she found herself standing before the side entrance to the Glen-bow. It was long past nightfall. She could hear the vacuums of the night custodial crew, the honk of passing cars on the street. Aimee glanced at her phone: 10:52 p.m.; far too late to call her mother. And she wouldn't be able to sleep even if she went over. With a sigh, she pulled out her key fob and swiped the door to buzz herself inside.

In minutes she was ensconced in her office. The scent of mildew wrapped her in a cloak, the faint whir of the fans running in the depths of the basement a steady hum. The unsettled emotions—the terror of that truth she didn't want to face: that she might really be going crazy; that this may indeed be a mental break, one she couldn't control—all disappeared as she picked up a cleaned, but unrepaired artwork. It was a Warhol print from 1963: synthetic polymer paint and silkscreen ink on canvas. The mud had dulled the bright whites of Elizabeth Taylor's celebrity smile, though the darker, brighter colours remained firm. It was a simple repair, and soon Aimee was matching the undamaged pigment with her own acrylic mixture. She painted a series of lines along a test board, then leaned back to wait. Colours changed ever so slightly when pigment was dry, and she needed to be sure.

"That looks good."

Aimee turned to the door, expecting to find Steve or one of the other night security guards watching her, but the door was closed. She ran a hand over her face. *Should head home to get some sleep,* she thought, *I'm starting to hear things.*

"Yes, surprisingly good actually," the voice added. "I like it. Like it a lot."

Aimee squeaked. She turned the other direction to discover Andy Warhol lounging on one of the stools, one leg thrown jauntily over his knee.

"Andy Warhol," Aimee murmured. She usually enjoyed her unexpected visions, but tonight she was unusually sensitive to her mind's tricks. "I wasn't expecting you." She frowned. Why would he show up if she wasn't trying to call him to mind? That wasn't how it worked.

The ghost unfolded his legs, stepping off the stool with the ungainly motions of a stork. "Could have used you in the studio," he said, nodding to her work. "Would have saved so much time, having someone who was able to match colours like that."

"Thanks." She stared at him with wary eyes, focusing on the edges of his form—not quite solid—which grew, like layers of smoke, into opacity near the centre. Could she make him disappear? Aimee narrowed her gaze and focused. Long seconds passed.

Andy stayed.

"You've got an eye for colour," he said.

Aimee put the brush back against the canvas, silently cursing. She *used* to be able to get rid of them, but lately it seemed like her visions were the ones in charge. "Go away," she muttered, but the apparition came closer. "I don't want to talk."

"Are you art school trained?" he asked.

Aimee scowled.

"I said, are you trained?"

She glanced up. "Yes. I took a post-graduate restorations degree at Queens University."

"No, not restoration," he said, waving away her words with his hand. "I mean, are you an artist?"

"I was," Aimee said wearily. She lifted the brush, adding another daub of paint to the canvas and spreading it in thin layers across the surface.

Andy stood beside her, nodding. "But not anymore?"

"No, Andy. Not in a long time."

She leaned in, scanning for damage. Andy cleared his throat.

"Yes?" Aimee said.

"There's a spot there," he said, pointing to a smudge of grey near the corner. "Just a small one, but still."

"Thanks," she muttered.

Aimee loaded the brush again, covering the faded marks. Every so often she peered up at the apparition through a fringe of lashes. Blue jeans and boots, a black turtleneck and leather jacket. She could see he wasn't real if she looked right at him, but if she ignored him, the vision took on solid form. *Next time, I'll try that with George,* she thought grimly.

"Ah. That's very good," Andy said with a laugh. "Almost better than the original."

"Hardly," Aimee snorted. "It's not your work anymore."

Bright laughter followed her statement. She lowered her brush, setting it into the tray alongside the paints.

"What?"

"You must be kidding," Andy snorted.

"About what?"

The ghost ran a hand through the grey tousle of his wig, leaving bits of it standing on end. "I hardly touched any of my work. They were factory produced. Factory made. I was part of that, of course." He tapped his temple, giving her a mischievous grin. "But I didn't necessarily create them with my own hands."

"Right," Aimee muttered. "I knew that."

"Of course you did. And don't feel bad," Andy said, reaching out to pat her shoulder. "I forget myself sometimes."

She shivered. There was no pressure to his touch, but she felt colder somehow. George's ghost flickered in the back of her mind. George had never tried to touch her, but what if he did? Would she feel that? She wrapped her arms around her, fighting the ice that seemed to grow inside her.

Andy stepped back from the canvas, inspecting it from another angle. "That's the secret, you know. It's the connections we make." The ghost's smile widened. "It's what we do with them that matter. Not the actual person who puts the brush on the page—you or me, or anyone else—but it's how we create: Artists, poets, writers."

Aimee frowned, remembering the argument—real or imagined—with George about her meeting with Barrett Cardinal.

"But what if those connections mean hurting someone we love?"

"Then it happens," he said.

"It doesn't bother you to hurt someone you care for?" she asked. "Not by purposefully being cruel or anything, but by connecting with someone else."

The ghost's expression shifted. He no longer seemed like the slick pop art deal-maker most people knew, but an aging artist wearing a ridiculous wig. "Oh, I know a little bit about that," he said.

Aimee could feel the name on the tip of her tongue, but Andy answered the unspoken question before she could even say it.

"Jed never understood my need to be with other creatives: Artists, actors, street kids and the like. To experience life, all parts of it. The good and bad. I wanted to know it all."

A line appeared between Aimee's brows. "You sound a bit like George."

"George who?"

"Westerberg. My late husband."

Andy laughed. "You mean George Westerberg, the Canadian ex-pat?"

"Yes, that's him."

"Ol' Georgie!" Andy threw his head back, laughing happily. "Guy was a firecracker back when I knew him. A drinker and a fighter, even if he was the art world's latest up and comer! Always off on some crazy scheme, drinking until all hours then showing up at the studio to argue with me about the meaning of life. Never thought I'd see the day he settled down."

"He did," Aimee said dryly. "Twice, actually."

"That surprises me." Warhol smirked. "Congratulations, I suppose."

"Thanks, but not all of our marriage was happy."

"Are they ever?"

"Some are," she said with a sigh. "My parents' marriage certainly was."

"But not yours."

She sat with that thought for a long time, silent as the old pain filled her chest, then eased as something *else* appeared. Hard truth. While she and George's passion had been a wildfire, it had burned as much as warmed them. There were too many painful moments to ignore, too many troubles dotted in amongst the laughter and joy and sexual exploits. Aimee's shoulders slumped.

"Most of the time things were fine, but George wanted what he wanted. And since I was younger than him, he just assumed I'd be the one who'd give in." She reached out to straighten the line of brushes as she spoke. "He never really understood me or my needs. I had things that I wanted too. Hopes and dreams, but George never gave me space to do them. Just expected me to put them aside."

Andy leaned forward, his bony elbows resting on skinny knees. "So what's stopping you from doing all those things now?"

"I—" Aimee frowned. "I honestly don't know."

"Artists do what they need to do." He straightened his jacket and gave her an enigmatic smile. "You should too."

—

When Aimee stumbled out of her office mid-morning, she found the Glenbow buzzing with activity. Workmen carried sheets of drywall past her and hammering echoed through the hallway. Aimee skirted them and plodded slowly up the busy stairwell to the main lobby. Sometime in the last hour, the morning staff had arrived. Bright bands of sunlight poured through the front windows, the first clear day in a month. She squinted against the glare.

"Morning!" Niha said. "Heading out to grab a coffee?"

"Heading home, actually." Aimee forced a smile. "I worked late."

"Late," Niha laughed. "Honey, it's almost ten in the morning. You worked all night!"

"Yes, but I got the Warhol finished."

"Really? That's awesome."

Aimee stretched her back. "Thanks. If you could let Luis know, that'd be great."

"I will," Niha said, "but you should get some sleep. You're going to make yourself sick if you don't."

Aimee stumbled to the front door. "Just tell Luis. Alright?"

By the time she walked the five blocks to the condo, Aimee was so tired she could barely think. She struggled with the key in the lock, only discovering after a minute of cursing that she was using the cabin key rather than the apartment key. She switched keys and staggered through the door. The lights were still on, the answering machine flashing.

No sign of George.

She pressed play and pulled her jacket off before dropping it on the floor. The machine beeped, and a well-known voice echoed from the speaker.

"*Hi, Aimee. It's Bear. I was wondering if you had time to talk again. I know, I know, I said two interviews.*" Warm laughter broke through his words and she smiled at the sound. "*But after I wrote up some of the things you said, I thought we should talk again. Three times the charm, right?"* Aimee kicked off her shoes, staring at the answering machine as she waited for him to continue. *"I'd feel better if you took a look at what I wrote in your chapter before I go any further. I was serious about letting you have a voice in how you're portrayed. Anyhow, if you have a minute I thought we could get together again."* He cleared his throat. *"I guess what I'm trying to say is I liked talking with you the other day and I'd like to do it again."*

Heart pounding, Aimee glanced furtively around the foyer, but it was empty. George was gone. Alone, a knowing smile curled her lips. *Bear liked talking to me.*

The answering machine beeped, pulling her back to the present. She waited through two more messages: due to its position on the mountain, the cabin in Banff was safe from flooding, but David figured it would impact the price, given that the gardens were completely waterlogged. The second was from her lawyer. Jacqueline was demanding that Aimee pass over a list of items she considered "family heirlooms". Would Aimee have time to look at the list, as a sign of good faith?

Aimee wilted under the new request. It felt like there was a never-ending litany of them.

"Fuck you, Jacqueline," she muttered, and hit delete.

—

The wedding was a small, private affair, held in the backyard of their newly purchased cabin on the weekend before Aimee headed to Queens University to finish her graduate degree. Aimee wore a white sundress and sandals, George, a linen suit. The only people in attendance were Claudine, and a handful of friends. It was, Aimee thought, the best day of her life.

She'd been wrong.

When they returned from a dinner at the Banff Springs Hotel, there was a message waiting on the phone.

"Leave it," George growled, his hands roving over Aimee's thin dress to cup her breasts. "I want to get this off you."

She swatted his hand away with a giggle. "I want to hear," Aimee said. "Lots of my friends couldn't come. They'll still want to send their congrats."

"Suit yourself," George said, tugging her against him. He bit her shoulder and she shivered. "Just don't expect me to listen."

"Hold your horses," she giggled as she pressed the play button. "We've got all the time in the world to screw around as horny newlyweds."

There was the buzz of the tape rewinding and then a woman's voice: "*This message is for a George Westerberg. I'm not sure this is the right number...*"

George's hand against Aimee's waist was suddenly too tight.

"Shit!" George snapped, releasing Aimee and fumbling with the answering machine.

"*If this is him,*" the woman continued. "*I want to let you know that Jacqueline told me you were remarrying, George. I didn't believe it at first.*"

"George?" Aimee said. "Who is it?"

"*I couldn't believe that you'd treat me like this. I thought we had something. That I meant something to you.*"

"How does this fucking thing work?!" he barked, pushing buttons at random.

"*So if this is your number, then let me say this: you're a liar and a bastard, and, well, I hope this new wife of yours screws you over the same way that you—*"

With a jerk, George tugged the cords out of the wall and the machine fell to the floor. Aimee stared at it, broken, on the hardwood. Her mind was reeling: Jacqueline was George's daughter. She'd refused to attend their wedding; she hated Aimee and had made no bones about that. But who was this other woman?

Aimee's gaze lifted. "George?"

He shook his head. "I need a drink."

He turned away, but Aimee stepped in front of him.

"Don't," she said. "Not today." Her voice broke. "Not on our wedding day."

George took a low breath as if steeling himself for something unpleasant. The jovial humour was gone, something else hanging between them.

"George, please."

His face contorted. Pain? Or something else. Aimee didn't know. All she could read was anger.

"I said my vows," George said grimly. "And I meant them. But I hope you don't think I was a saint before I met you."

Aimee swallowed against a lump in her throat. Her palms were moist and she wiped them against the side of her thin silk dress. "I just— Who was she?" she stammered. "How does she know your daughter? Why would she call you? Why?"

George reached out, running a finger down Aimee's cheek, wiping away the tears that had begun to fall.

"That was the past," he said quietly. "It's over."

"But I—"

"You are my future, Aimee. You. No one else." He pulled her close. "You understand?"

She nodded. "Yes."

George smiled, his hands moving up over the bare skin of her shoulders to cup her chin. "I love you," he whispered. "You're my muse."

Aimee opened her mouth to argue: muses changed like whims. She'd known enough artists to realize that truth. "But what if—?"

His voice grew dark. "You're mine."

He leaned down, kissing the rest of her fears away, Aimee clinging to his shoulders. They were married. His mouth against hers was all that mattered, and by the time he pulled back, her arguments were long forgotten. She took a gasping breath, the room spinning.

"I love you, George."

He grinned devilishly before he grabbed her wrist and tugged her to the stairs. "Good," he growled.

And Aimee could almost forgive the fact that his fingers were so tight she had a circle of bruises in the morning.

—

The answering machine appeared in Aimee's slumbering thoughts, the vague sound of voices lingering in the half-waking state as the day crawled past. Her mother, Claudine: *Cherie, I'm getting worried here! I haven't heard from you in days. Call me. Please!* Bear's voice once and then again: *Niha told me you'd gone home early. You alright? Give me a call back.*

His words invaded her dreams with secret imaginings. Behind closed lids, the two sat in the empty coffee house—or was it the cabin in Banff? In the dream, Bear reached out across the table, but Aimee didn't just take his hand. This time she leaned in and kissed him. A tug pulled him closer and soon they were in each other's arms, Aimee finally released to do the things she'd always wanted to…

Aimee's lids fluttered open to find the bedroom drenched in mid-afternoon sunshine. She searched the corners of the room, but it was empty, George's ghost nowhere to be found. She sat up, running her hand over her face and groaned. If she didn't get up now, she'd never sleep tonight.

There wasn't any point in going into work. Flex time meant that her hours accumulated and Luis was adamant about maintaining them. Aimee already had more built up than any other person at the Glenbow. She looked guiltily at the blinking light of the answering machine. Aimee knew that her mother wasn't above showing up unannounced if she was worried, so she called Claudine back, lying about the rush to repair the damaged artwork, and then chatting about useless things—the weather and gardening—and assuring her mother that she was doing fine. Then only Bear's message remained. A flash of her dream appeared, and her cheeks burned. She wanted to see him again, but needed time to pull herself together before she called him back.

In the end, she ran errands. She'd destroyed her last pair of runners slogging through the mud that caked the roads of downtown Calgary, and gum boots were only going to be acceptable work-

wear for so long. Shoe shopping seemed an innocuous enough way
to spend the day.

As Aimee stood next to the sales rack, scanning the leftovers
from last season—even these seemed out of her price range—an
elderly woman stepped up next to her.

"Sorry," Aimee said. "I'll get out of your way."

The woman smiled. "You need to bury him," she said.

Aimee blinked. "What?"

The woman stared. "He's never going to leave you alone otherwise."

Aimee glanced over her shoulder, but she was the only person
in the store besides the saleswoman. None of her ghosts lingered in
the corners. "I don't know what you mean."

The woman laughed, the sound strangely young coming from
her wrinkled body. "Oh you do, my dear. You do. He's here with you
right now."

A thrill of terror ran up Aimee's spine. *George.* She peered around
the room again, but it was empty as far as she could see. "Who is it?"

The old woman nodded knowingly at a rack of purses nearby.
"Him. Grey hair, light eyes. Broad shoulders." She snorted. "Looks
a bit peevish."

It was on Aimee's tongue to admit to George's ghost, but he
wasn't there, so far as she could see. Besides, she didn't know this
woman and wasn't sure she could trust her.

"It's not an accident he's here," the woman continued. "You asked
him to stay."

Aimee's scalp crawled. "*Don't go. Stay with me, George. Stay.*"

"He's not going to leave on his own," the old woman added. "He
can't."

She pointed to a nearby rack and Aimee followed her knobby finger. The purses hung in a rainbow spectrum, the area around them
bare. George was nowhere to be seen. A new thought intruded:
Aimee was George's widow. She was always 'a little off' as people
liked to say. Perhaps this woman was playing games with her. *Maybe
she knows Jacqueline.* Could this be another way for George's daugh-

ter to show Aimee was mentally unstable?

"Look," Aimee said sharply. "Do you know me somehow? Because if this is a joke, I'm not enjoying it."

The woman frowned. "You don't see him?"

Aimee's gaze flickered sideways. No ghost. "This isn't funny!" she said.

"But he's right here, dear."

"Stop it!" Aimee stepped backward, bumping the rack behind her. Purses swirled. This was impossible! Insane! She *imagined* her ghosts, didn't she? They didn't really exist. Her gaze darted around the shoe store. No ghost to be seen! "I don't know what you're talking about."

"Him," the woman repeated. She pointed to the rack. "The one following you."

Aimee needed out. She couldn't deal with this right now. Not when she was finally starting to put her life together.

"I don't know what you're talking about!" she said, fighting her way through the tangled purses. The straps felt like fingers. "I need to go!"

"But—"

Aimee jerked free, several purses falling to the floor. "Stop it! I don't want to hear!" she cried as she dodged her way to the door.

"Miss?" the salesclerk called. "Are you alright?"

The old woman followed Aimee's retreat. "He's following you," she called. "It's you he wants. You alone. I thought that you'd want to know."

Aimee didn't stop running.

—

Aimee clung to the phone's receiver, trying ineffectively to ignore Niha's prying eyes.

"It's not a date," Aimee said into the receiver. "It's just another interview."

There was a pause before Bear answered. "I never said it was."

Aimee felt her cheeks flush. She was relieved he wasn't here to see it. "I just wanted that clear beforehand," she said. "In case there was any question about that."

Niha rolled her eyes.

"Oka-ay," Bear said. "Not a date. No problem."

There was a pause.

"Right," Aimee said. "So as long as we're clear, then yes, I'll go."

Niha grinned and gave her a thumbs-up just as Luis came through the doorway.

"Sounds good," Bear said. "So dinner around seven alright?"

"Seven's fine."

"Any place in particular?"

Aimee frowned. She hated making these plans. "You decide. There are a bunch of restaurants downtown. We could walk some-place. I'll just work until you call."

"Perfect," Bear said. "And thanks again. I really appreciate the help with the book."

"Not sure I've been much help."

"Yes, you have, Aimee. And thank you for that." His voice grew quieter. "I've really liked getting to know you."

Aimee bit the inside of her cheek to keep from smiling. That *definitely* sounded like something you'd say on a date. She cleared her throat, forcing her voice to stay calm. "Oh, okay. Well, bye."

"Later then."

She hung up the phone and turned to hand the receiver back to Niha. Luis waited at her side, his eyes dancing.

"So it's 'not a date' then," Niha said with a coy smile.

"Not dates are the best kind," Luis added in a sage voice.

"The very best kind," Niha agreed.

Aimee groaned, heading back to her studio. "It's like you two are in kindergarten."

Laughter followed her retreating back.

—

Aimee worked on a faded Frida Kahlo painting for most of the afternoon. It had a trail of bleed marks along one side where the flood
waters had reached the box where it was being stored. Armed with
a fine brush and purified water, Aimee lifted the murky flecks of
mud and blended away the worst of the water damage.

At her side sat the ghost.

Frida lounged on the stool across from her, quietly inspecting
her work as Aimee worked to fill the long hours until seven neared.
Aimee's stomach growled. It had to be close to dinner time, and her
body hummed in anticipation. *Bear will call soon*, her mind whispered, but she refused to check the time. As if echoing her thoughts,
the apparition turned to the clock, sighing before rearranging her
shawl.

"You waiting for someone too?" Aimee asked.

Frida nodded.

Aimee took a clean strip of cotton, soaking it in water. "Diego,
I take it?"

Frida gave another long sigh, her shoulders slumping. "Yes."

The single word said far more than any explanation.

"Do you think he'll show up?" Aimee put the brush back to the
canvas and dabbed carefully with a cloth.

"If he wants to."

Pain wrapped Aimee's chest. She knew that feeling. "Is it another
woman or his work?"

Frida chuckled. "You understand then."

"Yes," Aimee said wearily. "A little."

For a few minutes she worked in silence, the ghost watching.
Bits of Frida Kahlo and Diego Rivera's love story floated through
Aimee's mind. Very little of it was truly happy: two artists struggling
to find a way to coexist. Marriage and divorce and remarriage, and
another divorce. Almost as bad as me and George, Aimee thought.
As if hearing her, Frida looked up. She glanced at the clock again.

"Why do you keep waiting for him?" Aimee said. "Why not just
go?" She imagined every place she'd go if nothing—nobody, no
obligations—held her back. Surely long-suffering Frida deserved

at least that.

"Because I love him."

Aimee's brows knit together. "But you're always waiting. What do you get out of it?"

Frida shrugged. "I have my own life, my own mind, but my heart—" She laughed, though the sound was bitter rather than happy. "My heart is his, not mine. It never was."

Aimee's hands tightened around the paintbrush. "You should leave him behind," she said, confused by her sudden anger. "Just go. Live your life." She pointed at the ghost with the end of the brush. "Be your own person, Frida. Not his."

The ghost laughed, her face growing brighter for a moment, like a candle had been lit beneath the faded skin. "O-ho, you are young, child, to think you can make that choice." She leaned closer. Aimee could see flecks of gold in her dark eyes, could count the fine line of dark hairs between her brows. "What you say is true: you cannot live for someone else," Frida said. "But you cannot always live for yourself either."

"Yes, you can," Aimee argued. "You could make a choice to move on. You could!"

I could.

Frida shook her head. "Not true. Your heart chooses its match, not your head." She looked over at the clock. "And my heart has never really been my own to bid. There were two terrible accidents in my life: one was the streetcar that took my body. The other was Diego, who took my heart and soul."

There was a footfall behind them and both women turned as one. Aimee almost expected Diego to appear, but her heart contracted in shock at the figure which waited in the doorway, hands on hips.

"George!" she gasped. "What in the world are you doing here?!"

Mind reeling, she turned back to Frida, but the other ghost was gone. George shouldn't be here in the basement. It made no sense! This was her place. He'd never visited her office when alive. Not even once.

"You're seeing him again, aren't you?" George growled as he stalked across the room.

Aimee swung back around, heart banging against the walls of her chest. "What?"

"You're cheating!" he bellowed. "Don't deny it! It's him!"

Aimee struggled off her stool, knocking the dish of water to the floor with a clatter.

"Who are you talking about?" Her gaze darted around the room. None of this made sense!

"You know who! Barrett Cardinal, the writer you keep talking about."

The name jerked Aimee out of her panic. She stared at George in confusion. "Yes, I'm meeting him," she said, "but it's about a book. Your book, George. I told you that. This is another interview."

His jaw tightened. "So this is what we've come to?"

Aimee let out a choked laugh. "Come to? You're dead. You've been gone for months! I don't even know why you're here now."

"I'm not gone!" George roared. He reached out as if to grab her arm but Aimee stumbled out of his way. "I never left!"

"No," she gasped. Suddenly the words of the woman at the shoe store felt like a warning. "No. That's not right! You're dead. You're—"

"I'm standing right HERE!"

His shout of fury sent her running. She grabbed her coat and bag, dodging past the apparition and into the hallway. She didn't stop until she reached the stairs. In her purse, her phone began to ring and she dug it out with shaking fingers.

"Hello?"

"Aimee," Bear said. "I'm waiting up front, but I can wait if you're not ready yet."

She glanced back down the dark stairwell. In the distance, a shadow moved.

"Yes, I'm ready. Let's go!"

—

Dinner had been almost completely free of chatter. Aimee'd eaten slowly, fork in one hand, the pages Bear had written in the other. She hadn't commented as she read, just paused now and then to make notes in the margins or ask a question. Based on those questions, Aimee appeared open to his assessment and far less controlling than Jacqueline had been. When she finally straightened the papers and handed them back to him, she was smiling.

"Hal is really going to be happy when he reads this," she said. "You've polished George up a bit." She smiled. "Put him into his nice clothes and brushed his hair."

Bear laughed. "That wasn't my intention."

"I know, but your language, the words you've used. They make him more than he was." She took a sip of her coffee, grinning at Bear over the rim. "Believe me, Hal will be ecstatic." Her smile faded. "Even Jacqueline should like it."

"And you?"

Aimee took another sip, long lashes fluttering against her pale cheek as she considered his words. When she looked back up, her expression was guarded. "I think you've done a very honest job."

Bear smirked. "That does not sound like you liked it."

Aimee set the cup down. "No, I do," she said. "It's just—"

"Just what?"

A line appeared between her arching brows.

"What, Aimee? I want your honest opinion."

"Do you?"

"I do." Bear nodded and put his hands down on either side of his empty plate, grimacing. "I've worked under some pretty tough bosses. I promise I can take it."

The smile returned. "It's nothing like that," she said. "It's how you write him loving me." She shook her head.

"What about it?"

She ran her finger along the rim of the cup, as if considering her words. "I've been thinking about it since George died. He and I and what we had." She tapped the papers. "What you've written is more romantic than it really was. George and I weren't star-crossed," Her gaze darted up to him, imploring. "We just fell together, so to speak. You know?"

"No, I don't."

"When I read your version of the two of us, it sounds so passionate, like a perfect love story." She lifted the cup as if to drink, then set it down again. "It wasn't like that at all."

Bear leaned closer. He'd written what people had told him—even George Westerberg's daughter had described Aimee as a jezebel with whom George had fallen headlong into passionate, unrequited love.

"Then how was it?" Bear asked. "Tell me."

Aimee smiled wistfully. "It was much duller. Much more mundane."

"That's not what other people have said about you two."

"They weren't part of it," she said. "They just watched and gossiped."

"Then tell me."

Aimee didn't answer. She watched him instead, the seconds dragging out uneasily.

"It's the same deal as before," Bear said. "You'll see everything I write." He lifted his open palms. "Don't like it? I won't put it in."

Aimee nodded. "That seems more than fair."

"I just want the truth. All of it."

Aimee shook her head sadly. "I'm not even sure what the truth is half the time, but I'll tell you my side."

And with that, she launched into a long story of their beginnings, of Aimee as a newly-graduated artist working in George's studio; their intense attraction. Her stream of words grew jerky as she tried to explain how this wildfire romance had turned into a ten year marriage. How she'd taken a graduate degree and George's eye had begun to wander in their months apart. Her time as his muse and how it had eventually ended. What had driven them to separate for almost a year, and why they'd finally come back together again. Why she'd stayed despite all their troubles.

"When you marry an artist, you're only along for the ride,"

Aimee said. "You're just a piece in a larger puzzle. I didn't get that when we were first married. We had fights—terrible ones!—about absolutely everything. I wanted to be everything to George." Her voice broke on his name. "And I wasn't. I wish I could have seen that early on. Understood it. It's just how George was. And I never really knew."

Bear swallowed hard. He had the sudden urge to hold Aimee, to hug her, to protect her from the fool that hadn't valued what she might have given him.

"Did you ever understand him?" Bear asked quietly. "Or did you only see it after—" He struggled for a better phrase than 'he died' but Aimee flinched all the same.

"I learned," she said, "but too late. Our last years were better." She rolled her eyes. "Less dramatic than the first ones."

Bear reached out and touched her arm. Not a long touch—just a brush of fingers before he let go—but he needed to assure her.

A blush rose up Aimee's neck and she smiled. "We learned to be friends eventually."

"How?"

Her face grew sad and she turned to stare out into the crowded restaurant, waiting, it seemed, for some answer that the milling faces could give.

"Someone had to be the grown up," she said.

—

Aimee and Bear walked side by side, the sounds of downtown Calgary a background hum. It was drizzling tonight, but nothing like the flooding sheets that had burst the riverbanks weeks before. Aimee lifted her face, letting the mist rest on her cheeks, bead on her lashes. She breathed slowly, at ease. A thought rose in her mind. She felt happy tonight. *Peaceful.* The pain wasn't gone, but she could feel something else now too. Talking with Bear was like discovering a buoy to hang onto in the middle of a raging storm. His questions helped her make sense of things. Made her *want* to move forward.

Gave her hope.

Reaching the condo, he paused, and offered his hand.

"Thank you again," he said, enclosing her cold fingers in his warm palm. "I couldn't write this book without your help, Aimee."

"I'm glad to help out," she said. Another part of her wanted to add *George would have wanted me to*, but she held that part back. The handshake lingered a moment too long.

Bear was the first to let go.

"I'll write this up and get back to you again," he said, sliding his hands into his pockets. His face was flushed and Aimee bit back a smile. He was reacting to her presence and the thought warmed her. "I have to check into details for a few other chapters," he said. "I'd like to get your continued input on that, if you're willing."

"Mm-hmm," she murmured, though her attention was elsewhere. Dotted with moisture, Bear's dark hair curled around his head in a corona of curls, backlit by the streetlight. He looked like a Renaissance painting of an angel with a halo of golden light, something that—at another time—she might have wanted to paint. It was one of O'Keefe's details containing the seed of joy.

"I'm sorry for taking so much of your time," Bear added. "I know you're busy with the flood clean-up and repairs."

"Bear, I enjoyed talking to you." Aimee wanted to brush her fingers through his damp curls, but she touched the sleeve of his jacket instead. His gaze flicked down, staring at her hand for a moment, then back up. His expression had changed.

"I had a good time tonight," he said in a low voice.

Aimee nodded. "I did too."

Bear leaned closer. He smelled warm and clean, the faint hint of cologne lingering on his clothes. "You're easy to talk to, Aimee." His gaze changed, eyes drifting to her mouth, then up. His brown eyes were so dark they seemed almost black. "I feel like I understand you."

Her eyes widened as his fingers tightened over hers. "You do?"

"More than you know."

His hand over hers was the push, the last weight that tipped

Aimee forward. Without thought to how or why (or, more likely, why not), she stood on tiptoes and kissed Bear full on the mouth.

CHAPTER EIGHT

Bear had been aching to touch Aimee all evening, but he hadn't expected her to be the one to initiate a kiss. He groaned as her narrow arms looped over his shoulders, pulling him down to half the height difference between them. Her small breasts pushed against his shirt, her tongue scraping along his teeth and into his mouth. His body reacted in a sudden rush of need. Bear had been attracted to Aimee since before he'd known her name, but thinking it, and dealing with the onslaught of physical sensation, were two different things entirely.

He pulled her closer as the kiss dragged on, heat growing between their mist-dampened clothing. Clinging together, the two of them stumbled sideways, bumping into the foyer wall. Bear's gaze flicked to the entrance panel. They hadn't hit any buttons, had they? The thought was lost as Aimee's lips slid against his, insistent and needful.

"Please," she gasped. "Please."

What was she asking for? Bear leaned down, kissing her again. The position was just uncomfortable enough that his neck ached, but he didn't care. He could barely think. The fire between them grew until he was certain that one or both of them must be burning. Aimee gasped as he kissed his way down her neck, only stopping when the stooped position became too impossibly awkward. With him at well over six feet, and Aimee well under it, there was no way this was going to work.

"Please, Bear," she moaned.

With a muttered swear, he slid his hands underneath her hips and lifted her up against the wall. Aimee squeaked before breaking into a sudden burst of laughter.

"This okay?" Bear panted. "I'm just too tall."

"And I'm too short," Aimee laughed, wrapping her legs around his waist to hold her position. She leaned in kissing him hard, and his knees went weak. God, but he wanted her!

"Aimee," he groaned, words lost against her mouth.

This was too public a place, and the timing was all wrong, and he shouldn't be doing this and— *Oh, Jesus fuck does it feel good though!* his mind shouted in outright rebellion. With Aimee balanced between him and the wall, Bear was free to touch and feel. His hands slid up her ribs to her breasts, kneading gently. She was in motion against him, her hands twirling his tangled hair, her lips slanting beneath his, her legs twisting as she held her acrobatic position. Bear couldn't breathe. There were stars behind his closed lids, but he wanted to drown in her. To have this moment, and nothing else. All rational thought was gone.

Suddenly Aimee's teeth nipped at his lip, and Bear jerked in surprise. He opened drugged eyes to find her staring into the corner of the small entranceway. Her eyes were wide circles of fear, a line of white visible around the green. Her hands had turned to claws against his shoulders.

"Shit," Bear grumbled. He turned, expecting to find someone watching, but the room was empty.

"No!" Aimee said in a hoarse whisper. "It's not. It's not!"

Bear turned back to her in surprise. She dropped her legs to the tiled floor, staggering back, and he reached out to straighten her shirt. "Aimee? You alright? You look like you saw a—"

"Don't!" she cried, the single word too loud in the small room. Bear stepped away from her on instinct, hands lifting, but she wasn't watching him. Not at all. Her gaze was skittering left, right, then back. "No, no, NO!" she shouted. "It's not like that at all!"

Bear took another step back. She was talking to herself—or so it seemed—but that didn't explain the look of terror on her face.

"Aimee, are you alright?" He touched her arm, and she jerked away from him so fast he stumbled.

"I have to go," she gasped. Her face was pale, the heat of the moment drained away. "I'm sorry. I can't—" She turned to glare at the side of the room, then back to Bear. "I just can't."

"I shouldn't have kissed you," Bear said. "It was my fault. I thought—"

Aimee's face contorted in pain. "It's not you, don't you see?" she choked. "It's me. I'm a mess! It's true what everyone says." She laughed, but it sounded like crying. Like the sound she had made at the Gainsborough Gallery. "I'm fucked up, Bear."

"Hardly." He smiled gently. "We're all a little screwed up. I know I've—"

"Just stop!" she shouted. She put her hands over her ears, pressing her eyes closed. "I'm not!" Aimee's face contorted as she struggled to compose herself. After a few seconds she opened her eyes again.

Bear waited, watching her warily. During his interview with Jacqueline she'd hinted that Aimee might have mental issues, but to see it in action was unnerving. "Aimee?"

"I just can't do this right now," she said, her words coming haltingly. "I can't. Not here. Not now." Tears glistened along her lashes and began to fall. "You should stay away from me," she said. "It'd be better that way. Just stay away."

And with that, she tugged her keys from her purse and bolted for the door, leaving him standing alone in the empty street. A shiver ran up his back, hair crawling over his scalp. Where he'd been burning moments before, he now felt like he'd been doused in ice water. He turned, scanning the barren foyer.

It was icy cold, empty.

—

Days passed, then a week, and another. Hounded by publishing deadlines and troubled by Aimee's odd behaviour, Bear spent long hours writing about George Westerberg's life, an artist he begrudgingly admired for his genius, but disliked for his personal failings. Bear researched George's work, his writings, his family, then wrote some more. Whispers came through the pages of interviews, suggesting that Aimee Westerberg might not be as stable as she seemed. Various friends had noted her volatile relationship with George, public fights at galleries and restaurants, and several had mentioned her strange artistic process that George had notably called "crazy" to more than a few close friends. It left Bear feeling protective of Aimee as well as wary of pursuing a relationship. What was going on with her? What strangeness fueled her artwork?

Day by day, she never left his thoughts.

Bear distracted himself with work as the broken downtown of Calgary slowly healed. In his free time, Bear volunteered to clear basements of destroyed memories, to shovel the layer of mud that filled every crevice along the Bow river, and later to hand out sandwiches to those working alongside him. Memories of both Aimee and his childhood filled his thoughts each day. She'd seen something that night. He didn't know what, only that her behavior had thrown things off between them. Unlike Jacqueline, he didn't entirely believe it was simply mental illness. The rest of Aimee's life seemed stable enough to suggest it was a vision or ghost of some kind. Nonetheless, the idea unsettled him. It wasn't because he didn't believe in visions—Bear himself had seen things during ceremonies, and his dreams were filled with messages that appeared days later in real life—but because she didn't seem to be able to control it. There was something a Tsuut'ina elder had once said to Bear that he mulled over now: *Life is not independent from death—it only appears that way.*

Were life and death connected for Aimee? And if so, how closely?

The chapters on the last decade of George's life grew and expanded. Bear polished and altered, added details and clawed them back. His "cleaned up" version of George Westerberg regained some of the stubbled shadow and sharp temper that endless art world friends had described in detail. The man on the page grew into the bombastic art world darling who had a bright streak of genius matched by a wicked temper. He drank too hard and worked like a person possessed, but could always be counted on to show up to support other artists, backing them even at severe personal cost to himself. (There'd been a two-year unofficial blackout on George's art career from the New York Times when George had struck a reporter for commenting that Basquiat was nothing more than a drug using vandal.) The real George, Bear realized, was found between these inconsistencies. He could be kind and cruel, patient and horrible. Yes, he'd had endless affairs, but his description of Aimee in CBC interviews, and numerous newspaper articles, was nothing less than enamored and devoted. In a word, the man was an enigma.

Bear's editor was euphoric when she read the latest draft, giving Bear a new list of angles and details to investigate. All of them involved reconnecting with Aimee.

"The daughter has signed off on her section of the book, but I need you to make sure his widow is okay with her chapters too," Bear's editor insisted. "I don't want to end up with a lawsuit on my hands."

"I told Aimee that she'd have final say on those chapters," Bear said. "She will."

"When? I'd like to get this project to copyedits."

Bear flinched. He'd dreamed of Aimee more than once in the time since they'd kissed. They were in a foggy forest and she walked ahead of him in the mist. He kept calling her back to him, but she never turned around and eventually she disappeared into the fog's grey embrace.

In the dream, he stopped. The trees were lonely sentinels, bare-branched and skeletal. Bear looked from side to side. Where *had* Aimee gone? And why had she left him here? The hair stood up on the back of his neck as he realized he wasn't alone. There were silvery figures moving through the trees, their bodies formed of mist. They circled around him slowly, getting closer by the second. *Aimee's ghosts.* In the moments before he woke, the clouds morphed into demons with long nails and teeth, ready to kill him.

"I'll talk with Aimee soon," Bear said. "I promise."

"Make sure you do."

Eventually, there came a July morning when he realized that to delay calling Aimee a moment longer would mean passing the threshold between uncertainty and loss. Without hesitation, he picked up the phone and called the Glenbow. The familiar voice of the receptionist answered.

"You've reached the Glenbow. Niha speaking. How may I direct your call?"

"Is Aimee Westerberg around?" Bear asked.

"I believe so," she replied. "But she may be working right now. Could I ask who is calling?"

"Bear. Barrett Cardinal, that is. I'm the writer who called before."

He heard a sharp intake of breath and half expected her to hang up the phone. Instead, her voice changed, growing softer. "Mr. Cardinal. I was wondering what happened to you! Seemed you were calling all the time and then nothing."

"I've, um…" Bear pinched the bridge of his nose. "I've just been really busy on this book. Deadlines and all that." He cleared his throat. "But I need to talk to Aimee. Is she available?"

Niha laughed. "I'm screening her calls," she said. "She doesn't like being bothered when she's working, but it's you, so I'll ring down. Hold on."

The mellow strains of elevator music piped through the handset. Bear watched the clock. The longer this took, the less likely she'd take his call. *Then what'll I do?* He couldn't just show up. Not after how long had passed. What could he say to her? *I was worried you might have mental issues?* Even thinking the words made his chest tighten. Unnerved by her behavior or not, he'd been a fool to delay so long. Now he'd lost his chance with her.

Suddenly, the nightmare of Aimee in the fog made sense. She was leaving him behind.

There was a crackle, and Niha's voice returned. She sounded less chirpy than before. "Aimee's a little tied up right now," she said. "But she said she'd call you back. Could you leave a number?"

With a resigned sigh, Bear complied. *Waited too long*, he thought sadly. *Now it's over.*

—

It surprised Bear to receive a phone call just as he was coming in the door a few hours later. Aimee's voice was quiet but firm.

"Niha said you called."

"Yes," Bear said. "I need to apologize. I got backlogged with some of the research on George. But I promised you that you'd have a chance to read through the parts that include you. I'd like to do that, if you have time."

"Email them. I'll read the chapters and get back to you."

"I was hoping that we could sit down in person. I really liked doing that. Are you open for dinner again?"

There was a long silence.

"I don't know if that's wise."

Bear winced. This wasn't going well.

"Aimee, if this is about the kiss, then I'm sorry," he began. "I shouldn't have overstepped by—"

"It's not about the kiss."

Another lingering pause.

"Then what?"

She laughed tiredly. "Oh Bear, that'd take a long, long time to explain. And I'm pretty sure you wouldn't understand."

"Try me."

She sighed. "I don't even know how to begin."

His fingers tightened on the receiver. "Then start at the beginning. Or start at the end. Just start." Bear closed his eyes, trying to draw in details from the sound of her breathing, quiet and fast, in the receiver. From the sound of her voice, there were things she wasn't saying.

Aimee's reply was a whisper: "You sure?"

"Please," Bear said. "I want to know as a friend."

"Then I think this has to be in person."

The printed pages of the most recent chapter sat on the park bench between them, the text lost in the bright reflection of sunshine. After weeks of rain, the world had exploded with green. Aimee stared out at the water, muddy brown, but receding, and the tangled mess of broken branches it left in its wake. There was a twisted bedspring on the banks, torn—who knows from where—and deposited downstream. She stared at it. Who'd once slept there? Whose dreams had appeared above those twisted wires?

"So what do you think of the new chapter?" Bear asked.

Aimee blinked herself back to the present. "Sorry, what?"

"The chapter," Bear said, tapping the papers. "What do you think?"

"It's good," she said. "Really, really good."

Bear groaned. "Oh no. That bad?"

She smiled at his tone. Bear made it easy to be out. To pretend she was okay. He hadn't pushed her to explain, and she hadn't quite found the nerve. But it had to happen sometime.

"It really is good," she said. "I liked how you built him up, then brought him back down to earth again. George—" Her tongue caught on her dead husband's name. "George would have liked it."

"Well, he won't be reading it," Bear said. He winked. "You might."

Aimee dropped her eyes, a flush of heat warming her cheeks. She had to stop this right now. Otherwise it was going to be even harder. Her gaze drifted out to the pregnant swell of the Bow river and its broken banks. Life was returning after the flood, but the damage would take years to undo.

"I wanted to tell you some things in person," Aimee began. "I need to explain what happened the other night when—" She looked up, needing to see his eyes when she said it. "—when I lost it."

His dark brows were tugged together in concern, but there was no judgement that she could see, just worry. She could connect to him in ways she hadn't been able to with George. There was no competition between their artistic skills as there'd been with her late husband's work. No comparison. Bear just was, and so was she. *Bear's a good person,* a voice inside her noted. *He deserves better,* another countered. Aimee clenched her hands together as she struggled to quiet the thoughts. Her fingers ached with the pressure, but she didn't release. She needed something to hold onto.

"It started a long time ago. It was when George and I first—No wait. It was before that." Bear was watching her as she spoke, the groove between his brows deeper than it'd been moments before. "Even when I was a child I used to—" She closed her eyes, throat aching. *I'm insane!* her mind screamed. *You should see that!* She knew she ought to tell him outright, but the words wouldn't come.

The feeling of Bear's fingers, warm and solid, atop her clasped hands, brought her back to the present. She opened her eyes to find he'd leaned closer on the bench. He smiled down at her. "When you were a child?" he prompted. "What?"

"We moved, and I was so lonely. I began to see things. Invented them, I mean."

She waited for him to recoil, to let her go, but he remained. His fingers stroked over her clenched fists. "You imagined things?"

"Yes or no," Aimee said with a shake of her head. "They seemed real to me. I didn't have a lot of friends."

"Neither did I."

"Really?"

"Uh-huh." Bear nodded.

Aimee didn't answer, just sat watching him.

"That's why I started writing," he said. "I needed to share my thoughts and when Margaret—she's my sister—didn't feel like listening to my rambling, I wrote the stories down. It became a habit and that led, eventually, to university and then to a career, but it all started by being a pretty lonely kid living out in the boonies."

She laughed shakily. "That surprises me. You never seem to have trouble talking to people like I do. I figured you would've had lots of friends."

"I've learned how to make small talk, but I was pretty shy when I was young."

He squeezed her fingers, and she opened her hands, letting her fingers go limp in his embrace. She wanted to do more, but the rest of the story remained.

"Tell me more about the things you see," he said quietly.

Aimee frowned and looked down, unable to hold his gaze. "When I got a little older, my father died, and I found myself in that same sad place. No friends," she said. "I'd always loved art, and I took it in high school and university. Around that time I started to imagine people—artists mostly—when I was painting." She looked up at him, waiting for the look that would end it. "I told you about that part before. About channelling my artwork. But the part I didn't say is that I see and hear things sometimes."

There was a long pause. "Things like what?"

"Like an artists' voices, when I'm restoring. Or people. I've been doing it more lately. A lot more." She swallowed hard. "I can't always control it."

He gave her a crooked smile. "Sounds like what writers do when they're writing. God, I can't shut the voices off sometimes." He threaded his fingers through hers. "Sorry, this is your story. Keep going."

She stared at him a moment. "This doesn't freak you out?" She laughed shrilly. "It scares the hell out of me."

"Why?"

"Because George—" Her throat closed tight, tears fighting their way to the surface. And there it was, the thing she couldn't say.

"George what?" Bear said gently.

Aimee blinked furiously, fighting for control. "I see George sometimes too."

His hands, stroking her fingers, went still. She could see the moment Bear realized what she was saying. That this wasn't just a momentary vision that spurred on the creation of a piece of art. That this was psychosis, plain and simple.

"You see him like, for real?" he said carefully. His fingers hadn't pulled back, but he wasn't moving either.

Aimee cringed. "It's when I'm upset, or when I'm someplace

where George used to be." She turned to stare out at the muddy banks of the river. There were tangled bits of detritus twisted around everything. That's how she felt, tied to the past. Trapped by it. "I can't control it anymore, and you should know that." She looked back at him, pulling her fingers free. She crossed her arms. "I like you, Bear, but we shouldn't do this."

He frowned. "Do what?"

"Be friends. Be whatever else we could be." She bit her lip, fighting the urge to run. "I'm fucked up. Anyone can see that. Haven't you heard the rumours that I've lost it?"

He put his hand atop hers. "I don't care what people say."

She choked back a teary laugh. "Don't care?"

Bear's hand slid back into hers, holding gently. "Active imagination? I get that. I told you about spirit quests and you didn't run off. Ghosts? My mom talks to her guardian angel all the time. Tells Saint Anthony to bring back her lost purse and bingo daubers whenever she misplaces them. Dreams and spirit warnings? My sister uses them to guide her life more than any financial report." Bear's voice dropped. "You've been through hell, Aimee," he said quietly. "But I'm here. Okay? I'm listening."

Aimee nodded, heart in throat. "Okay."

—

With the chapter red-marked, and new comments added to the margin, Aimee headed for home, Bear at her side. She kept waiting for the moment he'd pull away, but after tucking his papers into a satchel, he offered her his hand and they walked the muddy banks of the Bow side by side. Nearing the condo, Aimee paused, and Bear matched her stride.

"I'll go from here," she said. "Last time…"

Bear smiled. "You imagined him there."

Her lips pursed. Was that almost-truth close enough? "Yeah," she said. "Too many memories."

The wind swirled, bringing with it the scent of water and green things, Aimee's hair twisted and twirled in the breeze and Bear reached out, brushing a curl back behind her ear.

"I'd like to see you again," he said.

Aimee nodded. "Do you mean after you finish editing the next chapter?"

The corner of Bear's mouth quirked up. "No, though I'd like to do that too. I mean to see you, Aimee. Just you." He smiled, and her heart lurched. "Because we both want it."

She looked down at their hands, blushing.

"I'm not expecting anything. I just want to talk with you—about you—not about George and the life you shared. I want to get to know who you are. You, Aimee. For real."

She looked up. "But why?"

He leaned in and brushed a kiss against her lips. It was faint and tender. Nothing like the first intense kisses they'd started together in the foyer of the apartment building. This kiss held a hesitancy that surprised her, as if Bear was afraid she might run. *Should I?* When he pulled back, her heart was pounding so hard she felt faint. She reached out and caught herself against him, holding tight. He made her feel alive.

"Do you want to go out this Friday?" Bear asked.

"You mean on a date?"

He grinned. "Exactly."

For a moment she was certain she could feel George waiting in the shadows: watching, judging. She could imagine him pacing in the darkened condo, waiting for her to return, ready to scream and rail the way she'd once done after his absences. But she tamped down the thought, willing to risk George's venom for a chance at happiness, no matter how fleeting.

She took a hesitant half-step closer and smiled up at Bear. His face reflected the same nervous excitement. "Yes," she said. "I'd like that."

—

Bear was still grinning as he walked in the door of his house. From the distant bedroom came a loud baying, and Leo came skittering to a stop in front of him, barking and yipping.

"Yes, Leo," Bear laughed. "I'll walk you in a minute."

He strode through the kitchen, dropped his coat and the ragged pile of papers on the table, and pushed open the back door. The dog surged down the back steps, dancing in his awkward, overgrown canter. Bear laughed as he stepped outside, letting the porch door slam shut behind him. The Husky's boundless energy was sometimes the only thing that kept him going, but today he felt like he matched Leo for happiness.

A date, his mind whispered. Aimee had said the words even before him.

Out in the yard, the Husky did his business behind the shed, then tore around the perimeter of the yard with the energy of a dog half his age. He sniffed and sprinted from one spot to the next, pausing in front of Bear to bark happily before doing it all over again. Bear grinned. Today felt like a new beginning, the kind he'd looked for since he was a child.

There were some parts of Bear's childhood on the Tsuut'ina reserve that he hadn't enjoyed—the poor infrastructure for one, generational poverty and a system designed to oppress for another—but there were many more aspects that he loved about his childhood. He'd grown up in a multi-generational home, tethered by love and a fierce sense of family. His great-grandmother, as one of the traditional knowledge-keepers, had connected him to his tribe's history and the world at large. But his most beloved memory was the bond he felt to the land and animals. He remembered being a child, wading through waist-high grass in the summertime and deep drifts in winter. He learned to sit silent on the prairie until he became part of the landscape too. There, he watched deer move through the valleys, following their footsteps and his heart's desire to wander. Moving to the city years later, he'd found himself in an alien world, but the connection remained. As Bear learned, nature was there, if you only knew where to look. The silver and glass towers of downtown Calgary hid microcosms of nature, the river valley teeming with life. Even little spots like the grassy areas near culverts and the forgotten bands of untilled land between the divided highways held their magic. Few, however, could see it.

It struck him that Aimee was someone who'd understand that.

Still smiling, Bear left Leo to his backyard exploration and headed back into the kitchen. He set his cell phone on the table alongside his coat, belatedly noticing that there were five missed calls on the screen. The first few he listened to with half an ear: one was his editor asking him for an updated date for the latest draft; another his sister, Margaret, calling to see how he was doing, then two messages pitching a new cable service. The last surprised him. The number was unknown—*blocked*, Bear realized—but the voice was familiar.

"Hello Mr. Cardinal. This is Jacqueline Westerberg-Kinney calling. You interviewed me a few weeks ago." Bear lifted his chin in surprise. He already had Jacqueline's carefully noted replies to his questions. In fact, they were already transcribed and included in key points in the book's middle chapters.

"I'm calling because I have some new information," she continued. Jacqueline's voice was cultured, calm, with a hint of ice. Bear remembered talking to her at the retrospective for George Westerberg. She was on Hal's arm at the time and had shaken his hand, smiling in her cool, socialite fashion. Bear knew people like her. They rarely gave him the time of day until they knew who he was.

"And I'd like to talk to you about the details." There was a pause. "This is *not* something I can do on the phone."

Bear frowned in concern. *Details? About what?*

"If you're willing to meet face to face, I'd be more than happy to compensate you for the flight. Contact my secretary and he'll be able to arrange for a meeting later this week." And with that the message ended. No goodbyes, no questions about whether or not Bear wanted to meet with her again, not even a number. Just dead air.

Bear listened to the message a second time, then hit save. He skimmed through his contacts—no secretary or contact number for Jacqueline Westerberg-Kinney—she'd never given him one.

"Figures," Bear snorted in annoyance. He scrolled through the rest of his contacts before deciding on Hal Mortinson. Seconds later, his phone was ringing, Bear's hand sweaty in anticipation.

If George's daughter had something to tell him, and was willing to fly him out of country to say it, then it had to be important.

—

"To new beginnings," Aimee said, offering her glass to be touched.

"To our first date," Bear said, lifting his glass. "Let's toast it."

The thin sound rang out as their glasses met. Aimee took a sip of wine, watching him over the rim of her glass and smiling. "So if this is the first date, what exactly were the other times we met?"

"Practice?" Bear said with a laugh.

"Practice. Yeah, I can go with that."

The restaurant was dim, and Aimee was glad. Though excited, she was still unsettled with the idea of being here. She knew she should start moving forward with her life, but guilt was an anchor. Aimee was caught halfway, and no one seemed to understand how that made her feel. Her mother had been pestering Aimee ever since she'd admitted she was going out on a date. Niha was practically hysterical. Pushing the thoughts aside, she drank deeply, almost missing Bear's next words.

"We're not going to talk about George tonight," he announced.

She lowered her glass. "We're not?"

"No. And nothing you say is going into the book." He leaned closer, dropping his voice. "I know that's probably a given, but I just wanted to say it out loud. This is just us being us."

She laughed nervously. "Well, that's good. Right?"

"I think so."

Bear's mouth quirked up in a crooked grin. He had a great smile—almost perfect, white teeth, with just a tiny gap between his front ones—but it was the way it lit up his face when he smiled that Aimee loved. There was no smirking, knowing looks. It was an open smile, she decided. A real one.

"I want to know about you," Bear said. "About what you do. What you love in life."

She glanced away and began fiddling with the edge of her napkin, hoping that the dim interior of the bustling restaurant hid her unease. "I honestly don't know anymore." Her cheeks felt warm but she didn't know if it was because of the alcohol or his presence. "I haven't really thought about that in a long while."

"Why?" Bear asked.

"I don't know."

"Then tell me what you used to love." He winced. "I mean, besides George."

And there he was. As if her dead husband had pulled up a chair and sat down at the table next to him. Aimee could imagine George pouring himself a drink. He'd be angry and sullen, ready to take offence or—

Don't! her mind hissed. *Don't let him in. Don't bring him here!*

She took another swallow of wine and forced a smile. "I used to love painting," she said quickly. "I used to love losing myself in the process."

"What did you paint?"

She laughed. "Nothing really."

Bear waited, unspeaking.

"I mean, that's what they looked like. They were abstract. Colours and lines. Shapes." She swallowed down a wave of melancholy. "I used to paint how I felt. I could catch onto an emotion and draw it out. Make it bigger. Stretch the feeling of joy and feel it grow into something more."

"Sounds amazing." Bear leaned one arm on the table, shifting forward so that he was angled toward her.

"It was," she said. "I miss it."

"Why don't you pick it up again?"

Aimee shrugged. "It's not that easy. You have to be in flow. Right now, I'm not."

Bear's eyebrows furrowed together. It made him look older. "Is it like writer's block?"

"Sort of," Aimee said, folding the napkin as she spoke. "But not about words. It's more about being in the right place. The right time to let the art happen."

Bear reached out and touched her wrist. "So tell me how that happens. I want to know."

He was barely touching her, his fingers feather-light against her pulse. If she went back to fiddling with the napkin, she'd break the contact, so she stayed still, letting the pinprick of contact drag on.

"For me, it's about being consumed by the moment," Aimee began. "It's anything creative: painting/drawing/acting—"

"Writing?" Bear asked.

"Yes, exactly. Everything and anything at all. It's about really living, rather than just existing. It's catching the hum and pattern of the moment and setting yourself on fire with the potential of now." She laughed shakily. *I probably sound crazy when I talk like this,* she thought. But Bear stared at her, enraptured.

"That's what you mean by flow," he said slowly. "That feeling you get doing it." He grinned. "I get that when the words just get away from me. And I can write—but never fast enough—and it feels like I'm channelling something else. Not even really composing at all."

Aimee grinned, wondering if he knew how good it felt to be understood. She opened her hand and slid her fingers into his. She was cold, but he was warm. "I think all creative acts are like that," she said. "You have to burn every bit of yourself out in the process. Leave nothing behind but your art and a hollowed out shell."

Bear laughed. "A hollow shell? I'd rather be a happy man with a lot of money in the bank."

Aimee shrugged. "I don't care. It's the act."

Bear's hand stroked over the bones in her hand, teasing the invisible hairs until gooseflesh rose. She shivered.

"You love painting," he said quietly. "I can tell."

"I used to love it. I don't paint. Not anymore."

"Not at all?"

"No, I restore." Aimee's smile grew brittle and then disappeared altogether. "I enjoy it, but it's not the same."

"I'd like to see some of your work. Your paintings, not the restorations. If you'd let me see them, that is." The sound of his words, gentle and quiet, had Aimee blushing. There was an intimacy to painting—even with restorations—and she rarely painted, except when alone. Barring George, very few people had been privy to her studio.

"Maybe someday, but I don't—" Aimee's words stumbled to a sudden stop. She fished through her bag, coming up with her cell phone. "Hold on. I do have a photo of one. It's a watercolour I did years and years ago. I photographed it for the framers." She slid the phone across the table to him. "I gave it to my mother for her birthday."

Bear's eyes widened to see a dreamlike image that seemed to be both the sea and the sky at once, the hues rolling and changing whenever he looked at it from a different angle. There were no straight edges, but hints of something that could have been a boat or perhaps a person emerging from a flare of light caught his eyes. He leaned in closer. Something about the watercolour reminded him of a Turner print he'd once seen.

"That's amazing."

Aimee rolled her eyes. "It isn't."

"Don't brush it off," he laughed. "It is!"

"Hardly."

Bear turned the phone. "Come on, look at it. It's beautiful! Every bit as good as anything painted by Geor—"

His name, half-spoken, brought the conversation to a screeching halt. Bear's smile wavered. "Sorry. I never meant he wasn't good. I just—" He dropped his chin bashfully. "I like yours better. It's more—"

"You don't know art," Aimee interrupted before he could say more. She reached out and took the phone from him, dropping it back into her purse without meeting his eyes. She didn't want the comparisons. *Hated them.*

"I may not know as much about art as you, but I know my eyes." She grimaced. She could feel George coming back, the moment's laughter gone.

"Take the compliment, Aimee. The painting is beautiful."

"No. It's not," she said glumly. "It's good, but not good enough." She lifted her glass and drained the rest of the wine. The room felt too warm now. She wanted out.

"There's a quote by Ira Glass," Bear said. "You heard of him?"

Aimee shrugged, staring at the napkin, wrinkled before her. She wished she hadn't come, but it was too late now.

"It's about the gap between what we want our artwork or writing to be," Bear said, "and what we know is good. And there is that gap, Aimee. A gap that makes us all feel inadequate. You're not the only one to feel it."

She peeked up at him through a fringe of curls. "A gap."

"Yes, like a standard we never quite meet. We want to be at that level, but we aren't good enough. Not yet."

She gave him a sardonic smile. "Well, that's depressing."

Bear reached out, offering his hand. She stared at it, uncertain.

"And what Glass says about this gap is that we have to be the ones who close it. We need to find our way to the quality we want. We have to learn to be okay with being novices first. We have to accept our failings."

Aimee reached out, resting the tips of her fingers against his palm, barely touching. Even so, the warmth spread.

"How?"

"We create and we create, and we create some more," Bear said. "And eventually—sometime in the future, long after we begin—we are finally able to do something that reaches the mark. Something that makes us really, genuinely happy." He chuckled. "I'm not that good yet. There are so many things about my writing that bother me, but I'm still working on it. Still trying. And I'll reach the mark someday." He winked. "So will you."

Aimee slid her hand forward, clasping her fingers around his. "I think you're already there."

CHAPTER NINE

Bear glanced down at the littered interior of his truck and winced. His vehicle wasn't more messy than normal, but its usual state was enough to leave him sweating. The seat was covered in dog hair, floorboards littered with paper coffee cups. After the high-end restaurant, his truck looked like it belonged at a truck stop. But it was too late now. He'd made the offer.

When they'd walked outside, Aimee'd looked up at the low-hanging clouds and groaned. "Good Lord, is summer *ever* going to start?"

"Someday, but not today. You need a ride home?" Bear had offered, not even thinking of the consequences. Now he cursed himself. He pushed Leo's dog blanket over the back of the seat—out of sight, out of mind—and forced a smile.

"Sorry about the mess."

She shrugged, sliding across the bench seat until she was up next to him. "Don't care."

Bear kicked two cups under the chair. "Having a dog's like having a kid," he said sheepishly. "I should've cleaned it up before—"

She cut off his words with a kiss, wrapping her hands over his shoulders.

It was like lightning—a flash and then a boom—deep down in his gut. Her lips slid against his, full and open. Bear caught his hands in her hair, tilting her chin to deepen the kiss. *Aimee*. She tasted like wine—sweet and spicy—and he was drunk on her in seconds. He hadn't felt like this in years. *Ever?* he wondered.

Bear knew he should consider the repercussions of doing this.

She was the widow of the man whose biography he was writing, after all, but as she moved over and straddled his lap in the tight confines of the cab, George Westerberg was the last thing on Bear's mind. Aimee's fingers danced against the skin of his shoulders, down his chest. Where skin met skin, sparks flew. Bear groaned, and the kiss grew needy, teeth grazing his lips in her haste.

Outside, the stormy rain grew in intensity, drops buzzing against the roof, flooding the windows. A faint blur fogged the glass. Small sounds and gasps rose and faded into the rush of rain. In the back of his mind Bear struggled to put this wild woman writhing on his lap together with the wary widow he'd first met. Breathless, he broke the kiss to suckle the soft skin of her throat. Aimee tipped her head back, gasping.

"God, I've been aching to kiss you again since that night in the foyer," she moaned.

Bear looked up, dazed. "Really?"

She laughed. "Of course. You couldn't tell?"

Bear struggled to think, but his memory was of her running away from him, talking to herself as she did.

"I dunno," Bear said. "You seemed upset by the whole thing." He hoped this was the right answer.

Aimee's fingers slid down his chest until they rested on the flat plane of his stomach. Bear's muscles tightened in anticipation.

"Can you tell now?" she said with a warm smile.

"God, yes."

And then she was kissing him again, and whatever he'd been about to say was lost. *Aimee.* Everything about her left him off-centre. It was like trying to hold onto a hurricane. He had no idea which way her winds would blow, but for now—*here and now*—he was holding on as tight as he could. Time lost meaning as their bodies danced. Fingers, lips, hands, and the growing heat that spread from touch to touch. A horn blared somewhere nearby and they jerked apart, panting.

"Not the best place." He laughed as Aimee crawled off his lap. Bear wiped his sleeve across the beaded window. His truck was one of the lust in the restaurant's parking lot. He'd no idea how much time had passed since they'd climbed inside, but the rain had long stopped. Aimee straightened her blouse, and smoothed her skirt. She'd lost her shoes somewhere along the way, Bear noted.

"I think you should probably take me home," she said, pushing a tangle of curls away from her face and toeing on her high heels. He watched her with dark, desire-filled eyes. She was a different Aimee again: not the wary, high-strung widow, nor Salome, ready to seduce. She seemed calmer, quieted in a way he hadn't ever seen before.

"I liked tonight," Bear said. "Talking and learning about you." He reached out and ran his fingers along her jaw. She turned into the movement, lashes fluttering closed. "I liked kissing you," he whispered.

Her eyes fluttered open and she smiled. "I liked that too."

Bear started the truck and hit defrost. As the mist faded, the world outside returned.

"I'll take you home," he said. "But I'm going to call you. You can decide whether or not you want to screen my calls again."

Aimee giggled.

"If you're not doing anything tomor—" Bear groaned. "Shit!"

"What?"

He popped the truck into gear, easing from the curb and into the stream of late-night traffic. "I've got a meeting with Jacqueline Westerberg-Kinney. I'm heading out on the red-eye." He glanced over at her. "I'll call you when I get back and we can…" His words faded.

Aimee's arms were wrapped tight around herself, her expression closed.

"What is it?" Bear asked.

"Nothing," she said with a shake of her head. "I'm just ready to go."

"Is this about Jacqueline?"

Aimee's mouth twisted in annoyance. She gazed out the window at the passing cars. "Bear, I had a nice night," she said stiffly. "I liked our date." Her gaze flicked over to him, her eyes dark and sad. "But I sure as hell don't want to wreck it by talking about George's daughter."

"Got it."

Bear reached out, and touched her arm. This time she didn't take his hand.

———

Aimee came through the door of the condo wearing a half-sad smile. Her lips were swollen, her body burning with the vestiges of desire. The last moments with Bear—when he'd mentioned the meeting with Jacqueline—had been awkward, but it didn't slake her thirst for him. Her heart had been dry and shrivelled for too long, and she could feel it unfurling like a seed, touched by the sun, watered by kindness.

Aimee dropped her keys on the counter, lips curling as she remembered Bear's goodnight. He'd kissed her again, so gentle she'd barely felt it. He'd put his mouth against her ear, murmuring "this was nice," and she'd almost broken her own pledge and invited him in. She headed toward the bedroom, smiling at the thought. She hadn't felt this good in ages. This wasn't a quick fling. She could sense that Bear was more settled than that. Aimee pushed open the bedroom door, and stepped in without turning on the lights.

George lumbered out of the darkness, half-empty bottle of bourbon in hand.

"You goddamned BITCH!" he roared.

Aimee shrieked.

"You think I don't know where you've been? Who you've been fucking!"

The apparition crossed the room with the rolling gait of a boxer about to throw a punch. Alcohol fumes burned her eyes. Why was he here?! She hadn't been thinking of him at all.

George seemed to grow in size as he neared. "It's that goddamned writer you've been seeing!" he announced with a belligerent sneer.

"That bloody bastard thinks he can slink in here and fuck my wife behind my back."

"No," Aimee mumbled, stumbling backwards. Her foot twisted under her. "You're not here. Not real."

"You answer me, damnit!"

She struggled with the doorknob, afraid to turn her back to the vision. George's face swam in the darkness, twisted by rage. He looked oddly young tonight.

"ANSWER ME!"

"You're not real," she choked. "You're not—"

Without warning, George slung the bottle at her. She jumped aside with a scream. The bottle slammed into the mirrored dressing table, shattering the mirror into a thousand jagged shards. George raged on, his voice growing in intensity, but Aimee could only stare at the glass at her feet. There was no bottle, no alcohol, but the mirror itself was destroyed. Aimee's eyes grew wide, struggling to understand.

Not real. Not real. Not real, her mind chanted. But she knew it wasn't true.

"You think you're so fucking smart and that I wouldn't know, but I do! I DO!" George's words flowed over her like a television set too loud to hear properly. "And I won't stand for it! I'll kill you before I let you slut around behind my back!"

"No!" Aimee was trapped by the horror of the glass, the slivers of light caught on its surface. This moment. This change. It hadn't happened before.

George reached out, and icy fingers encircled her arms, clamping down like a steel band. How many times in life had he grabbed her like this? Shaken her until her teeth rattled? In death it was so much worse. Aimee screamed as the sensation of a thousand frozen daggers lanced her wrist, stabbing up her arm. It was like touching a live-wire that froze her to the core. The pain threw her into motion and she tore away. Out the door, down the hall, across the kitchen, and out of the condo. Her mind was a white flash of terror, reeling with a single, coherent thought.

It wasn't just her imagination. Nor was this just a ghost.
Aimee had a poltergeist.

—

Claudine Tessier paced the floor, her face a mask of fierce protection.

"You have to talk to Father Mackenzie," she repeated. "There's no other choice."

Aimee shook her head, exhaustion and the downward spiral of fear leaving her drained. She'd come to Claudine's as a last resort. She hated that she'd been forced into this, but what choice did Aimee have?

"I'm not talking to a priest," she said wearily. "He'd just say I was nuts. Get me committed." She didn't mention that Father Mackenzie had been a source of conflict when Aimee had been a teenager, talking to imagined ghosts as she painted, and Claudine—newly widowed—had worried there might be more dangerous reasons for Aimee's strange behavior. "I haven't forgotten how that went last time."

"That was fifteen years ago, Aimee. He thought he was helping you."

"He thought wrong."

Teenaged Aimee'd reluctantly agreed to talk to Father Mackenzie, but only if her mother had come to the meeting too. Father Mackenzie hadn't thought Aimee was possessed. He'd told Claudine he feared she was schizophrenic. Aimee remembered the weeks that followed their "chat" as she tried to convince a line of psychiatrists that she wasn't, in fact, experiencing a psychotic break. She'd never gone to church again. Her mother's perceived betrayal was the final wedge between Claudine and herself.

Aimee grimaced. "I don't want Father Mackenzie involved in this at all."

Her mother did another two rounds of the living room while Aimee stared at the walls. There were photographs of her everywhere a line of pictures from grade school, pig-tailed and smiling shyly; her graduation photo, her unruly, red hair curled demurely beneath the mortarboard.

"You need to talk to someone, ma petite. This isn't normal. It's dangerous."

"I can't, Mom."

The last in the line was a photograph from Aimee's late summer wedding, George smiling at her side. A frisson of fear ran up Aimee's spine. It felt like an invitation for him to arrive.

"Why not? Father Mackenzie would be able to advise if—" Her mother turned in surprise as Aimee clambered to her feet and walked unsteadily to the wall. She lifted the picture from its nail and set it, face down, on the bookshelf nearby.

Aimee slouched back down on the couch. "Not going to church," she said, closing her eyes. She was tired, but sleep held dangers she couldn't even consider. *The mirror had broken on its own.*

She felt, rather than saw, Claudine settle down next to her. "I know someone," her mother said in a gentle voice.

"Please don't."

"Not from church," her mother continued. She cleared her throat, her words coming out in a half whisper. "Someone else I know. She might be able to help you."

Aimee opened her eyes to find her mother watching her. The lines of Claudine's face were etched with worry, her visage so pale her lips were colourless.

"Who?" Aimee asked.

Her mother reached out and patted her hand. "A friend."

—

The limousine driver was waiting at LaGuardia when Bear passed through the customs gate into the main arrivals terminal.

"Mr. Cardinal?" the uniformed man called. He carried a white placard with 'B. Cardinal' emblazoned in black letters. Bear looked up in surprise.

"That's me."

The man strode forward, reaching for Bear's bag. "Ms. Westerberg-Kinney arranged for your transport," he said, taking the handle to the case. "I'll drive you."

"But I—"

"Ms. Westerberg-Kinney is eager to meet with you as soon as possible," he said brusquely. The man turned, heading toward the doors to the private parking section of arrivals.

"Fine, but I still have to book into my hotel," Bear said. "I want to change before our meeting."

"She suggested you use the guest house at the Kinney Estate," the man said, giving Bear's rumpled clothing a cursory once-over, "if you needed to freshen up."

Bear followed the driver out the doors into the slanting afternoon light. Moist air hit him like a soft blanket. No matter how many times Bear travelled outside Alberta, the difference between the sharp dryness of the air always caught him by surprise. A layer of sweat rose on his face.

The driver was moving up the sidewalk and Bear jogged to catch up. "I haven't even told Jacqueline I've arrived," he said in exasperation. "I don't want to show up unannounced."

A weary smile flitted over the driver's lips as he set Bear's bag in the trunk of the limo. "It's already arranged, Mr. Cardinal. I've been waiting for your plane for an hour."

The man climbed into the car and with a muttered swear, Bear followed. The rich, Bear had discovered, expected to get their way, and today he was too tired to argue.

In minutes the limousine was speeding along the looping roads out of the city, into the lush suburban sprawl, and the grand estates of the rich. The interior of the limo was filled with luxuries and Bear scanned the contents with disdain. A small fridge contained foil-sealed packets of nuts with sea salt and organic honey, Godiva chocolates, and bottled of imported glacier water. The speaker system hummed with surround-sound, while a flat-screen television offered hundreds of channels. When Bear pulled out his phone, he discovered a Wi-Fi link which made his home systems seem dodgy.

"Jesus," he muttered. Having grown up in a home that still had a primitive wood-burning stove rather than central heating, this kind of excess spoke to the two extremes of modern society. Bear didn't fit into this world.

When they turned up the gated driveway to the Kinney Estate, Bear's jaw was clenched in irritation. He knew from his research that Jacqueline Westerberg-Kinney was the first person who'd contested George Westerberg's will, knew also that Aimee stood to lose almost everything George had once left her simply to pay the lawyer's fees. Seeing the long drive with the three-storey Cape Cod home in the distance, the multi-car garage, and separate guest house where the limo headed, Bear felt a sudden wave of disgust. It wasn't fair! Jaqueline was rich, and Aimee stood to walk away from a ten-year marriage with absolutely nothing. Jacqueline, on the other hand, didn't *need* the money.

He dropped his bags in the wide foyer of the guest house, choosing purposefully to stay in his wrinkled clothing, and headed to the porch of the main house. He rang the bell, and a white-clad maid answered.

She eyed his outfit dubiously. "Yes?"

"I'm here to meet with Ms. Westerberg-Kinney."

"Please wait here." Before he could step inside, the woman closed the door in his face and disappeared.

Bear shook his head in irritation. It figured.

—

The house was a small post-war bungalow located in one of the sprawling suburbs of southwest Calgary. The neighbouring houses had changed over time—jarring additions and bright colours altering the flavour—but the house where Aimee and her mother stopped seemed unexpectedly out of time. The rock-dash stucco was the same as it had been sixty years before, the manicured flowerbeds and caragana hedges that lined the sidewalk were as crisp and neat as if they'd been planted that spring rather than decades earlier. Claudine put the car in park and rolled down the windows. She turned off the engine, but didn't move.

"I told her you'd be here around one," Claudine said. "It's five after."

Aimee twisted a long strand of hair around her finger as she stared out the window. A neighbour was mowing his lawn, and he raised a hand to wave. Aimee turned back to her mother. "But you're coming in too. Right, Mom?"

Her mother lifted her purse from the back seat, not holding Aimee's gaze. "I don't think so," she said, pulling out her wallet and counting out four crisp, fifty dollar bills. "I'll just wait here in the car," she said as she pushed the money into Aimee's hands.

"Mom, I can't take this."

"Just take it," she said waving away the money. "Goodness knows, it's the least I can do. And Magda has to feed herself somehow."

Aimee folded the money in half. "But why can't you come in? I want you there."

Her mother shrugged. "Because it's your business."

"Mom, c'mon."

"No. I—" Claudine fished through her purse, finally pulling out a makeup compact. She flicked it open and powdered her nose. "When I went to Magda, she knew things, dear."

"Things?"

She snapped the compact closed, meeting Aimee's eyes. Her face was grim.

"Things you might not want me to hear if it was me listening in."

"Oh."

Her mother squeezed her hand. "I'm right here, waiting," she said with a smile. "Go on, *cherie*. Go talk to her. Open up your heart. What can it hurt?"

Aimee didn't want to know.

She stepped out of the car, heart pounding. The lawn-mowing neighbour was now at the far end of the lawn but he waved again. Aimee ignored him, striding purposefully toward the house. Flowerbeds brightened either side of the front steps, a garden full of gnomes, glass bulbs, and pink flamingos standing at attention. If Aimee didn't know, she'd assume this was the home of someone's grandmother. Before she could lose heart, she rang the doorbell.

Maybe she's not home, a voice inside her whispered. *I'll count to ten and if she doesn't open the door then I'll—*

The door swung open, and Aimee gasped in surprise.

It was the woman from the shoe store.

—

From the inside of the sprawling mansion came the sound of a woman's raised voice. The tap of high heels rose, and the front door swung open.

"Bear, darling!" Jacqueline said, greeting him with the forced enthusiasm of a born liar. "Mary didn't realize who you were," she laughed, stepping back. "Come in, come in. I'm very sorry to inconvenience you." Her smile stayed in place while her eyes grazed his clothing. "Did you want to freshen up?"

"You seemed in a bit of a rush," Bear said, "so I thought I should hurry."

"Right," she said, "of course," as she turned away and walked back into the house. "Thank you for coming."

The walls were painted a gleaming white, furniture and accents in ochre and black: pale wood floors gleamed beneath the austere gaze of long windows, with wrought iron details on the lighting sconces and balustrade. Bear passed a line of paintings, his gaze catching on one in particular. He recognized the broad black lines. *An original Kline*, he realized in shock. Rows of photographs marked his passage into a house which looked more like an art gallery than a home.

Reaching a sun-filled sitting room, Bear turned in a circle, scanning the walls. There was a glaring absence of colour.

"You don't have any of your father's paintings," he said.

Jacqueline's tinny laughter followed the statement. "Oh, Daddy's work is lovely, of course, but doesn't quite fit with my minimalist aesthetic." She sat down on a white leather couch, patting a near-by chair that seemed to be formed of silver tubes and black vinyl. "Come, Mr. Cardinal. Let's begin, shall we?"

He sat down gingerly, wondering if this seat, too, was a work of art.

"You said in your message that you needed to talk," he said. "I'm afraid I can't quite understand what the rush is. Is something wrong?"

Jacqueline's expression settled into a smug smile. "I heard from Hal Mortinson that you were nearly finished."

"Hardly," Bear snorted. "A first draft is a long way from done."

"All the same, I needed to talk to you before you submitted it."

"Why?"

The clock on the mantle ticked quietly.

"Because," she said slowly. "I heard you'd been interviewing Aimee."

"Not a secret. I've been interviewing everyone associated with your father."

She raised a narrow brow. "True, but it worries me."

Bear pulled a pad out of his pocket and crossed his legs, balancing it on his knee. "Why is that, if you don't mind me asking?"

Jacqueline's smile cooled into distrust. "I have no issue with Aimee," she said. "But I do have a vested interest in what the world thinks about my father."

Bear smirked. Now that was a lie, plain and simple.

"You don't keep in touch with Aimee?" he said genially.

"No."

He tapped his pen against the pad. "I would have thought…"

Jacqueline reached into her pocket, pulling out a slim case, distracting him from his question. She popped it open, revealing a line of narrow cigarettes. "Thought what, exactly?" she murmured.

"Nothing in particular," Bear said. "I just noticed the coolness between you two. Any reason?"

Jacqueline lifted a cigarette and tapped it against the case before she lit it. Her hands, Bear noticed, were trembling as she brought it to her lips. She took a long drag, closing her eyes for a second before she blew out a line of smoke and answered.

"They always acted like Aimee was the love of Daddy's life," Jacqueline said.

"They?"

"The press. The art crowd. You know. People who talk about such things." A cruel smile crossed her face then disappeared. "She wasn't."

Bear scribbled a note. "No?"

"Oh, she was young and pretty, I suppose, in that sort of easy, art-school sort of way." Jacqueline rolled her eyes. "God, she was all over him at events. Embarrassing really."

Bear made another note. This part he knew was a lie. Various friends of George Westerberg—many of them artists themselves—had described George pursuing Aimee with a focus that was almost predatory. How he'd insisted they move in together weeks into their relationship, married her months later. How he'd flown out to Kingston every weekend of her graduate studies to be there in case she caught anyone's eye. Then there'd been the exorbitant gifts. The public displays of affection (and even more public fights from supposed slights.) From day one, George had insisted that every single article that mentioned him *mentioned her* as his wife.

"That's interesting," Bear said. "I understood that George had been the one that pursued her."

Jacqueline laughed. "Oh, I'm sure Aimee would like you to believe that, but no. She's smart. Mean. She went after him knowing what he could do for her career. Knowing how easy he was to manipulate, if you knew the right buttons to push."

Bear lifted his brows in question.

"You know. The whole seduction thing." Jacqueline sighed. "Please, I'm sure you've heard the rumours."

Bear put down his pen. "Sorry, but I haven't." He forced himself to smile though he wanted to shout at her. "No one's said anything of the sort. In fact, everyone I've talked to seemed to believe George was genuinely in love with Aimee. Almost obsessively. More than one has said she was the love of his life." Bear dropped his voice. "No disrespect to your own mother, of course."

Jacqueline blew a line of smoke to the side, expression grim. "He was fond of her, perhaps," she said in a brittle voice. "But she was hardly the love of Daddy's life." She tapped the ashes of her low-burning cigarette into a carved crystal dish. "Aimee's just—Oh, you know," she snapped. "She's common."

Bear leaned back, watching her. "From what my sources have said, your father didn't think so."

Jacqueline took another puff on the cigarette, the smell of tobacco nauseatingly sharp. Her lips were pursed as she retorted: "Daddy was manipulated by her." She crushed the cigarette out into the bowl, leaving a dark smear across the crystal surface. "Looks like you have been too."

Bear met Jacqueline's kohl-lined eyes. Fury sparkled in her pale-blue gaze.

"I'm only basing my assessment on what other people have told me," he said, lifting his hands. "There's nothing I've seen to suggest Aimee was in it for the money." He bit his tongue to keep from mentioning that Jacqueline had ensured that. "And there's no evidence to suggest that your father wasn't in love with her." He shrugged. "I know. I asked a lot of people who knew them. I've read several of his journals, spoke to numerous friends." He paused. "Even your sister-in-law, Vivienne, said as much."

Jacqueline leaned forward, her bony hands clawed on her lap, the pose of a snake about to strike.

"Funny," she hissed. "You never asked me."

—

Aimee opened her mouth and closed it again, the need to run surging through her. She couldn't breathe or move.

The woman reached out, patting Aimee's arm. "I was wondering if you'd come." She winked. "I dreamed of you again last night, standing here on the step."

"You did?"

"Yes. *Him* too." She stepped back, gesturing to the interior. "I'm Magda. Please come on in, Miss...?"

"Tessier," she said, distracted, before following the woman's retreating back. "But I'd prefer you called me Aimee." She cast a nervous glance back to her mother as she closed the door, but Claudine had gotten out of the car and was chatting happily with the neighbour. No help to be had there.

She heard the old woman's laughter rise in the other room. "He's not happy you've dropped his last name."

Aimee followed the sound, finding herself standing in a cluttered room which felt more like a nest that a living room. The floor was scattered with the layers of carpets, piles of faded newspaper teetering in one corner, a wicker basket full of brightly coloured balls in the other. The walls were decorated with a mishmash of prints, paintings, and wall-hangings. Knickknacks cluttered every shelf, photographs lining the tables. A multitude of details drew Aimee's attention, but she turned to the woman in confusion.

"Sorry, who's not happy with me?" she asked, perching precariously on the edge of a couch strewn with at least twenty luridly-coloured cushions.

"Him," Magda said cheerfully, her eyes on the space next to Aimee.

Aimee peered next to her, expecting George, but for now, at least, she couldn't see him. She turned back to the psychic. "What do you mean?"

"You still have them with you," she said matter-of-factly. "Don't tell me you haven't noticed."

"Noticed, what?" Aimee choked.

"Why, your ghosts, dear. You're drawing them in." She sighed. "I'm surprised you haven't seen them yet. I can see this one clear as day."

Aimee glanced over again. She could faintly sense a shape beside her, but she forced her gaze back to the elderly woman who'd taken a seat in a nearby chair. "It's my husband, George," she said. "My late husband. I try not to think about him. Try to keep the thoughts away."

Magda laughed, the sound warm and kind. "Is it working?" She reached out, taking Aimee's hand. "Or does he come back?"

"Sometimes it works," Aimee said, pulling her hand away and crossing her arms on her chest. "Sometimes it doesn't."

Magda smirked. "There's a reason it happens, you know."

"Why's that?"

"Did you ever lay in the dark when you were a child, thinking about all those monsters under your bed?"

Aimee nodded.

"The longer you do that, the nearer they come," Magda said. "Those fearful, black things we know we shouldn't think about, but we do." The woman's voice dropped, and the room seemed to shift along with her tone. It no longer seemed like a comforting nest, but dark and sinister. "That's what you're doing. You're calling them. Luring them toward your light."

"Them?" Aimee choked.

"Yes. There's the man here. Perhaps he's your husband; I don't really know. But there are more of them. Many more," she said with a hard laugh. "Lordy, they hardly all fit in the room."

"But how? That's impossible!"

"You're an open channel, Aimee, and you're calling them into the light. It's like what I do, but without my control." Magda turned, nodding to the space next to her. "Look. You're doing it even now."

Aimee turned to see that there was a man next to her—a shadowy form—and he was growing clearer by the second. With a gasp, she bolted from the couch and backed towards the door.

"How's he doing this?" she cried. Around her, ghostly figures began to fill the room like mist. "No! I don't want him here! I don't want any of them!"

Magda's laughter echoed around her.

"It's too late to stop them, Aimee. Your ghosts are already here."

—

Bear stared at the address in his hand. "I don't know what I'm supposed to do with this."

Jacqueline gave him an icy smile. "You do what any good writer would do," she said, standing up from the couch and brushing away the faint marks of ashes from her lap. "You go find the truth."

Bear looked back at the paper, and the single name. "But if it's true, this changes everything. You stand to lose even more of your inheritance."

Jaqueline rolled her eyes. "It's never been about the money."

"But your father's legacy—"

"—is *not* going to be the troubled artist and the one 'great love' of his life who saved him." She spat the words. "I'd rather the truth came out than people believe *that* line."

"Then why?"

Jacqueline made a sound of disgust. "If this is true, then Aimee Tessier is a liar." Her lips twisted in a mocking smile. "And the world deserves to know that."

CHAPTER TEN

"What did she say?" Claudine asked for the tenth time.

"Nothing."

"Nothing? I hardly believe that." Her mother pulled the car away from the curb and drove slowly down the side street. "You tore out of there like the devil was at your heels."

Aimee didn't answer.

"Besides," her mother added. "Magda always says something."

"Fine. She didn't say anything I didn't already know," Aimee grumbled.

The street met a larger thoroughfare clogged with a steady stream of cars. They paused, inching forward until the cars parted.

"But she did say something. Yes?"

"I don't want to talk about it," Aimee said. "Can we just go?"

Her mother hit the gas and the car accelerated. Aimee's hands clutched for purchase on the seat.

"Go where?" Claudine asked. "Back home? Back to the condo? Back to Magda's?"

"Back to the condo," Aimee snapped. A car sped by, honking and her mother swerved. "Christ, Mom! Please watch where you're going!"

Claudine tittered with laughter. "Stop being so jumpy. City driving always puts you on edge. Just relax."

"It's your driving, not the city."

"I'm doing just fine. It's all attitude, you know." The exit ramp appeared and her mother crossed two lanes to meet it.

"Signal lights would help," Aimee groaned, but Claudine igɴᴏᴜᴇᴅ hᴇ̶r.

For twenty long minutes, neither Aimee nor her mother spoke. The radio chattered incessantly about flood recovery and government programs. Housing prices were dropping everywhere affected. *The cabin in Banff*, Aimee realized, *isn't going to sell for what it's worth*. The taxes alone would be enough to sink her, yet another debt she couldn't manage. The mere thought of asking Jacqueline to help had her fighting tears.

Goddamnit, George! Why'd you have to go and die? A part of Aimee longed to go back two years and warn herself and George of what was coming. The security she'd felt—that she'd come to expect—had been torn away so suddenly that Aimee still hadn't adapted to it. (If one part of her wondered if this was why she kept seeing George, she ignored it).

The radio program switched to a sappy song about a man and the woman he loved, who didn't love him back. Aimee reached out and flicked off the radio.

"So, are you going back to the condo to stay?" Claudine asked.

"No. Just to pick up a few more things," Aimee said. "Do you mind if I crash at your place for a couple more days?"

"Are you going to talk to Magda again?"

"Mom…"

"I don't mind if you stay, ma petite, but I think you should talk with her. She understands." Claudine glanced over at her and the car shimmied. "These troubles won't go away on their own. How long has this been going on?"

"A few weeks."

"Magda could help with that."

Aimee slumped lower in the seat, watching the buildings flash by. She couldn't explain, and couldn't escape. "If I talk to her again, will you drop this?"

Claudine laughed. "Yes. I suppose so."

It took half an hour longer to weave through the mess downtown. Construction crews blocked streets, while industrial vans and restoration company trucks clogged the entrances to many buildings. Calgary was rebuilding, but it was far from finished. Nearing the apartment, traffic slowed almost to a stop. The streets looked so different from the other night when Bear had dropped her off, and they'd kissed.

Biting the inside of her cheeks to keep herself from smiling, Aimee pulled out her phone and tapped in a text:

Miss you, Bear.

She sighed, remembering their last moments when he'd stepped away and waved, and she'd wished for a moment that she had invited him upstairs, no matter what the consequences. Aimee tapped in another message, hitting send before she could think better of it.

Looking forward to seeing you again.

She stared at the screen, waiting.

There was no answer.

—

The condo lobby reeked of cleaning solution and mildew. Aimee coughed and covered her mouth.

"Mon Dieu!" her mother said, wrinkling her nose in distaste. "I thought you said the apartment didn't flood."

"It didn't," Aimee said as they walked down the hallway, "but all the condos on the main floor did, and the underground parking. The whole place is a mess."

She sighed in relief as they reached her front door. Closed. She hadn't remembered if she'd shut the door or not. At least she'd had that much sense. Stepping inside felt like walking into a tomb: cold and empty. Aimee glanced at the thermostat, frowning when she saw that it was set to the regular temperature.

"Have to get the super in to look at it," she muttered.

"What's that?" her mother asked.

"Nothing," Aimee said. "Just troubles with the heat again." She rubbed her hands over her arms, shivering.

"Well, you gather up what you need," Claudine said. "I'll clean up the glass in the bedroom."

"You sure?"

"Yes, I'm sure. You're the one having trouble with George's ghost, not me." She gave Aimee a quick hug. "You do what you need and I'll deal with the mess. You go on."

Aimee emptied the meagre remains of groceries out of the fridge, and gathered up a suitcase of clothes, darting in and out of the bedroom as quickly as possible. Barring the broken mirror above the dresser, the room looked completely untouched. Her mother ran the vacuum over the carpet, humming to herself. Aimee stepped past Claudine, and dropped her bags at the front door, waiting for her mother to finish. Reaching the foyer, she noticed that the answering machine was blinking. She pressed the button.

"*Aimee, David Arturo here. Haven't seen you around Banff in the last while, and needed to report a bit of trouble with the cabin.*"

"Not now," Aimee grumbled. She didn't have time or money to deal with this.

"*Nothing serious,*" David's message continued. "*Just looks like some kids must've gotten inside. I took a couple through, and there was, uh…*" He laughed. "*The craziest thing, really. There was water running in the upstairs bathroom, like someone'd been up there, showering. Doors were all locked, but there were smudges on the mirror. Words. I um, I wiped it away before anyone saw, but it was kinda creepy.*" He laughed again, but it sounded strained. "*Like I said, stupid kid stuff, but it's a little unnerving. Anyhow, if you could give me a call when you get this, I'd like to change the passcode on the alarm.*"

The phone beeped at the end of the message. Aimee stood staring at the machine as if it could provide an answer to her unspoken question. *Why are you doing this, George?* She felt a vibration deep within her purse and with shaking hands, she lifted out her phone. There was a text message from Bear waiting onscreen.

Got your message, he wrote, *but I'm going to be in New York for a few more days.*

Aimee frowned as she typed in another text: *Everything okay?* His reply came back a moment later.

A few things have come up.

Aimee had just started to write a response, when his next message came through.

Got to run. Bye.

She stared at her phone for a long moment, heart pounding. Years of marriage to George had made her an expert at reading the emotions hidden behind benign statements. (She'd had to in order to survive George's temper.) There was no question in her mind: Something was up with Bear.

A man's growling voice interrupted her thoughts. "Don't like the idea he's screwing around with someone else, do you?"

Aimee jerked her head up to discover George's ghost leaning against the door frame, arms crossed on his broad chest.

"Jesus!" she gasped. If anything, George had grown more solid since she'd last seen him. Heavier, more intense. She stared at the edges of his form, searching for the hint of absence, but he was as solid as the table next to which he stood.

"Mom?" she called tremulously.

The vacuum continued to buzz. Aimee stared at the apparition's hair—it was almost brown today with only a hint of his grey—and though his face was less lined, it was far more angry. *He looks younger*, Aimee realized, and that thought terrified her. This George wasn't from her memory. She'd never known him this way.

"You going to answer me?" George asked. "Or just stare?" He took a step closer, and Aimee backed away until she was standing with the exit door to the condo at her back.

"Go away, George. I don't want to talk to you."

He smiled darkly. "Who d'you think he's fucking behind your back? Some assistant of his? A friend, perhaps? A little piece he's keeping on the side?"

Aimee's eyes sparkled with anger and tears. "He wouldn't do that."

"You sure?"

"Yes, I'm sure. Bear wouldn't cheat."

"Maybe not, but you are!" George took another step closer. "You've been trying to get him in bed with you for weeks. You think

I don't know that, Aimee?"

"So what if I have? You're dead! It isn't cheating if your husband's dead!"

"You BITCH!"

The ghost spun back toward her and Aimee yelped, darting out of his way. George's jaw was a hard line, hands rolled in fists. This version of him looked more like the strapping young man who'd partied his university days away, laughing and drinking with the East Coast art crowd. Aimee'd never known him, but she'd heard the stories. Fights in bars. Fights with other artists. A string of arrests that only money and Margot's affluent connections had hidden away. This George had been mean.

"Mom!" Aimee shouted. "I think we should go!"

The vacuum turned off, and George glanced back toward the bedroom at the same time her mother's voice wafted forward. "Just a minute, Aimee dear. Almost done."

The vacuum started again.

"Mom, please!" Aimee shouted, panic rising. "We need to LEAVE!"

"Not a chance!" the ghost snarled. He reached for Aimee and she dodged him again. "I'll have an answer from you!" George said. "No fucking WAY am I tolerating you sneaking around behind my back!"

"You're not real," Aimee said in a shaky voice. "You're not real. You're not real. You're not—"

He lunged again. This time she was too slow and he caught her by the arm. Aimee screamed. Shards of ice seemed to embed themselves in her flesh, her body consumed by a cold that reached to her core. "I'm every bit as real as you are!" George roared. "And I want a goddamned answer! How long have you been fucking him?!"

"Mom!" she screamed, struggling to escape his talon grip. "George is HERE!"

"Mon Dieu!"

George released her as Claudine stepped into the room; the vacuum fell from her hands. "Notre Père, qui es aux cieux. Que ton nom soit sanctifié..." Her mother's voice rose in prayer as Aimee swung open the front door. She kicked the bags out of her way, tumbling into the hallway. The prayer was cut off with the bang of the door swinging shut on Aimee's heels. A sound like a hurricane rose from within, the door reverberating from inside.

"Run, Aimee! RUN!" Claudine shrieked from the other side of the door.

"Mom! Open up!" Aimee turned and rattled the handle, but it was locked. Locked! "Come on! You need to get out!"

Trapped inside, her mother began to scream.

—

Bear stood in front of a sagging Brooklyn apartment building, his gaze on the graffitied brick and sad, slumping window frames.

"You want me to wait?" the cabby called.

The offer caught him off guard and Bear turned around, frowning at the man who hung half-out the car window. "Yeah," he said, fishing out a twenty and pressing it into his open palm. "How much will that buy?"

The cabbie shrugged. "Five minutes," he said with a grin. "Ten at most, unless I get another call."

Bear nodded. "Thanks, man."

He headed up the steps, his mouth steeled in angry lines. It was an expression that had served him well in high school, when he'd been one of the few Indigenous students in the advanced placement program. If it worked on jocks, Bear thought, let's hope it'll work on drug dealers too.

The front door was locked, a good choice given the area. The apartment's intercom panel was in questionable repair: beneath the line of buttons, the speaker hung partly askew, wires dangling. Bear checked the name on the paper, then pressed 5-0-4 with a silent prayer to avoid electrocution. Thirty seconds passed before a woman's voice answered, younger than Bear had expected.

"Yeah?"

"Hi, hey," Bear said, unexpectedly nervous. "I'm sorry to bug you but I was wondering if we could talk a min—"

"Not buying," the woman snapped and the speaker went dead.

Bear pressed in 5-0-4, waiting. A minute passed. He punched it in again.

"I said I'm not interested!"

"Don't hang up!" Bear rushed. "My name is Barrett Cardinal. I'm an author from Canada. I'm writing a book about George Westerberg and I need to talk. Please! Just for a moment."

There was no answer and Bear was just about to retype in the code when the door suddenly buzzed, the lock releasing.

"Fine," the voice on the intercom said. "You have five minutes."

—

The doctor had left minutes before and the hospital waiting room was empty save for Aimee and the police officer who was interviewing her. Constable Singh was a middle-aged woman with a weary expression, dark, hooded eyes, and a broad-shouldered body. She exuded patience as Aimee turned away time and again, her thoughts on her mother, battered and bruised in the other room.

"If you don't know exactly what happened," the officer said, "then just tell me what you remember."

"But I honestly don't know!" Aimee sobbed. "I was in the hallway."

The officer nodded. "The police who arrived on the scene said that the door had been locked from the inside. You couldn't get in until you found your keys. That true?"

"Yes. They were in my purse. But it took me—" Her voice broke and her forehead crumpled. "A couple minutes probably. I don't know. It felt like forever. Mom was screaming, and I—" The words wouldn't come. Aimee felt something break deep in her chest, tears tumbling over in panicked gasps. The officer waited out the bout of sobbing, making quiet sounds of solace until Aimee could breathe again.

"Do you need to take a break?" Constable Singh asked.

"No. I'll be okay in a second," Aimee wiped her eyes, and took a slow breath.

"Would you like a moment?"

Aimee shook her head. "No. Let's keep going."

The officer nodded. "Alright. Let's go back a bit," she said. "What happened when you two first arrived at the apartment?"

Aimee chewed her lower lip, forcing herself to put things in order. To make the impossible sound plausible. She couldn't tell the truth and allow herself to be committed for her own safety. Not when the ghost could simply show up at the hospital and torture her there too!

"We weren't staying long," Aimee said. "I just came by to pick up my stuff."

"What for?"

"I needed a few things to wear." Her voice broke. "I'm staying with my mother."

"Why?"

"With the flooding, the whole condo smells," she said. "I needed to give it a couple days to air out."

"Did you both go inside at the same time?"

"Yes. We came in together. My mother was helping me clean. While she went to the bedroom to vacuum, I emptied the fridge, and grabbed some clothes."

"You weren't together in the same room?"

"Not most the time. Like I said, she was in the bedroom. I was in the kitchen, and then the foyer."

"Then what happened?"

"There was a message on the machine, and I started listening to it and the vacuum was going, and—" Memories surged, pushing Aimee's words away. She stared at her hands, willing them to stop shaking. She took a slow breath to speak, but the tears were at the surface. Sobs tore from her, drowning Aimee in grief.

The officer rubbed Aimee's shoulder until the bout passed. "We can stop anytime, you know, I can come back if—"

"No!" Aimee cried. "I just want to finish this."

"Are you sure?"

"Yes, let's keep going."

"Alright. Your mother told police you called out to her," Constable Singh prompted.

"Yes."

"Why did you scream?"

"I thought that—I thought I saw—" She burrowed her face in her hands. This was the impossible part to explain. "I don't actually know what I saw."

"We need a statement, Mrs. Westerberg. You're going to have to try."

"It's Ms. Tessier," Aimee said in a rough voice. She lifted her face and wiped her wet cheeks. "My husband is dead. I'm a widow." She needed to say it. To believe it.

"I'm very sorry, Ms. Tessier. I'm just trying to get a clear sense of what happened. Your mother said she was in the other room and she heard you call out for her. She said you sounded scared."

"I thought I was alone, but I wasn't." A frisson of fear rose up Aimee's spine. Her tears had begun to dry, but a different sort of terror now lodged in her chest.

"There was someone inside the apartment besides your mother and you?"

"Yes."

"Any idea who it was?"

Aimee took a shaky breath. "I thought it was George," she answered, her hands twisting together in her lap. If she let go, she'd fly apart into pieces, like the mirror on the floor. *He's real!* Her mind screamed. *Real! And he attacked Mom.*

"George?"

"My husband. My *dead* husband," she added, the words breaking into halting sobs. "That's who it looked like. Except it wasn't George." Aimee's voice was high pitched, terrified. "It *couldn't* be him, right? George is dead. He's gone. That just doesn't make sense!"

"But this man looked like him. Correct?"

Aimee cringed. This wasn't *really* lying, was it? It was sort of true. Or at least as true as she could get to without being committed.

"Yes," she said carefully. "Only he was younger. Stronger. Like George looked in old photographs." She buried her face in a wad of tissues, blowing her nose loudly. "It—He surprised me."

The officer nodded, flicking through her notes. "Now, Ms. Tessier, to be clear on the events: You and your mother came to the apartment. She was doing some cleaning, and you were packing, and when you went back to the foyer, you saw someone in the apartment. That right?"

"Yes," she replied, not holding the officer's gaze. "That's right."

"And this is the same man who attacked your mother?"

"I don't know—I mean, I didn't see—" Tears rolled down her cheeks and Aimee rubbed angrily at them. "Whoever it was, he was angry." She rubbed her upper arm where the line of bruises encircled it. "And Mom said to run, and when I did, he slammed the door." Aimee hiccoughed. Would this be the moment they locked her up? Would they commit her for this? Because she was going crazy, no doubt about it!

"Your mother said the lights were off when she came in the room. Someone threw her against the wall. She doesn't remember anything after that point. That's why it's so important we get a clear chain of events. What happened after the door shut?"

Guilt tightened around Aimee's chest. "I tried to get back in to help her," she cried. "But I couldn't! I swear I tried! And by the time her screaming stopped, the neighbors had called the police. I couldn't find my keys. God! It felt like forever before I got the door open and when I came inside—" Aimee's words disappeared into heaving sobs as the image of Claudine, crumpled on the floor, appeared in her mind. She pressed the wad of damp tissue to her mouth, fighting the panic that had been rising ever since the door had slammed and she'd been forced to listen to her mother under attack. Aimee knew she'd been the one responsible. She couldn't protect her mother. Couldn't protect anyone anymore.

"I couldn't stop it from happening," Aimee choked. "I was too late."

The police officer flipped shut her pad, sighing. "Thank you for your time, Ms. Tessier," she said. "If you think of anything else, just give me a call."

"I'm sorry," Aimee sniffled. "It was me he was after. I'm sorry I couldn't—"

"Why do you think he was after you?"

"I don't know! He just was!"

"Please, Ms. Tessier, just stop," the woman said, her voice gentler than it had been before. She reached out and patted Aimee's shoulder in an awkward attempt at comfort. "It's never the victim's fault. You probably stumbled in on a break-in. You were lucky enough to get away, and lucky that the guy—whoever he was—didn't do something even worse." Constable Singh stood from the chair, stretching her back. "Your mother is lucky that you were able to get that door open. We'll dust for prints. I figure he must've left by the same door you came in. And then we'll find him."

"But what if you don't?"

The officer shrugged. "Install an alarm, and don't worry." She hooked her fingers in her belt loops. "This sounds like a crime of opportunity, and perps like that rarely go to the same place twice."

Aimee nodded, fighting the urge to scream.

If she knew anything for certain, it was that George *would* be back.

—

Bear sat on the centre of the sagging couch, his writing pad open on the table next to him. Pages upon pages were now full of writing, a single name—*Brandy Suarez*—now matched by a story. Across from him sat the young woman in question, while a little girl of four set up a line of dolls on the cushions at his side.

"Tasha," her mother sighed. "Mr. Cardinal does *not* want to play dolls with you anymore."

The little girl lifted her chin, lower lip jutting forward in defiance. "Does too, Mama."

Bear grinned, moving his arm as she set another doll at his side. "It's alright," he said. "I grew up with a sister and I have a niece a few years older than Tasha." He winked at the little girl. "She used to put bows in my hair sometimes, so I've had lots of practice." He brushed his hands over the back of his neck where his hair ended. "Not sure it's long enough anymore though."

The little girl giggled. "That's silly."

"Honey, please," her mother said. "Mr. Cardinal and I need to talk a little more."

"I'm pretty much done," Bear said, turning to Tasha's mother. "Thank you again for your time."

"It's no problem at all. I'm glad you came."

Brandy Suarez was beautiful and younger than he'd expected her to be—twenty-eight or twenty-nine at most—with a lush mane of black hair, and full lips. Golden hoop earrings hung from multiple-pierced ears, her t-shirt and yoga pants barely containing the lush sexuality of her figure. Bear recognized her shapely form from a series of prints and one large painting he'd seen of George Westerberg's New York series. They'd been created in the years after his drawing of Aimee. But she wasn't the 'untitled' woman any longer. She and her daughter, Tasha, were the reason Westerberg's will had been such a complicated mess. The little girl was the recipient of the mysterious trust fund which no one seemed able to explain.

The little girl looked up at Bear. "Do you know how to braid hair?" Tasha asked. "I have a brush."

"Not well," Bear said. "But I can try."

"Tasha," her mother groaned. "No more dolls."

"I'll get some barrettes!" she announced, bounding from the room.

The young woman slid her chair closer. "I hope that nothing I said to you about George messes things up with Tasha's fund. I'd like her to go to college someday; do something with her life."

"I'm not a lawyer," Bear said. "But no. I'm pretty sure that the trust Mr. Westerberg set up for Tasha isn't going to change because of any of this. You'll still be cared for." He glanced around the room. It was decorated with second-half castoffs and mismatched furniture. The sight of it angered him. Tasha Suarez had every bit as much right to George's estate as his legitimate daughter did.

"Besides," Bear added. "Mrs. Westerberg-Kinney was the one who gave me your name. She wouldn't have told me if she didn't understand."

"But what about George's widow?" she asked in a quiet voice. "She never knew. George insisted on that."

"I don't think that Ms. Tessier will want to challenge anything to do with the trust." He shrugged. "I don't know for sure, of course, but it just doesn't seem like her."

Brandy's expression tightened in concern. "So, you are going to tell her?"

Bear let the thought sit for a moment before answering. There was a choice—there always was—but he hadn't even considered the alternative. Jacqueline was determined to prove that Aimee wasn't the love of George's life, and Aimee was determined to preserve George's legacy. What did Bear want from the entire process?

The answer came to him in an instant. He wanted what he always did when he wrote: *The truth.*

"I think she deserves to know," he said slowly. "Even if it hurts. It's better in the long run."

Brandy frowned. "I guess."

"And as long as you're okay with it," Bear said, "I'd like to include your side of the story too." He tapped the notebook. "It's another chapter in George Westerberg's life. No better, no worse than the rest," he said with a weary laugh. "I just want to tell the truth."

"Then you should know it wasn't always like this." She nodded to the shabby room and peeling wallpaper. "It was better before. George made sure of it."

"Before?"

She picked at the peeling polish of her fingernails. "Things were easier before George died. He used to send me money. I had a nicer place then. An apartment downtown, with a park next door. Tasha loved it. But after he died, I had to be smart."

"You moved here instead."

"Not 'cause I wanted to," she hastily added. "It's just the money stopped, and what little I had put away wasn't gonna go very far. I couldn't very well ask George's family to help." She nodded at the open doorway where her daughter had disappeared a moment before. "Tasha's what matters. She's the reason I keep going." She sighed. "But I still miss George, you know?"

She turned away from Bear, staring out the scoured window to the street. Her hands were clasped tight in her lap, her throat bobbing.

"I never wanted to hurt anybody." Her words were so quiet Bear almost missed them.

"I didn't think you did."

She turned back to him and smiled sadly. "George never said anything bad about Aimee, you know? We were just something on the side." She tipped her head and her earrings twirled. "A little New York flavour, when George needed—"

Her words came to an abrupt stop as Tasha skipped back into the room. "I found them!" she squealed.

Bear lifted the nearest doll. "Let's see if I can remember how," he murmured as he plaited the hair into a quick French braid. "Aha! Done. There you go," he said, handing it back. "But you have to put in the bow yourself."

"Thanks, Bear!"

"Mr. Cardinal, Tasha."

Bear smiled and eased himself up from the low couch. Brandy followed, wringing her hands as he gathered his notepad and slid on his jacket. The cab would be long gone, but he needed some time to think. Decide what he wanted to do next. A walk to the nearest busy street would help with that. Jacqueline wasn't going to be happy with this story either. She knew about Brandy, but not about the daughter, or the trust fund. He followed Brandy to the door, rolling the various ways it could play out over and over in his mind.

"Can you tell her something for me?"

"Jacqueline?" Bear asked, pulled from his thoughts.

"No. Not her," she said. "His widow, Aimee."

Bear didn't answer right away. "I guess," he said slowly.

Brandy nodded to her daughter. "Tell her that the first name George suggested when Tasha was born was Amy." Tears glittered along her lower lids, her voice dropping quietly. "And I loved George. I really did. But I couldn't let him call her that."

CHAPTER ELEVEN

Aimee moved around the hospital room on tiptoes. Visiting hours at the Foothills hospital were long over, but she'd been talking to the officer at seven, and the nurses had given her the go-ahead to stay afterwards. The room purred and hummed like a contented cat. Machines whooshed in time to their own tempo, filling it with a steady pulse. There was no hint of George—he'd always hated hospitals and doctors—and Aimee briefly considered staying all night, but she knew there was no time to waste.

She had a meeting planned with Magda first thing tomorrow.

Aimee slid her jacket on, then placed the handwritten note on her mother's bedside table. She leaned over the bed and pressed a kiss to Claudine's wrinkled forehead.

"Night, Mom."

Claudine's face was mottled with bruises, her throat hidden beneath a white collar. The sight of it was enough to bring a fresh wave of tears.

"Love you," Aimee whispered.

Her mother stirred. She opened groggy eyes, fumbling to grasp Aimee's hand. "Where are you going?" she asked in a hoarse voice.

"I've got to put the apartment back together," she said tiredly. "The super asked me to call him as soon as I got back in."

"But George!" her mother gasped. "Won't he find you?"

"George follows me, so it doesn't really matter where I am." She blinked back tears. "I can't go anywhere he won't be."

Her mother's face contracted in pain. "Oh Aimee!"

"I'll be fine," she said, though it felt like a lie. "I'm going to Magda's tomorrow. If George shows up, I'll deal with it." She forced a smile. "Don't worry."

Two heavy tears rolled down the sides of Claudine's face. "I'd rather you stay here," she said slowly. Her pupils were dilated with the effect of the pain meds and Aimee could tell it was an effort for her to stay awake. "You could sleep in the chair."

"I can't. I need to get ready."

"You could," Claudine said, her lids fluttering closed for a second, then opening again. "Stay, ma petite. For me."

"I'm sorry, Mom, but I'm going to have to deal with this at some point. Might as well be now. Besides," Aimee said, "I haven't felt George around since he attacked you." She squeezed her mother's hands. "It's okay. Promise."

"Okay." Her mother nodded, and closed her eyes.

"I'll come back tomorrow," Aimee said, tiptoeing across the room. "I'll tell you what Magda says."

She pushed open the door, almost missing her mother's parting words. "Just be careful."

"I will," Aimee said, then slipped out of the room.

—

Calgary never slept. The ring roads and thoroughfares buzzed with traffic, a chain of fireflies passing in the night, as Aimee took the cab back downtown. She paid for the ride, and stepped out onto the street, looking both directions. There was a handful of rowdy, late-night revellers having a smoke outside a bar a few doors up, and a man digging through a garbage dumpster in the alley. These were the people Aimee usually avoided when she came home late, but tonight they gave her a degree of comfort. She hesitated just outside the doorway to her building, until one of the men at the bar looked up, and caught her eye. He shouted out an obscene invite, and Aimee stepped inside. She didn't want trouble.

But I'm inviting it by coming back.

A shiver ran up her spine. She wondered if she should have gone back to her mother's house instead, but she knew that George's ghost went where he wanted, did as he pleased. If there was going to be trouble, she might as well face it here.

"Just got to stay focused," she said, tapping in the code and heading to the elevator. "Keep my thoughts on what's real."

The cables groaned as the elevator began to lift. Aimee leaned against the wall, her anxiety rising along with each passing floor. The decision to come home had felt like the right one when she'd made it in the antiseptic safety of her mother's hospital room. It had felt like she was taking control. Now she wondered if it was crazy.

As she reached her floor, the phone in her purse buzzed, and she reached to grab it just as the doors opened. She stepped out of the elevator, and looked down at the screen. A text message flashed.

You still awake?

"Bear," she breathed. She glanced up and down the hallway, terrified that George would see her waiting. The corridor was empty, everything the same except for the police notice taped next to the door to her apartment.

With trembling fingers, Aimee tapped in a reply: *Yes. Just got back from the hospital.*

She hit send.

Hospital??? What the hell is going on?! You okay?

Aimee let out a sharp laugh, covering her mouth to muffle the sound. She sat down against the wall, unwilling to go inside while she was texting Bear, but not ready to end the conversation.

It's a long story. I'm fine. My mom is in the hospital. Stable now. Things have been CRAZY here. She paused, and added one last note: *Really miss you.*

The screen blinked as Bear's reply began.

Miss you too. Need to talk to you again. See you again. Sorry. I'm in danger of sounding lovesick tonight. Been a long couple days. Miss you like crazy.

Aimee's smile spread until her cheeks hurt.

That's good, she wrote.

Bear's next text came a moment later: *You free tomorrow?*

She felt a blush rise up her neck to set her face on fire. She glanced up at the door to the apartment. Then answered.

Is this a real date or a work date?

There was a longer than usual pause before he answered, and Aimee stared at her screen wondering if she'd lost the connection. Suddenly it appeared.

A little of both, but I promise that it's going to end with me kissing you.

Aimee grinned. *I guess that's alright then.*

Bear's reply came a moment later.

Hope so. Goodnight, Aimee. I miss you.

"Miss you too," she whispered.

With a relieved sigh, Aimee turned off the phone and stood. The door to the apartment waited, closed and foreboding.

"Alright," she sighed. "Let's do this."

—

Aimee pushed the door open with her toe. It swung inward, creaking loudly.

She waited.

Oh, please be gone. Please be gone. Please, please, please, please…

Five seconds passed in silence. Then ten.

When nothing moved, she took a tentative step forward, fumbling blindly for the switch. She crept in from the security of the hallway, but left the door ajar in case she needed to make a quick escape. The condo was cloaked in shadows that seemed to crawl upward from the floor, scuttling over ceilings and perching in corners. Her hand blindly searched the bare wall. In the second before anxiety choked her, Aimee's fingers found the light switch by the door. She flicked it on and the bulb flared to life.

The foyer was exactly as it had been when the EMTs had carried her mother out, Aimee weeping at her side.

"It's fine," she whispered, "just fine."

She scanned the room: the broken coffee table, upended chair, and smashed pictures hinted at much darker events. Even the over-head light barely chased the shadows away. With a wince, Aimee let the front door fall closed behind her and took another step inside. Her heart lurched as the door clicked. She turned back, but it wasn't locked, just latched.

"It's okay. I'm fine." She cleared her throat, speaking louder. Making her actions real, if only to herself. "I'm fine," she repeated. "I'm just getting my things. Cleaning up." She didn't say anything about sleep. She feared that would never happen, at least not here.

Aimee picked up the first broken frame from the floor, staring at it for a long moment. She and George, St. Tropez, two years before. With a sigh, she carried it to the garbage.

Time to move on.

An hour and a half later, the apartment was almost returned to its earlier state, the last of the glass vacuumed. Three garbage bags of broken frames and damaged items sat near the front door. By then, Aimee's fatigue had become a palpable thing, tripping her at random moments, leaving her staggering. The third time she came into the bedroom to get something—but couldn't recall what it was when she arrived— she slumped down onto the bed fully clothed.

Just going to rest for a minute, she thought, her eyes fluttering closed. Within seconds she fell into the deep, dreamless sleep of ut-ter exhaustion. The few hours until morning passed in what seemed like only moments. The dark shadows faded, replaced by thin bands of watery light as the city came back to life. Aimee stretched and sat up, stiff and cold.

The room was empty, the specter of George gone.

—

Early the next morning, Aimee drove slowly down the narrow street. It was luridly bright after the weeks of rain. Green swaths of grass abutted muddy sidewalks, a riot of colours exploding in flowerbeds. *The entire world felt different*, Aimee thought. She too had been altered by the last month. She pulled over to the curb and stepped out onto the sidewalk. As the car approached, the elderly woman lifted her head. The wide sun hat she wore tipped back, casting her face in shadow.

"Good to see you again, Aimee," she said with a warm grin. "I've been waiting for you to return."

"After last time, I wasn't sure I wanted to."

"Well, I'm glad you came all the same," Magda said. Her teeth flashed white in the smoky half light which shaded her face. "He's still following you."

The hair on Aimee's head crawled at the comment. She peered behind her, but all she could see was the quiet suburban street.

"I wasn't sure if he was still there," Aimee admitted. "After what happened with Mom, I was hoping he'd gone."

"Oh no. Not gone," Magda snorted. "Not by a long shot. He's tired himself out, but he's still there. He's lurking on the edges of the light even now. Skulking, if you will. Waiting to see what you'll do next." She stood and slapped her pant legs, dust and bits of grass flying up from her hands to dance in the air.

"Why?"

The old woman shrugged. "I'm guessing the outburst with Claudine tired him. Depleted his reserves."

"You know what happened then," Aimee said, shoulders slumping.

"Oh yes," Magda said brightly. "Your mother called this morning. I think she's as emotional as I am." She laughed. "If only where you're concerned."

"You said he's depleted, but not gone. Do you think George will return?"

"No doubt about it."

"You mean he'll get stronger again? Be real again?"

"Yes, of course," Magda said cheerfully. "He's feeding off your energy, after all."

Feeding off me, Aimee mind chattered. The sun, the heat, the sound of a lawn mower buzzing in the distance all rushed together, leaving her weak and breathless. She wobbled on her feet.

"You alright, dear?" Magda asked. "You're looking a bit peaked."

"Yes...no." Aimee shook her head. "I don't know. I just need to deal with George."

Magda nodded. "Then we should begin."

—

Magda's foyer and other overly-decorated living room were much as Aimee had remembered, but this morning the house was filled with the warm scent of coffee and fresh bread. Aimee's mouth was watering even before Magda brought in a tray of coffee and scones and set them on the table.

"Eat and talk," Magda said. "And we'll see what we can do."

Magda started with questions about their past, and the way they'd met, laughing as Aimee admitted she'd been George's student and later muse.

"Aha! That explains his obsession," Magda chortled. "He's still following you. Still madly in love."

"But it wasn't always like that. I mean, we had troubles too."

"Troubles?"

"Normal things. I wanted to marry," Aimee said. "George didn't. Same with children." She shook her head. "George always seemed to get his own way."

"But you *did* marry. I wonder if you know how much power that gave you over him."

"Power? I really don't think so." Aimee shook her head. "You wouldn't say that if you actually knew George."

"Perhaps." Magda shrugged. "Or perhaps you just couldn't see his obsession with you. He's tethered to you for a reason."

"George was always the wanderer. Not me." Aimee frowned. "I don't think you realize how difficult things could be."

"Then tell me."

Aimee launched into another story as Magda refilled her cup, her stories a shuttle passing back and forth through the loom of the years. Aimee's stomach was full, her eyes heavy, when she finally came to George's death. The weight of the months since he'd died hung in the room, Aimee's voice hoarse from disuse and emotion.

"I asked him to stay," she said, wiping away a wayward tear. "Begged him."

Magda frowned at her words. "Oh dear."

"But it was too late," Aimee continued. "He was already gone, and I was left behind to pick up all the pieces." She reached for the tissues at her side, dabbing her face. "And now everything's broken. The will, the cabin, the lawyer's fees. *Everything*."

"So now you're dealing with his reappearance, and the other…"

"Artists?" Aimee prompted.

"Yes. Other than those visions, how are you coping?"

Aimee slumped against the couch, letting the cushions support her limp body. "I miss George every single day," she said weakly.

"But you're still working. You're still—"

"People tell you that when someone dies it gets easier with time," Aimee snapped, a long dormant anger reappearing under the heavy layer of grief. "But that's just a lie to make themselves feel better. It doesn't get easier. It's just that you learn to cope better. The pain is the ocean, and you learn to swim it or you go down in your own grief and drown."

"Go on," Magda urged, passing her another tissue.

"I've learned to swim, because I have to. I have friends and some family. I have bills to pay. Things I need to do. I have a life, for what that's worth." She gave a teary laugh. "It feels like I'm going crazy. I used to imagine George with me—I do that sometimes with the artists whose work I'm repairing—but with George it's different. I need him, you see? I miss what we had. I ache. Every minute of every day. And no amount of crying will make it go away."

Magda's sinewy hand reached out. At first, Aimee thought she was going to touch her lips, to stop her from speaking, but her forefinger came up and paused in the centre of Aimee's forehead.

"And *that*," she said in a low tone. "Is what feeds him."

"What?"

Magda pulled her hand back, but Aimee could still feel the warmth, like a dot, in the centre of her forehead. "Your grief," she said. "Your pain." Magda tapped her chest with her wrinkled fist. "*That*, right there. He feels it. It calls him to your side." Her eyes flitted sideways and she squinted. "Calls the others too."

"So, what do I do? How do I get rid of him? Them?"

Magda tipped her head to the side, as if listening to something far away. After a moment she nodded. "Do you really want to?"

Aimee pulled back, frowning. "*Of course* I do! I wouldn't be here otherwise!"

"So you say," Magda chuckled. "But you wouldn't even give me the time of day when I spoke to you in the store."

"That, well, you surprised me. And I thought there might've been other reasons for you to talk to me. I wasn't certain I could trust you. Now I do."

The old woman's lips curled into a knowing smile. "If you want to get rid of George, you must move on. Let him go." Her eyes narrowed into slits: "You need to find your *own* joy. Not his."

Aimee's heart sank. "But how? George has been my entire life for a decade."

"And now he's not. So, do you want to be happy?"

"Yes, of course."

"Not 'of course,'" Magda chided. "Tell me, how. What do you want, exactly?"

"Well, I—" Aimee stumbled. "I want to be happy. To take pleasure in things the way I used to. To enjoy my friends the way I used to." She blushed as Bear came to mind. "To find love again. But sometimes it just seems really hard."

"Why is that?" Magda asked, though the mischievous look hadn't left her face. "What's holding you back?"

"Because," Aimee said with a shaky voice. "I still miss George. I miss him with every single breath I take, every fiber of my being."

At her words, the room darkened. Both women looked up in surprise. It was as if the entire house had sucked in a breath and now held it, waiting. "Do you feel that?" Magda whispered. "He's caught hold of that emotion. He's pulling himself back to you."

Before Aimee could respond, a voice—*a different voice*—interrupted, angry and other worldly.

"*Aimee.*"

"Sweet Jesus," Magda gasped. "They can't usually do that."

"Do what?!"

"Make sounds like that."

"Is that bad?"

"It's not good. I think he might be stronger than…"

Magda's words disappeared as the room abruptly darkened. It was as if a cloud had passed in front of the sun, only the shadows came from everywhere and nowhere at once. From all corners of the living room a murky form coalesced. It drew together like clotting blood, thickening in one corner of the room as the tendrils of shadow drew together like snakes.

"No," Aimee whimpered. "This can't be happening!"

The elderly woman rose from her seat, her eyes darting here and there. "Oh yes," Magda said with an angry laugh. "It is."

"*Aimee!*" The voice was louder now, insistent. The figure in the corner had began to twist and ripple into a human shape. It wasn't just shadow but form with the first hint of colour. Blood seemed to pulse just under the surface of the walls.

"It's George," Aimee cried. "He's found me again!"

"Yes, he has," Magda said grimly. "But he's not allowed to stay."

The elderly woman stood from the couch, placing herself between Aimee and the ghost. Her voice rose in a litany of prayers in a language Aimee didn't speak. They were loud and powerful, seeming to echo from all corners of the room rather than from the old woman. In their aftermath, George's shape loosened and then faded. The swirling nest of shadows scattered, disappearing into corners of the room and along baseboards, absorbed back into the sunny home with its cozy interior. Outside the window, it seemed that a cloud moved out of the path of the sun. The couch was drenched in sunlight once more, the voice gone.

Magda gave Aimee a stern look. "He might be tired right now, but he's very strong, dear. It's going to be a fight to untether him from your life."

Aimee stood, grasping the old woman's hands in trembling fingers. They were warm where Aimee's were ice.

"What do I do?" she whispered. "How do I break the chain?"

"We'll smudge your house, and give you some prayers, but that's only half of what needs doing."

"What's the rest?"

"You must face him. Show him he's not welcome." Magda pulled her into a hug. "Most importantly, you must find a way to rediscover your joy. That part I cannot help you with."

—

With a bundle of sweetgrass and sage in her purse, and a hennaed incantation inscribed on both palms, Aimee left Magda's bungalow and drove slowly back downtown. At each stop light, she turned her palms over. Layers of symbols borrowed from Aimee's Roman Catholic upbringing and religions she didn't recognized ringed the edges of each hand; the center of her palms were marked with words from Aimee's own life, each line of text spiralling to the center where a single handwritten line repeated over and over again, a litany.

You didn't know how to be faithful. I forgive you and release that memory.

You never understood my own art was worth pursuing. I forgive you and release that memory.

Your rages terrified me. I forgive you and release that memory.

You never protected me from Jacqueline's hatred. I forgive you and release that memory.

The studio was never mine. I forgive you and release that memory.

You didn't care for your health, even though your death destroyed any stability I had. I forgive you and release that memory.

I grieve the children we could have had together. I forgive you and release that memory.

The student / teacher affair was inappropriate. I forgive you and release that memory.

You loved me as a muse, but never understood me as my own person. I forgive you and release that memory.

On and on the words went, filling her open palms with the re-pressed grief and pain she'd uncovered in the last months. Many of the phrases had emerged from questions Barrett Cardinal had asked her and she wondered how different her life would have been if she'd never met him. But the truth couldn't be hidden any longer. Today, her skin wore these indelible messages as her heart had for years. She hoped it would be enough.

Reaching her parking spot in the garage, she sat for a long mo-ment, undecided. If she went back upstairs, she'd be inviting a con-frontation. George had appeared in Magda's house today—a place he'd never been before! Alone, she wasn't sure she could manage.

The other option was work.

A brisk walk took Aimee back to the Glenbow where she spent the afternoon reorganizing the remaining damaged paintings and prints and restocking pigments, her gaze dropping to her palms time and again. *I forgive you and release that memory.* As she pe-rused a Jackson Pollock painting with minimal damage, the art-ist appeared. Pollock was falling-down drunk, his shirt soiled with sweat, chin stubbled. She stared at him in concern. This ghost was too much like George for comfort.

"Wha's that?" he mumbled, gesturing to the painting she held.

"Sorry. What?"

"That," he said. "The paint—" He burped. "Painting there." He staggered to her side, jabbing at her with a knobby finger, the nail ringed with dried black paint. "What is it?"

"It's a painting of yours."

"Of mine?" He snorted. "Looks like shit."

Aimee narrowed her gaze, wondering why he was here and if she should be concerned. This wasn't going to work if she couldn't even control the artists she imagined. "Well, you painted it," she said tartly. "Not me."

He doubled over with laughter.

"Doesn't mean I can't call it shit."

"Fine," she sighed, moving to continue with the inventory. "It's shit. And the Glenbow paid three and a half million dollars for it." She rolled her eyes. "Happy now?"

Pollock, however, was far from finished. Bottle in hand, he shouted at her: "No, I'm not happy. It's a waste."

"Maybe for you, but it's a good investment for a museum."

He coughed. "Museums. Shit! That's no good reason."

Aimee lifted an eyebrow. "Art's a commodity. It's not just about creation."

"Bullshit!" he said, swinging his arms wide. "You've gotta live in the moment, not play some stupid art game. You've gotta follow your muse! Let it out. Let it live!"

"Muse, hmm?" She looked pointedly at the bottle. Pollack's drinking reminded her too much of George's demons. How many times had she asked him to go to rehab? That too, she thought sadly, should be inscribed on her palms.

"Yes, the muse," he said, drinking again. "We all have one."

"Maybe so, but not all of us get to indulge it." Aimee lifted a narrow brow. "Now, if you'd excuse me," she said as she stepped past him yet again. "I have work to do."

The ghost wasn't deterred.

"You think you can just turn it on and off," he said, stumbling along beside her, "but the muse doesn't work that way. The muse doesn't take orders." Pollack stopped to take another drink, and belched loudly. "Art doesn't work like that. You've got to find your own way." The words droned on and on, harassing her as she worked. Aimee carried the last of the paintings to the crates, carefully organizing them. When she'd ignored his ramblings for as long as she could, she finally turned to him and glared.

"Wha'?" he asked, then wiped his mouth of the back of his hand.

"I don't want you here," Aimee said firmly.

Pollack stared at her. "But you called me."

She didn't consciously try to repel or ignore him, just lifted her hands so that the writing faced him. She took a deep breath, thinking of Magda's advice.

"Begone, Jackson. Go back. Return to the light," she said calmly. "What're you doing?"

But even as Pollack spoke, the image shifted imperceptibly in quality. It was like a sunbeam dimming, and then without warning he was abruptly gone.

"Jackson?" Aimee whispered.

Nothing.

She turned around, searching for any telltale signs: abandoned bottles or phantom brushes, but the room was empty. With a relieved laugh Aimee sat back down and stared down at her hands and the curling lines and symbols Magda had painted.

"Gone," Aimee said to the silent room. "Just like that." If it had worked on Jackson, it would work for George too. *It should, shouldn't it?* She just needed a chance to find out.

From inside her purse came the sound of ringing. Aimee dug around until her fingers found her cell phone. A bright spot of colour bloomed on her cheeks as she saw the caller ID. She smiled as she answered.

"Hello, Bear. I was wondering when you'd call."

—

Bear paced the street in front of the Glenbow as he waited for Aimee to come out to meet him. Words, explanations and lies tumbled through his mind, but none of them felt right. He couldn't lie to her without damaging their burgeoning relationship, but he couldn't very well tell her the truth either. Bear had come home with the best intentions, but now that the moment was at hand he found himself caught.

Would I want to know?

The door behind him opened and he turned. Aimee grinned as she caught sight of him. She pulled her hair from the clip at the back of her head and a mass of red ringlets tumbled around her face: a flame in the ashes of an ordinary day. She jogged forward.

"It's so good to see you," she said, reaching his side. Bear's heart tightened as she leaned in and gave him a quick hug. "I've missed talking to you the last few days."

"It's good to see you too. I—" For a moment Tasha Suarez appeared in his mind and his words stumbled. "I'm glad to be back," he said.

Her smile faded. "Something's wrong."

A sudden fear hit Bear like a fist to the gut: *What if it's a mistake to tell her? What if this new truth destroys us?*

"Not *wrong*, exactly," he said. "Different."

"Different how?"

"I've got news," Bear said. "Things I found out when I was in New York. Things about George. I thought we should talk about this before—Well, I thought we should talk."

Everything felt like it slowed in the moments after he spoke. Aimee's hair swirled in the wind. Far above their heads, clouds snagged the top of the skyscrapers, their pregnant bellies threatening rain.

"It's bad, isn't it?" she whispered. "Whatever you discovered."

Bear reached out, taking her hand. "It's not good, no. But I think you deserve the truth," he said quietly. "Problem is, I don't know if you'll *want* to know it."

Aimee pulled her fingers from his and stepped back, distancing herself. Bear's hands hung midair, waiting and outstretched. He needed to hold her close, but he could already see the repercussions unfolding.

"Please," she said. "Make it quick. Stop twisting the knife and just tell me what's going on."

He lowered his hands to his side. "I discovered some of George's secrets. Serious ones. I know why his will was such a tangled mess. He was hiding some of the recipients. But I want you to know that our deal still stands. I won't include these details in the biography if you don't want me to."

"I still don't know what you're talking about."

Bear stepped forward. The first raindrops had begun to fall from the leaden sky, marking the sidewalk with splashes of grey. "Is there someplace we could go?" he said quietly. "Someplace private? I don't want to do this here in the rain."

"There are still people working in the Glenbow. The custodial staff is just coming on shift." She nodded up ahead. "But my condo's only a couple blocks away if you don't mind the walk."

"Then let's go."

———

They strolled down the sidewalk side by side. An invisible barrier had appeared with Bear's admission, and he knew somehow it wouldn't come down again. Minutes later they were seated at her kitchen table, a steaming cup of tea which Bear couldn't remember Aimee brewing, sitting at his elbow. He stared at the mist rising off the boiling water, seeing it fade and disappear.

"You said you found something in New York," Aimee prompted. "Something important."

Bear wrapped his fingers around the cup. "Did you and George ever…" His words trailed away into an uneasy silence.

"Ever what?"

"Did you ever talk about children?"

Aimee looked down at her hands. They were covered in henna, Bear noted, and she stared at the designs for a long moment before replying. "Yes," she said. "But George never wanted them."

"If you wanted them, why did you let that go?"

Aimee swallowed hard. Her gaze flicked from her hands, to Bear, to the wall, then back. "Lots of reasons," she said. "He was older when we married. His art kept him busy. Too busy. Too much trouble." Aimee shrugged. "He and Margot had children and he didn't want to start all over again."

"That wasn't an issue for you?"

"Bear," she groaned. "I really don't want to talk about it. Alright?"

"Please, Aimee," he said fiercely. "Just answer me." His voice lowered. "It's important."

She took a sip of tea, and set it down again. Her words were tightly controlled and came out in halting jerks, as if a line drawn out from an uneven hand. "I guess I never thought about it much before I was married, and then when we were together, I kept thinking that George would give in eventually. George had a child already and he made it clear he didn't want more. We fought about it a lot. It became a very painful issue in our marriage. A sore spot, if you will. A few years ago, when I was in my late twenties, it finally came to a breaking point. I wanted a baby so badly but he refused outright. We separated for almost a year and one of the conditions he gave for coming back was that I'd never ask him again."

"Jesus. I'm so sorry."

"It's okay. We all make compromises." She laughed but it sounded brittle. "I loved George. Loved him more than anything, so I gave in." Her face fell, the mask of control softening. "I felt like it was a good choice at the time. But who knows? What's done is done."

"But you *did* want a child," Bear said gently.

Aimee nodded. "I did," she said. "Very much."

Bear pulled his notebook from his pocket, flicking open to the page of text. "When you separated," he said. "Did George stay here in Calgary?"

Aimee leaned forward, peering at the notes. "No," she said. "He went to New York that winter. Hal Mortinson had a show set up for him at the MOMA that January. Why do you ask?"

"This was 2009-2010?"

"That sounds about right. I'd have to check."

Bear put his finger on a date: November, 2009. "Aimee," he said grimly. "I found out a few things about what happened that winter." He met and held her eyes. "George met a woman in New York. Her name is Brandy Suarez."

Aimee's face paled to the colour of parchment. "Sorry, who?"

"When George moved to New York, he reconnected with someone," Bear said gently. "It was a model he'd painted some years before, and who he knew casually. It wasn't serious at first, but George and this woman developed a relationship—"

"No!" Aimee cried in shock, but Bear didn't slow.

"Miss Suarez became pregnant, and decided to keep the baby.

She had a little girl the following summer. Her name is Natasha Suar—"

Aimee surged from the table. "No!" she shouted. "Stop! It's not possible. George wouldn't do that! He didn't want children." Tears tumbled down her cheeks and she rubbed them hastily away. "You're wrong! You don't know how he was. He refused. Absolutely refused!"

Bear slowly stood, palms upraised. "I don't know how he was," he said, "but I know what I found."

"Well, your research has got to be wrong! There have always been rumours, but that's all they are. George would never do that to me. He'd never—"

"Miss Suarez had a paternity test so that she could claim child support," Bear interrupted. "The test was conclusive. George Westerberg fathered her daughter Tasha."

Aimee's eyes had grown to the size of saucers, glittering and bright. She was trembling. "No," she whispered, pressing her hands to her mouth. "No, it can't be. It doesn't make sense."

"I'm sorry, but it's true." His voice roughened. "I wish it wasn't, but it is."

When she didn't answer, he pushed on. "It's the reason the will was such a mess. After the lawyer presented George with the paternity results, George bequeathed certain parts of his estate to Tasha's care, but he didn't want you to know about it. They were hidden in the intricacies of the will, written in layers of legalese." Bear sighed. "He knew, Aimee. And he lied."

"His charities," Aimee murmured. "That's what they were."

"Yes. He hid the trust well. But eventually one of Jacqueline's lawyers discovered the nature of the charity." Bear's mouth twisted in disgust. "Jacqueline has been fighting the will for her own reasons. She hates Brandy Suarez, but she hates other things more."

"Me?"

"Not *you* exactly. But she despises the idea of your love story being the last chapter of her father's life." Bear felt the weight of the admission press down on him. "She'd rather that the truth—as unpleasant as it is—be in his biography, rather than a lie. She wants people to know who he was, rather than let them think your love was perfect."

Aimee pressed her fingers to her temples. "Why are you telling me all of this?"

"Because you deserve to know. You deserve to decide what story you want me to tell." He stepped closer, but Aimee backed away. He stopped. "I'll write what you want. You just need to tell me what that is."

His words were a flame to the fuse. Aimee flew into action, storming from the room. She disappeared down the hall, leaving Bear to follow. As he neared a partially-open door at the end of the corridor he heard her shouting.

"You fucking bastard! Where are you!? Come on! Talk to me NOW George!"

Bear pushed the door open and glanced inside. It was a large bedroom, decorated with paintings, but it looked like it was caught in the midst of a storm. Aimee tore handfuls of men's clothing from the open closet, tossing them into a pile on the bed. To it, she added one of the paintings, gouging the wall as she tore it off its hooks.

"You were such a goddamned liar, George!" she shouted. "D'you hear me? A fucking LIAR!"

"Aimee?"

She turned to him. "You wait!" she snapped. "You'll see what happens. George will show up, and then we're going to settle this once and for all."

A blade of fear ran along Bear's spine, leaving his hair standing on end. Hearing Aimee talk about ghosts was one thing, seeing her irrational and out of control a completely different experience.

"Show up?" Bear said. "What do you mean?"

She threw another painting onto the pile. "Come on, George!" she bellowed, ripping open a drawer and digging through. Boxers and socks were added to the growing mound. "I know you're here! Now come out and talk to me! You want me to see you? I'm waiting!"

Bear took a hesitant step into the room. The light seemed to dim, as if the brewing storm outside had begun to gather. "Aimee, please. I didn't mean to upset you. I only wanted to tell you the truth so you could decide if..."

Whatever he'd meant to say was lost. There, on the other side of the bedroom a figure had appeared. It was growing together out of shadow. Blood-like drips emerged from behind furniture and poured down the walls in black lines. There'd been creatures Bear dreamed of as a child—dark things, dangerous things—but they'd never terrified him the way this image did. The oily darkness clotted together, pulsing like a nest of snakes as it expanded into a man's form. From the deepest recesses of his memory, Bear felt the pull of the vision quest he'd done years before.

"You always thought you could just do whatever the hell you wanted," Aimee shouted. "Well, it doesn't work that way, George! I'm done with you! Done!"

The rippling black form surged toward Aimee, and Bear stepped in between them.

"No!"

The figure slammed into him with the force of a truck. Bear screamed as pain branched through his body like lightning. He felt himself heaved up off the ground, his limbs spread-eagled so tightly his joints threatened to pop. The pain was a force unlike any he'd ever felt. Aimee's cries filled his ears, but he barely noticed. He couldn't see, couldn't think. Screams tore from his throat, the agony expanding to reach every muscle and sinew in his body until—like the flick of a lightbulb—the release of oblivion took hold and he found himself lost in the dark.

A warm hand found his.

"*Be silent, Barrett,*" his great-grandmother whispered. "*You need to hide here until he lets go.*"

Who? he thought rather than said.

"*The darkness, child. He's trying to find you here even now. He'll kill you if he can.*"

But Aimee—

"*You cannot help her. She must face that demon alone.*"

CHAPTER TWELVE

Bear woke to the sound of Aimee sobbing.

His eyes opened a crack. She leaned over him, phone in hand. Flickers of a dream reappeared. His grandmother, dead for decades, had been with him. It had been someplace dark and warm. *A teepee?* he wondered. It felt like a winter camp on the prairies.

"What happened?" he groaned.

She dropped the phone with a clatter. "Bear! God! Are you alright?"

"Yeah," he said, sitting up and rubbing his forehead. "Feels like I just woke up from a bender."

"You've only been out for a minute," Aimee said, wiping away her tears. "I was just going to call for an ambulance."

"Good lord, don't," Bear laughed, then winced as a pulse of pain reached his temples. "Just a bump to the head."

"Are you sure?"

"I'm fine, Aimee. Really." He stood and Aimee followed. She pulled him into a sudden hug.

"I'm sorry," she said fiercely. "I should have warned you."

Bear ran his hands over her back, feeling her meld into the hard angles of his body: hips and chest and lips against his neck. Everything felt sore, but nothing was broken. "It's fine, and you did tell me about your ghosts. I just didn't know they were quite so… real."

"This isn't just a ghost though. It's George." She burrowed closer. Bear could feel her trembling in his arms. "He attacked my mother when you were in New York." A sob broke from her throat. "I'm sorry. I should have warned you."

"It wasn't your fault."

"But it was! I knew he'd react. I goaded him."

Bear pulled back, cupping her chin in his hands. "I'm fine. Okay? Fine."

She nodded, though a new wash of tears streamed down her cheeks.

"I remember following you to the bedroom," Bear said. "Of seeing something dark in the corner. Something shadowy." He frowned as the image faded. "Can't remember anything else."

"It was George. You stepped in his way. And he attacked you."

Bear's brows lifted in surprise. "Me?"

"Yes. Lifted you right off the ground and tried to tear you apart. You're not the first. That's what happened with Mom too. I was too surprised to get rid of him though. I just panicked and started screaming." Her arms tightened around him as she tucked her head under his chin. She shivered. "I forgot everything Magda told me," she whispered. "God, I'm so sorry. I was so upset. I should have remembered what she said."

"Who?"

"Magda's a psychic, though she doesn't call herself that. I saw her when you were away." Aimee leaned closer. "I'm so sorry you got pulled into this, Bear. I should've warned you."

"It's fine. I'm fine."

She lifted her chin to look up at him. He could see fear in the green depths of her eyes. "But he could have really hurt you."

"Luckily, he didn't." Bear caught hold of Aimee's fingers, turning her hands over so he could see her palms. "Is that what the markings are for?"

"Yes," she sniffed. "But I forgot to force him to leave." Tears glittered in her eyes. She looked around the room. "And that means he's going to come back again."

Bear shivered as a dream-memory of his grandmother returned, and along with it a warning. When George came back, Aimee would have to face her demon.

—

Aimee couldn't stop laughing. Bear's dog, Leo, would not stop licking. He was leaning up against her, pressing her to the window.

"Back, Leo. Back!" Bear shouted for the umpteenth time.

The Husky launched himself over the seat, disappearing into the narrow back seat of Bear's truck. Aimee smiled out the window, watching the green-gold prairie scenery whip by. The drive out to Banff had been her idea—she needed to meet with David Arturo—but Bear had immediately agreed to come along. He called it research; he'd never been to George's mountain home. Aimee considered it more than a weekend away.

It was a chance to stir up a ghost.

There was the sound of rustling behind Aimee's seat and the dog appeared on the other side, licking her other cheek before she realized he was there. She broke into another gale of laughter.

"You're a sneaky one," she said with a giggle.

"Bad dog," Bear sighed. He gave Aimee a worried smile. "Leo never acts like this, I swear."

"It's fine," Aimee said. "Totally fine."

After the confrontation in the apartment, Aimee'd expected George's ghost to reappear at once, but a week had passed and then another, and still he'd avoided her. She could feel the apparition hovering nearby, lurking in the shadows, and waiting. But the days stretched on and the henna on her hands darkened, then began to fade. She'd met with Magda, but the seer had shaken her head. "*He's a long ways from gone, dear. He's biding his time. Waiting for you to weaken again.*" She'd smiled knowingly. "*Happy these days, I take it?*"

Aimee smiled to herself, recalling nearly two weeks of growing calm. Even the parts of her life which had felt so chaotic weeks earlier had begun to settle. The final resolution of the will was one. With the revelation that one charity was actually a dispensation for an underage child who'd need support into adulthood, no one—not Aimee, nor Jacqueline—stood a chance arguing for more. The adjustments had been made and agreed upon. After lawyer's fees and estate taxes were paid, Aimee'd have a hefty nest egg that she could invest and use, if she was careful, for the foreseeable future, but not a large enough sum to be significantly life-changing. She would have no early retirement or jet setting lifestyle. But there *would* be a degree of security for her life. As the turmoil of the fight over the estate came to a close, a new realization arrived: though Aimee wouldn't inherit any significant amount of money, she wouldn't walk away with any crippling debt either. That felt like a miracle! With the newfound freedom she felt, Aimee had begun to feel the urge to create emerging from its years-long hibernation. She started carrying a sketchbook along with her, occasionally doodling on her walks. Lastly, and most unexpectedly, was a feeling she'd thought had died alongside George.

Love.

Yes, she thought, she was closer to happiness than she'd been in a very long time. And that alone was enough to get her heart pounding. Bear accepted who she was, both good and bad. He seemed determined to separate her from the memory of her late husband. Most surprisingly, he took the haunting with unexpected calmness. *Mind you, he's had first-hand experience*, she thought ruefully.

She peered over at the man next to her. He stared out the window, frowning. "I shouldn't have taken Leo along," he grumbled. "Sorry about that."

"It's really no problem," she said, touching his arm. "I love animals."

"Really?" He glanced over at her, then back at the highway. "You don't have a pet though."

"Oh, George wouldn't have them," she said, grinning as Leo inched his way up the back of the seat until his paws were firmly planted on top. "But I always loved dogs. My mom has a couple of Pomeranians. They're like little fur babies. God, she spoils them!" She reached out and rubbed her hands over Leo's fur. "They're not real dogs like you are, Leo," she said with a grin. "Just little guys."

Leo laid his head against the top of the seat and sighed, his tongue lolling. She glanced up and her gaze caught on Bear.

"What?" she said warily.

"Nothing."

"No, really."

"It's just the way you talk to him," he said, turning his attention back to the road. "Like he's a person. Like he understands." Bear grinned. "I like that. You know?"

Aimee nodded, leaning back against the seat and smiling. "Yeah," she said. "I know."

Outside, the mountains tumbled upward from the ripples of the foothills, growing larger by the minute. Soon she'd be home. *George's home*, a voice inside her whispered. Her chest tightened as the truck entered the shadow of the mountain.

Perhaps stirring up a ghost wasn't the best idea, but it was too late to back out now.

—

Aimee spent the afternoon talking with David Arturo about the costs for staging the cabin for sale. Jacqueline had begrudgingly agreed to pay for part of the staging, while Aimee's share would come directly from any profits she made on the deal. If it sold, the cost would be well worth it. When David finished his explanation, Aimee walked through the rooms that now looked like any other show home.

"Can we stay here," Aimee asked, "now that it's staged?"

"In the cabin?" David said. "After what you told me last time, I didn't think you'd want to."

"I didn't until now," Aimee replied, running her hand across a new kitchen table, set up to look like a family of four was about to sit down for dinner. She'd always imagined having children, though for years she'd resigned herself that it wasn't happening. She smiled and pulled her hand away as she took in the cozy scene. There were napkins folded into origami shapes, bright plates piled on woven place mats, polished cutlery gleaming. In the center sat a bowl of very realistic-looking artificial fruit. "But I'm staying in Banff and it seems silly to rent a hotel."

"Of course you can," David said with a nervous laugh. "It's your cabin, and you're renting the furniture." He looked furtively over to the entrance where Bear stood snapping pictures with his phone, Leo at his side. "But the dog…"

"The dog has a crate in Bear's truck," Aimee said dryly. "He'll sleep there, and we'll make sure he doesn't get on any furniture." She rolled her eyes. "I figured that much, David."

David smiled placatingly. "Right then. Any idea how long you and your *friend* will be here?" His tone said something else entirely. "You know, in case someone wants to come in and see the place?"

"A day or two at most," Aimee said. "I have to be at work on Monday."

"Right, perfect. Okay. No problem. I'll arrange for any new viewings to take place starting Monday." David tapped a message into his phone. "Hope you two enjoy the place. Lots to see in Banff, if you're going out; lots to do if you're staying in," he said with a knowing smirk. "I'll just get out of your hair."

Aimee fought the urge to tell him to mind his own business as he headed out of the cabin, leaving her and Bear alone. Staying in didn't sound so bad to her. She smiled as she recounted all the time she and Bear had spent together since his return from New York. They'd been on several dates and had almost spent the night together a number of times, but with Claudine slowly recovering at home, Aimee's free time had been at a minimum. Now that they were in Banff, Bear and Aimee were finally alone again. *Perhaps this is the time things will work*. A blush ran up Aimee's neck at the thought. She'd dreamed of all the things she'd like to do with him. Someday, she'd like to make those dreams reality. Though she and Bear had a much more stable beginning than she and George had ever had, that didn't mean her passion for him was any weaker. In bed alone each night, her body ached with need.

As if called from her thoughts, Bear appeared in the doorway, Leo on his heels. Aimee blushed as if he could read her thoughts on her face.

"You hungry?" he asked.

Aimee reached out her hand for Bear to take, the dog falling into place between them. "Famished." She slid her arms around him, grinning. "How about you?"

"Starving." He nodded to the staged table. "I'm so hungry I think I could eat one of those plastic apples."

"Don't think it's going to come to that," she laughed.

"Any ideas for restaurants?" Bear asked.

"I've always liked Maple. It's Canadian cuisine. Some of the best."

"Sounds great." Leo barked, and Bear chuckled. "Yes, buddy. We'll sneak you something out in a doggy bag too."

Dinner moved at a leisurely pace. Aimee couldn't help but notice the way Bear focused on her. His gaze, when she looked up from eating, or back from the room, always resting on her. A month ago, that kind of focus would have unsettled her, but tonight she felt reckless. She had been alone for over a year. In that time she'd been widowed, dragged to court, survived a natural disaster, found out her late husband had a secret love child, settled a messy estate litigation, and fought her way back out of the depths of depression. *So what if I want a little bit of happiness?* she thought. *Why can't I take what I want? Joy was hers to claim, wasn't it?* Bear wanted her as much as she wanted him. Of that she was sure.

By the time the cheque came, and they returned to the house to release Leo from his crate, she had decided tonight would be the night. She slipped off her jacket, hanging it in the empty closet, and joined Bear in the living room that looked like an altered version of the one she'd once known. Neutral paintings hung on the wall, a plush carpet softened the hardwood floor next to the fire, pillows and velvet throws covered the couch. She struggled to remember what it had been like when she and George had lived here, but the memories seemed wrong somehow, forced atop the new.

Bear had started a fire in the fireplace; he stood as she came into the room.

"Mmm..." Aimee said, warming her hands. "That's nice."

He grinned. "Reminds me a bit of camping. Hope Mr. Arturo doesn't mind the house smelling a little bit like smoke."

"David will be fine", she said, settling down on the couch nearby. "Leave me to handle him."

Bear chuckled. "You know, I think you can handle about anything life throws at you these days."

She giggled. "Let's not tempt fate."

Aimee expected Bear to come sit at her side—she had plans if he did!—but he grabbed a pile of papers from the end table and brought them to her instead.

"What's this?" she asked as he set them in her hands.

"It's the last chapter in George's book. I was wondering if you'd read it for me."

"Of course! I've been dying to read the ending."

"You know how it ends though." Bear said with a chuckle.

"I know, but—" She shook her head. "I suppose I just want to see it through your eyes."

"Fair enough." He sat on the couch next to her, nervously fiddling with the creases in his pant legs as she settled in to read. "Do you want me to give you space?"

"Goodness no," she laughed. Aimee patted his leg. "Relax. Stay here with me. It's only one chapter. Right?"

"It is, but I want your thoughts on it." He frowned. "Be honest, please."

"I will." Aimee cuddled in against him, and began to read.

Chapter 17: A Life Reimagined

In the winter of 2012 and spring of 2013, George Westerberg set aside the comforts of known success to embark on his most ambitious project: a return to his roots through an exploration of Canadian art. For the first time in a decade, he retired his exploration of the female figure, an approach notably expressed through portraits of his beloved wife and muse, Aimee, and shifted his focus to an equally challenging subject matter: the Rocky Mountains. Despite this change in subject matter, the through-line of his love for Aimee can be seen through-

out this final, unfinished series. In these paintings, their love is fore-most—a connection whose wildfire passions of more than a decade has finally grown to maturity.

George's passion for his wife is visible in vibrant sunrises over lofty peaks, explosive storms, and the excruciating beauty of rugged vistas...

As Aimee read, the uneasy feeling which had disappeared for the last weeks returned. She flipped through pages, reading paragraph after paragraph of their final year together, and the turmoil in the weeks and months following George's death. The flawed George Westerberg of previous chapters had been set aside for a new, larger than life figure, one whose personal failings were reflective of the times rather than of his own troubled life and bad decision making. A line appeared between Aimee's brows as she reached the mention of the will and the discovery of a child. Natasha Suarez's appearance was written away as George taking responsibility for a momentary lapse in judgement during a separation from Aimee—one that was due to career pressures, not actual marital troubles. In Bear's version, he didn't want to trouble Aimee, his dear wife, with knowing the truth.

Aimee's frown deepened as she read on. This final chapter would, without a doubt, be used in every gallery's catalogue, worldwide. Jacqueline would hate it, but many others would embrace these lies. Aimee had no doubt Hal Mortinson would use selected paragraphs as part of George's updated post-mortem biography. It would go into history books, be used to discredit the damage of a lifetime, leaving only a deified version of George Beecher Westerberg behind. Aimee's frustration rose to a crescendo as she reached a particularly false line.

Throughout the final months of George's life, his devoted wife stood by his side, ever ready to provide the much-needed support as he worked through his new process. Her guidance—

With a groan, Aimee looked up, unable to go on.

"Finished already?" Bear asked in surprise.

"No." Aimee pushed the papers into his hands and stood. Her calm had fled and a layer of annoyance now prickled under her skin. "I can't read this, Bear. I'm sorry."

He sat silently as she walked circles before the fire. The room had chilled in the time since she'd started reading and she put her hands out to warm them before pacing once more. Angry tears welled up in her eyes. *This isn't right!* Her heart twisted painfully. A month or two ago, this would have been *exactly* the chapter she would have wanted to read, but tonight it felt like a betrayal.

Bear set the papers on the couch next to him and cleared his throat. "I take it you're not happy with the chapter?"

She spun back. "Of course not! How could you think I would be?"

Leo sat up and whined as if sensing the unease.

"Relax buddy," Bear said quietly. He stood and came to her side. "I don't know. I just assumed—"

"Assumed what? That I needed to see his devotion to me?"

"No, I just—"

"Then why write George that way?"

"Because he *did* love you, Aimee, probably more than you realize. I've read his journals, seen the interviews he gave. You were his everything. Don't you see that? He loved you more than anything in the world."

"George loved the *idea* of me! He loved the pretty young wife who gave up her career to make him happy. But that wasn't true." Aimee pointed accusingly at the papers on the couch. "Do you think I like seeing myself as the perfect wife? The 'stand by your man' doormat that every fucking artist wants to marry?" Her hands were shaking, fingers icy. *Why was the cabin so cold?!* She wrapped her arms around herself. It *hurt* to see herself like this, portrayed as George's devoted muse and nothing else. What about the fight over the estate she'd been put through? What about the years of betrayal? Why weren't *those* mentioned? "I'm not okay with this chapter. I'd rather you cut me out entirely rather than publish it."

"But I don't understand. This is the part of your story Jacqueline doesn't *want* the world to see."

"I don't give a shit about Jacqueline. If you're going to tell the truth of our lives, then tell it. But this—" She glared angrily at the papers on the couch. "This might as well be one of George's portraits of me. A pretty picture of an empty person. Not real at all." Her voice broke. "I was more than that, Bear." Her chin lifted. "I *am* more."

"I know but—"

"But what?"

Bear gave her a lopsided smile. "I thought that was what you wanted the world to see."

"That I was spineless?!" Aimee snapped. Fury towards her late husband surged inside her.

"No. That you were *stronger* than George's failings."

"Stronger," Aimee repeated, her voice rising in surprise.

"Infinitely stronger." Bear opened his arms and she stepped into his embrace. "You *are* more than anything I wrote in there. You're strong willed, determined, and resilient. You are." The room felt impossibly cold despite the fire and he tightened his arms around her. "I know that."

She gave a bitter laugh. "Then why didn't you write the chapter that way?"

"Because his devotion to you was real."

"It wasn't," she said.

"No, listen." He rubbed circles on her back, holding her gently as she leaned against him. "George Westerberg could be awful, but he *did* love you, Aimee, probably more than you'll ever realize. That's how it looked, at least to me."

"But I told you how things were between us." She shivered. "George could be amazing, but he was also a misogynistic jerk. Women were his playthings. He *needed* people to love him; needed *me* to love him. He demanded everyone's adoration! God, I gave up so many things for him!"

"You did, but only for a time. Not forever." Bear brushed her hair away from her face. "I've seen you drawing again. I didn't want to say it, but I see the changes happening."

Aimee swallowed hard. "Be that as it may, I can't let you publish that chapter as it is."

"No problem."

She laughed. "Just like that? You're not going to fight me over it?"

"Nope." Bear grinned. "We had a deal. You make the final decision on how it looks. I've worked with harsher editors, I promise you."

She frowned. "How do you want the ending to go?"

"I want it to be true. I want an ending that gives George's story justice, but also tells the truth. If I'm missing things, then I need to fix that. I might be a little more objective about the research details, but you actually knew him, Aimee. You know what parts I've written are too much, what parts are too little. I owe you a chance to fix them."

"God, George would have hated that you were the one writing about him. Someone I care about. Someone who I have feelings for." Aimee laughed and around the room the shadows seemed to dance and move. "He'd be raging about it right now."

"You think?" Bear chuckled.

"Oh, I know he would." She slid her hands under the edge of his shirt, warming her fingers against his bare skin. The entire cabin felt like it was wrapped in ice tonight, but Bear was warmth and comfort. "I want you to write the truth."

"Then tell me."

"I want people to know George was flawed, just like everyone else. Yes, he was talented—incredibly so!—but he questioned himself constantly. I've been thinking about things the last while. George never thought I could hack the art world, but I don't think that's what was going on at all." She snuggled against Bear, tucking her head under his chin. "George couldn't stand competition from anyone. He never wanted a second artist in the house. I gave up everything—an art career, the possibility of children, my independence—and for what? A lie."

Bear cupped her jaw so she looked up at him. "There are going to be people who hate you for telling the truth."

"I know. And I don't care."

"You say that now, but I've seen hate campaigns against people who speak out."

She smirked. "If I can handle George, I can handle them."

Bear laughed. "You're okay with Jacqueline thinking she's won?"

"Oh, I trust you to still make our love come through. It was there too. I just want the world to see the *rest* of him." She stood on tiptoe, waiting for Bear to close the gap. "What did I say that first time I read your work? That you'd cleaned George up, I think it was. Maybe this time, just don't clean him up too much."

"Deal."

With that, Bear leaned in, his mouth bridging the space between them. This was another point of warmth in the icy room and Aimee allowed herself to be drawn into the kiss. The anger she'd felt minutes earlier had shifted and a new appetite had returned. She wanted him. Aimee wondered if Bear would delay sex yet again, but as the kiss dragged on, she felt things move into new territory.

He broke the kiss, breathing hard. "God, I've waited so long for this."

Aimee giggled. "You have?"

"Yes! But you've been so busy with your mom and I didn't want to interrupt and I was worried if you hated the finished book that it might screw things up between us and—"

She kissed him again, breaking the chain of words. Around the room, dark shadows shifted and pulsed in the corners, pulling together into coils of darkness. Neither noticed.

"You need to stop worrying," she said.

"But—"

Aimee set her hands against Bear's chest. "Stop. Just let things be." She reached for the top button on his shirt, unbuttoning it one handed. "I want something real, rather than a memory of what used to be," she whispered. "I want a *beginning* of a love story, not the bitter end." She leaned closer, mouth almost against his. "I want you, Barrett Cardinal."

After helping Bear undress, Aimee tugged off her clothes, dropping items piece by piece until she stood naked before him. Bear swallowed hard, trying to look away and failing. The play and dance of muscles under her skin was beautiful.

He ran his hands over her arms, watching her skin rise in gooseflesh. "God, Aimee. I want you."

"You waiting for something?" she murmured.

"Just surprised this is happening," he said.

"I'm not." Aimee's lips parted slightly, face flushed. "I've been dreaming about it for weeks."

Her voice was warm and Bear lifted his eyes to meet hers. She stared at him openly, her gaze tracing over the hard lines of his muscled frame. A small circle of heat was cast from the fireplace into an otherwise icy room. Bear pulled a throw blanket from the couch and spread it before the fire before leading her toward it.

Aimee took his hand and dragged him down next to her. A punch of energy hit Bear in the gut the moment they touched. Suddenly all he could think about was the fact that her palm was warm and her lips were full, and she was touching him—*touching him!*—and he wanted to touch her back. How long had he waited for this moment? Imagined it? Bear knew there was an answer, but he couldn't think past the nearness of her.

"Are you sure about this?" he asked in a tight voice. "We don't have to."

She grinned, leaning toward him, her breasts a soft weight against his chest. "Absolutely." Aimee traced his lips with her finger. "But a serious question here: Are you?"

"Christ, if you only knew."

"Then stop worrying."

He felt the floor under him waver, whatever he was going to say lost in the brightness of Aimee's eyes. Bear opened his mouth to assure her that he was—*Oh God, yes!*— but Aimee was faster. She slid her hands up the front of his chest to wrap her arms over his shoulders.

The motion unsettled their precarious balance and Bear tipped back, catching himself on his elbows.

"Careful," he said. "I don't want to fall into the fire."

She straddled his hips. "No? Not ready to burn yet?"

"Maybe just a little," he chuckled, sliding his hands up her torso to cup her breasts. Though he couldn't see her clearly, he could remember her unclothed and his mind filled in the details with light and shadow. The need to touch her—everywhere!—grew until it was a physical pain. He pulled her down and their lips touched, moving together at once.

The kisses they'd shared over the last month had lit the spark, but this kiss—naked on the carpet next to the low burning fire—blazed with intensity. Bear couldn't think for the taste of her, and his body quaked with each brush of her hips. She was sweet and warm, writhing on his lap, almost dancing in his arms.

A piece of firewood dropped, the light dimming as the tongues of flame faded to embers, wrapping them in velvety half-light. In the shadows, something moved. Bear's mouth left her lips to taste her skin: following the narrow line of her throat down to her breasts. He wanted Aimee with a desperate, wanton desire. He'd spent weeks trying to control his approach to loving her, to give Aimee the distance she seemed to need, to never press. But now that the moment was here he could hardly control himself from flipping her onto her back and having her then and there.

As if anticipating his thought, Aimee lay down between him and the faded glow of the fireplace. In the nearly solid black, her shape was barely more than a few curving lines, her long hair a bronze tangle around the oval of her face. A twinge of reminiscence rose: *Aimee en déshabillé.* Bear had seen the sketch at George's retrospective and it struck him that she'd lain like this for him once. Jealousy rose inside him, but he shoved the thought away. Instead, Bear slid closer, kissing her until the unwanted image faded and all that remained was touch and feel and taste.

Aimee, a voice in the wind called.

In the solid blackness of the room, Bear's actions grew bolder. His fingers searched for sensitive patches of dusky skin, judging his teasing based on Aimee's hitched breath and whimpers. His mind traced a picture of her desire with the forbidden wanderings of his tongue. He lingered, drawing out the torture.

"Please," she gasped, her fingers guiding him into place.

The sound of her voice ripped the last of his control away. Flashes of memory—kissing Aimee in the foyer, holding her hand as she cried—appeared behind closed eyes and he let out a pained moan as he entered her. Bear's body was rigid, his control wavering as his body begged for release. Each new sensation had surpassed the one before, but this moment of connection left him reeling, shaken to the core. He could hardly breathe for the feel of her around him and he broke the kiss to taste the skin of her neck, salty with sweat. His mind screamed for him to slow down but every single cell in his body was hell-bent on release.

Aimee's hips rocked beneath him, shattering his focus and throwing him into motion. The two fell into a steady rhythm. In the heavy darkness, the world narrowed down to sounds and sensations: the pop of a burning ember, the angry wind rattling the windows, sparks of ecstasy burning Bear's skin. Even the dancing shadows seemed alive. Aimee moaned aloud, her breath warm against his neck. His strokes quickened and her legs twitched in time to his thrusts.

"Faster!" she cried. "So close!"

Bear had been with a handful of women in his life, but this felt entirely different. Being with Aimee felt like he was flying, his body a bird, released. They moved together, their bodies in time. Without warning, Aimee cried out, her voice loud in the living room.

"Bear!"

The feel of her release propelled him forward and suddenly he was there with her—the two of them spinning over the edge together. Time stretched into eternity until he spiralled into half-consciousness. His heart was pounding, body slick was sweat. Their bare chests pressed up against one another, hearts pounding in time. After a moment Bear slid sideways, gathering her into the crook of his arms. The room was oddly cold despite the fire, and he shivered as the sheen of sweat dried.

"Love you," he panted. "Love you so much."

Aimee rolled closer and reached up to stroke his cheek. "I love you too, Bear. I think I have for a while."

The darkness around them roiled at her words.

"Me too."

Bear smiled and closed his eyes. The wind had risen into a storm. It was an angry roar pummeling the cabin, shaking the trees outside and sucking all heat away. Even the carpet beneath them held an icy chill, but with Aimee in his arms, that hardly seemed to matter.

Within minutes, Bear was fast asleep.

—

Aimee woke in the dark. Bear was curled around her, his body the sole point of heat in the bitter cold room. Shivering, she untangled herself from his body and pulled another throw off the armchair to drape over him. He murmured something inaudible then fell quiet as sleep pulled him back into its grip. Aimee dressed silently, her feet aching where they touched the hardwood. *Jesus!* she thought. *I'd forgotten how cold the mountains get at night.*

In minutes she stood in the brightly-lit kitchen, glaring at the thermostat on the wall. It was set on low. Sensible, Aimee realized, since no one was actually living here. She spun the dial, listening for the tell-tale whoosh of the furnace and ticking of the fan. She brushed her hands on her pants and smiled. "Done and done," she said as she turned around.

George stood behind her.

He loomed in the doorway, blocking her view of Bear sleeping on the floor of the darkened living room. In the split-second of recognition, a number of details pulled into sharp relief: The ghost was impossibly young tonight—late twenties at most—his body corded with muscle, his familiar face twisted in a mask of rage. This was the George she'd only heard about. The one who'd balanced on the sharp edge of addiction and anger. Virile. Volatile.

Dangerous.

"You cunt!" George barked.

Aimee gasped, her hands lifting to ward him off even as he lunged for her. "Begone," she cried. "Go back. Return—"

The incantation was cut off midway as George's hands tightened vise-like around her neck. Her breath caught in burning lungs and she flailed, struggling to release herself. *No!* her mind screamed. But this George wasn't the one she'd known. He wasn't the older man who'd loved her in his own flawed way, but a young George hellbent on murder. Solid, his body shifted like quicksand when she tried to catch hold, only to return to steel a moment later. His fingers clamped down on her windpipe, blocking her from calling from help, from sending him away.

"Die, you bitch!"

Aimee stared into his eyes, no longer fanned by wrinkles. Flashes of memory appeared: George asleep in bed next to her, mouth slack, softly snoring; then his grinning face, wrinkled in joy as he tugged her into his arms, laughing at some long-forgotten joke; and later his fingers brushing slowly over her skin in the moments after they'd made love, his murmured voice an incantation: *Aimee, Aimee, Ai-mee... What in the world am I to do with you?* Yes, they'd had years of turmoil, but there'd been love there too! She needed him to remember.

Aimee mouthed his name, silently begging: *George, please!*

The ghost smiled coldly, his fingers tightening in glee. This angry version of George wasn't the aged man she'd known. He was decades younger...and he hated her.

The lights dimmed, shadows crawling in from the edge of her vision. Pain spread from her throat down her neck. Her legs buckled and went limp, and she hung, doll-like in his unyielding grip. Aimee's eyes blurred and refocused, confused by the dimness that blocked her fading vision. Shadows had begun to fill the kitchen, pouring down walls, and rising up from under the table. And *that's* when she saw them.

They coalesced one after the other: Delacroix, fretting in his smoking jacket; Frida in her dress, cane in hand; O'Keefe watching her with sad eyes; Warhol pacing nervously while Pollack slumped drunkenly at the table; and many others she couldn't yet see, but could feel. Her ghosts neared, watching and waiting.

I'm dying, her mind announced. *And they know.*

That thought, above all, terrified her, because if she died, then she'd be trapped with George, and there'd be no way to ever get away. A surge of energy rushed back through her dying limbs and she flung her arms blindly, no longer grabbing at him, but at anything in the kitchen: drawers, the towels on the rack, and finally, desperately, the bowl of artificial fruit. Her fingernails caught the edge and it rolled sideways, apples spilling over the table, thumping down to the floor a half second before the ceramic dish that had held them came crashing down. It shattered at her feet with a resounding smash.

"Aimee?" Bear called groggily.

She was almost gone, and his words came from an ocean away, but she held them like a cord, drawing herself back to his voice. Frida stepped forward, and lifted her hand as if in farewell, and Aimee stared. The palms of her hands were marked with painted words, and that didn't make sense, except…

The palms are a hint! Aimee's mind screamed. A message.

With the last reserve of strength, she lifted her palms with their faded lines of text—all of George's broken promises, all of the disappointments in written form—as her mind recited the words her voice could not: *"Begone. Go back. Return to the light."* George blinked, the pressure of his fingers loosening.

"What the hell did you say to me?" he snarled.

She took a wheezing breath. "Begone," she croaked. "Go back. Re—" George's fingers tightened until she could no longer say the words aloud. *–turn to the light,* she thought.

"Aimee?" Bear's voice called again. "You there?"

"I won't!" George yelled. "I'm here! And I'm staying!"

Aimee closed her eyes, surprised to find that the room was still there behind her lids. If anything it was sharper and brighter. She focused on George as she raised her hands. Her hennaed palms glowed with golden light, shimmering on a shape that wasn't her husband as she'd known him, but his younger self. A virile man bent on killing Aimee. In the corner, Andy tutted to himself: "*I liked him well enough, but he was a bit of a loose cannon. Fighting and drinking. There were a couple years even the New York Times wouldn't cover his shows. Didn't matter that he was selling out. George Westerberg couldn't be trusted.*"

This was the version of George who'd returned tonight.

BEGONE! her mind roared. *GO BACK! RETURN TO THE LIGHT!*

She shoved her hands against the figure's chest, the light piercing through him. Streams of it caught on the other ghosts, their voices rising to join hers as she repeated the chant. *Begone! Go back! Return to the light!* The apparition roared, any semblance to George disappearing at once. A snakelike entity, made entirely of shadows writhed and screamed.

"NO!" the ghost bellowed, stumbling back. "STOP!" His fingers loosened again.

Aimee took a whistling breath and coughed, the midnight kitchen reappearing, the other figures fading back into shadowy ghosts. Through the open doorway, she caught a glimpse of Bear struggling to stand, his eyes wide with horror. The apparition still held her by the throat—Aimee's feet dangling inches above the floor—but his control was waning.

Aimee took a choking breath, filling her tortured lungs to the brim, her hands outstretched, palms burning like fire. "Begone!" she rasped. "Go back! Return to the light!"

The ghost wavered and her toes touched down onto the icy tiles.

"Begone! Go back! Return to the light!"

The figure before her shattered, pieces spreading out like an unsettled nest of moths, black shapes flickering into the darkness, and disappearing altogether. Aimee caught herself against the counter, as Bear came running, the blanket wrapped hurriedly around his waist. The room was full of ghosts, and they milled uncertainly around them.

"Is he gone?" Bear asked.

"George is," Aimee said, though she knew that the apparition wasn't truly the person she'd known, but some darker version of him. "But the others are still here." She lifted leaden hands, ready to release them.

And then someone spoke: "I'm sorry, sunshine, but I need to go." The voice was rough with age, achingly familiar. Aimee gasped, searching the crowded room for the source. And then she saw him.

Her husband, George, lay on the floor of the kitchen, near the back door where he'd fallen once, over a year ago. An old man once more, his lips were pale, his cheeks grey. *Dying*.

"No!" she cried. She took a step, and stopped. Around her, the ghosts waited.

"Let me go, Aimee," George whispered. "Please."

"But I don't understand." She took a trembling step forward, Bear following. "You're the one who stayed."

George struggled to sit, but failed. "I tried. I did. But it's time I left."

"Is it him?" Bear asked. "Is he back?"

"I don't know," she said. "I think this is him and maybe the other wasn't, or at least not the one I knew." She couldn't bring herself to come any closer. "George? Is that really you?"

The vision of her late husband smiled, fading into half-light. She could see him, but just barely. "It is," he whispered. "But I can't stay. The sun on the mountain... it's a bright cadmium yellow with just a hint of crimson in the edges. But it won't last." He smiled. "I need to go now, darling."

Aimee nodded, fighting tears. "I understand."

George's smile wobbled. "Be happy, sunshine. I love you. Always did."

She lifted her hands and took a calming breath. "Begone," she said slowly. "Go back. Return to the light." As she spoke, the ghost evaporated like smoke, fading until there was nothing left at all. When she lifted her gaze she was surprised to find the entire kitchen deserted. Every ghost, every artist she'd ever imagined, fled. "Goodbye," she whispered thickly. "All of you."

"You okay?" Bear asked.

Aimee stepped into the circle of his arms, setting her cheek against his chest. "Yes. You?"

He pressed a kiss to the top of her head. "With you here? Always."

CHAPTER THIRTEEN

Bear waited on the bench outside Central Park, smiling at the book in his hand. *George Westerberg: A Life in Brushstrokes.* He smiled to himself, relieved that the book tour was finally winding down. He could tolerate New York for a day or two at most. After that, it was torture. Interviews and panels, book-signings and, of course, another retrospective. Bear leaned back on the bench, kicking his legs forward and sighing. If he had to shake one more collector's hand, he'd scream.

But a job is a job, he thought. And this book was already doing well, hitting the New York Times Bestseller list for non-fiction in its first six weeks on the shelves. It was an honour that meant that the next project he undertook could be one he wanted. *Back to fiction again.* Bear squinted into the autumn sunlight, smiling to himself. The ideas were already bubbling.

He heard a child laughing happily and he glanced over at the park entrance. It teemed with businesspeople on lunch breaks and parents on picnics. But the figure he sought was nowhere to be seen. Disappointed, he flicked open the book, glancing through the preface, co-written by Jacqueline Westerberg-Kinney. He smirked. This was the polished version of what George's life had been. A moment later, Bear flipped to the final pages of the tome: the epilogue, co-written by Aimee Tessier. Bear grinned, remembering the argument *that decision* had started. He was glad he'd stuck to his guns. The book encompassed all facets of George's bombastic life and his story wouldn't have been complete if either one had been left out.

Happily, the critics agreed.

Bear closed his eyes, ignoring the buzz of Manhattan traffic so he could focus on the play of sunshine on his head and shoulders. Warm patches of light dropped through the open branches of the trees overhead, resting on him for a moment, then shifting when uprooted by a gust of wind. It was comforting. Like being at home in the mountains of Alberta, with wide open spaces, and a sky so big you could feel the weight of it. Bear's head nodded, thoughts flickering through his mind like the sun-dappled leaves. He didn't even notice the sound of footsteps nearing.

"You sleeping?" Aimee asked.

Bear jerked, his foot kicking out like he'd fallen. "Just resting my eyes," he said sheepishly.

"A likely story," she said, coming to sit at his side. She was smiling, but her eyes were bloodshot, face pale.

Bear slid his hand around her shoulders and she leaned up against him. He pressed his lips to her hair, whispering: "You okay?"

"Not really," she said with a teary laugh. "But I will be."

Bear nodded. "You want to talk about it?"

Aimee twisted her hands in her lap, not holding Bear's eyes. "She, um, she looks like him. Her lips and eyes. She's got his temper too. Screamed like a banshee when she dropped her ice cream." Aimee gave an unladylike snort. "Her mom's going to have her hands full when she hits her teens. Good lord."

"She's headstrong," Bear said, wondering what a child of Aimee's would be like.

"Yeah. You could say that."

Bear reached up, pushing a curl of hair away from her eyes. Aimee's lashes were in wet spikes, green eyes bright with unshed tears. It struck him that she'd probably finished the meeting with Brandy and Tasha some time ago, but had wanted to pull herself together before she came out of the park. "You think you'll see her again?" Bear asked.

"Maybe. If Brandy wants to." She leaned against Bear. "I'd like to," she said quietly. "She's a sweet little girl. Reminds me so much of George."

Bear tightened his arms around her, his own throat aching. He wanted so badly to protect her, but if the last year had proven anything, it was that Aimee Tessier could take care of herself.

"So the visit was a good thing then."

"Yeah," Aimee said, a hint of wistfulness in the tone. "It really was."

Beyond them, the traffic rose and fell, waves on an ocean of sound. Bear smiled to himself, thinking of home, and the woman he loved, sitting at his side. He knew, without doubt, they were one and the same. For a moment, a line from Aimee's epilogue flitted to mind. It was a quote from the sculptor Rodin, and today, with the return trip only hours away, it felt particularly true: "*The main thing is to be moved, to love, to hope, to tremble, to live. Be a human before being an artist.*"

If falling in love with Aimee had taught him anything, it was that joy was worth the messy parts it took to get there.

CHAPTER FOURTEEN
EPILOGUE

The painting that hung above the little boy's bed had never been repaired. "Mixed medium" was what his mother called it when he asked her about it. The ethereal shadow had once, in another life, been an oil painting of Mount Rundle at dawn. Shapes and colour blurred and blocked it, layers of paint and paper rippled across a surface which shimmered like water. All of it hinted at the textured, abstract technique for which his mother's art career was known.

"What is it?" the boy asked her.

"Whatever you want," she said. "That's how art works."

The boy's father had a different answer: "It's a secret," he said. "A message to you, from Mommy."

The little boy stared, wide-eyed, at the swirl of pigment, and shifting light. The patterns that ebbed and flowed with the boy's imagination. No matter how he stared, he could never completely decide what the picture was. And maybe, he thought, that was how his mother wanted it to be.

"What secret?" he whispered excitedly.

His father lifted the painting down from the wall, setting it carefully on the bed next to the stuffed bears, and the blanket where Leo slept.

"That the past is always here," his father said, tracing the shape of the mountain the little boy could never see. "But you can always make a new future." His fingers moved outward to the lines that Aimee had layered in on top, painting into, rather than repairing, the damaged scrape that covered one entire side of the painting.

The boy tipped his head and frowned. "I see a dog," he announced. "Next to that blue blob."

His father laughed. "Leo, hmm? He might be in there."

The boy's chubby hands moved over the surface, picking out shapes. "And here's you and Mommy and my room, and this part here is the house."

His father leaned in, kissing him gently on the forehead.

"And what about you?" he asked. "Are you in there too?"

The little boy nodded and smiled, his small hand, resting on a shape gouged deeply into the centre of the canvas: The top of the mountain where a single bright patch of cadmium yellow remained. It had been layered over with other colour, a bright flash of light atop a sea of shadow.

"That's me," he said with a grin. "Right there in the sun."

ACKNOWLEDGEMENTS

The writing of any book is a lengthy process, but the timeline for *Inescapable: A Ghost Story* was longer than most. I started this project in the months directly after the 2013 floods and worked on it, off and on, for almost a decade. In the years between inception and publication, many people shaped its form. My intense gratitude goes out to each and every one of them:

Thank you to my family for their undying support as I followed my dreams. Although my husband likes to joke that he "hitched his wagon to my rising star", the opposite is actually true. His art inspires me to write and paint and do everything that gives me joy! I'm so grateful to share a life together.

Thanks also to Stonehouse Publishing. I always believed this book would find a home, but to have that be my very first publisher is truly special! My profound gratitude goes out to Netta Johnson and the Stonehouse team, for their tireless efforts in bringing this story into the world. *Inescapable: A Ghost Story* is yours as much as mine!

Thank you to Moe Ferrara, my current agent, for her enthusiastic support and boundless energy, supporting my writing career. You are a gem, Moe! Thanks also to Morty Mint, my retired agent, for being a publishing mentor and dear friend. Morty was the first person to believe my books would be published and I've had his unwavering support every step of the way. You're amazing, Morty!

A huge shout-out to my fellow authors, editors, and artists, too numerous to list. Your encouragement keeps me writing! A special note of appreciation to the sensitivity reader who went through this book with an eye to details. Thank you. Thanks also to every reader who has picked up one of my books at a store or library and taken a chance on it. I wouldn't have a writing career without you!

One final note of appreciation: For my ghosts. I have many fond memories of gathering around my grandparents' supper table, listening wide-eyed to the stories of the uneasy dead, whispering secrets to those they've left behind. Many of these family legends have woven themselves into the pages of *Inescapable*; a few have given me hope that there really is something beyond this here and now. As my father once said: "I'm not sure what happens after death, but whatever it is, it'll be interesting." I agree.

ABOUT THE AUTHOR

D.K. Stone/Danika Stone is an author, artist, and educator who discovered a passion for writing fiction while in the throes of her Masters thesis. A self-declared bibliophile, Stone now writes novels for both teens: *Switchback* (Macmillan, 2019), *Internet Famous* (Macmillan, 2017) and *All the Feels* (Macmillan, 2016); and adults: *Inescapable* (Stonehouse, 2023), *Fall of Night* (Stonehouse, 2020) *The Dark Divide* (Stonehouse, 2018) and *Edge Of Wild* (Stonehouse, 2016). When not writing, Danika can be found hiking in the Rockies, planning grand adventures, and spending far too much time online. She lives with her husband, three sons, and a houseful of imaginary characters in a windy corner of Canada, Lethbridge, Alberta.